Black Cloud, Red Sea

Black Cloud, Red Sea

Game. Set. Execution

Arlinda Rotate

1st edition 2025

ISBN: 9798296570079

With thanks to everyone who made family life in the village of Grundisburgh such a happy time.

Page intentionally left blank.

CHAPTER 1

Hey," she gasped, pushing him up from below. "Move over, will you. I can't breathe."

"Sorry, chuck, I'm all in."

"Come on, you're crushing me!"

"But I'm spent," he said, still panting.

"For heaven's sake man!"

Bruce winced as he felt a nip in his side, followed by a second one which was sharper still, so he pushed up and rolled over.

She turned onto her side, stroked his cheek, and then snuggled up, tight against him. Screwing stark naked in a cornfield is hard to beat, she though as her eyes closed.

"Keep still," she said sleepily, "and hands off my bottom or I'll kill you." He raised himself on one elbow and looked down: she was already asleep. "Good idea," Bruce decided, lying back down and turning to warm himself from her body heat.

He briefly gazed up at the stars, then fell into a deep sleep. It was the middle of June. Heavy heads of corn swished in harmony, moving in the light breeze that drifted across the Suffolk countryside.

He awoke some time later, turned to lie on his back and stretched out his arm to find the wine bottle. He shook it. Empty.

"Misty," he whispered. "The wine is finito."

No answer.

"Misty. Hey, no more plonk."

Bruce reached across the blanket for her. But she was gone. So he sat up and arching his shoulders, glanced backward at the disused runway. His dusty pick-up truck was still there, but her Porsche was nowhere to be seen.

"Where...?"

Then he noticed the note stuck in the top of the empty wine bottle. He unfolded the paper and used the moonlight to read her "*Dear Bruce*".

> *... I wrote this before coming out tonight because I knew*
> *I couldn't tell you to your face.*
>
> *I'm leaving. It's over. I need a fresh start.*
>
> *I've got the job I've been chasing... secretary to Nicholas*
> *Fothergill, our MP, and when they vet me I don't want*
> *them finding your skeleton in my cupboard.*
>
> *Good luck and no hard feelings.*
> *We've had some good times.*
>
> *Love, Misty*

Well, well, what a surprise. The mighty Clarissa has given him the push, the big E.

Bruce held the note up again and re-read it. The words said the same as before, only this time they didn't sound like the end of the world.

He wadded the note up into a tight ball and fired it into the grass, then lay down on the blanket again and, if anything, felt rather relieved as he had been toying with the idea of ending things himself.

Despite the kiss-off he still felt great.

Clarissa, or Misty as he preferred to call her, was up-market class... proud and haughty; whereas he was the son of a photo-copier maintenance engineer, whose rather down-market tastes ran to fish and chips, and watching the stock-car racing at Foxhall.

She, however, came straight out of the top drawer... the daughter of Lord and Lady Seckford who owned a large agricultural estate in Suffolk and various multi-storey office blocks in central London. Yes, Misty was certainly well-heeled.

She was also lusty. Mixing with poncy, neutered sons of belted earls, had left her aching for some top-class action… then she met him.

It was a Friday evening just over a year ago at the annual May Ball, held out on the lawns at Seckford Hall, in aid of World Aid for Children. It was a hot night, in more ways than one.

Peter Barber, publican at The Dog in Grundisburgh, ran the bar as usual, and Bruce had help by ferrying crates around in his pick-up. It brought in a bit of useful cash, and he reckoned the exercise wouldn't do him any harm. When he had first seen her, she was surrounded by a gang of chinless wonders.

She spotted Bruce who was "devouring me with his eyes," as she told a friend the next day. "I liked what I saw, so it was game on," she confided with a giggle.

When the others departed for the noisy disco in the marquee, he made his move. Grabbing a tray of drinks, he joined her beside the pool. "Another drink, milady?" he suggested with a roguish smile.

Classy Clarissa turned eyes-on and, with lacquered nails, drew little circles on his shirt around each of his nipples. "Hey, Action Man," she said. "I need help. I can't find any action."

Bruce picked up the damsel in distress. "You want action?"

"Show me," she replied, her voice full of dare.

"I hope you can swim," Bruce cried as he stepped backwards into the pool.

Lord Seckford's daughter gasped as they hit the water. Gasping for air, Bruce and Clarissa surfaced, looking at each other. The message was loud and clear...

"What now, Lady Sexford?" Bruce enquired, hitting the mispronunciation hard.

Misty came back quickly.

"Your pleasure is mine, treasure."

Buttons popped, zips opened and silk was lifted high as the water in one corner of the pool rippled and bubbled vigorously.

It had been physical and it had been fun, but now it was over.

"Do-It-All" Dexy, flat-mate and self-made video whizz, had told Bruce all along how it would end: a sudden, clean break with no hard feelings. Well, maybe one or two.

Dexy had given the affair twelve months. And he was always right.

"You'll wake up one day and see things for what they are: an illusion," he had told Bruce on a monthly basis.

He lay stretched out on the tartan rug, still in no particular hurry to get dressed and go. "Just like you, Misty," he said. "Just like you."

This was a new ball game he thought: with the top seed in his life having withdrawn, he'd have to take a fresh look at the situation. Earlier flings came to mind and there had been some memorable times, ever since that residential tennis course in the early days, when Sharon Warmley drew his first ace in the empty dormitory.

Then there was Polly, the music lover from Stowmarket, and, of course, Fleur.

Fleur Hainault left school at sixteen to get married because she was pregnant. She had a second child before breaking with Waveney, the father, in violent fashion. He had battered Fleur a couple of times before they reached the Grand Finale, the day he knocked her to the floor for the last time.

Furious, she got up and slashed him across the arm with the kitchen knife she had been holding, then marched forward to strike him again but he backed off and left, never to return.

Bruce and Fleur had known each other from earlier times, since their athletics club days... in fact they had dated once or twice. With Waveney gone, Fleur asked Bruce if he'd like to move in. Yes, he immediately replied, he sure would... and he did.

Sharing the same bed was great, but there was more to it than that, much more as Fleur was good to be around. They talked of serious stuff like hopes and ambitions. And that was when his fears rolled in. Responsibilities. Demands and expectations. Traps, real or imaginary. It was all too much, too soon.

The split was triggered by nothing more than a petty argument in a supermarket and after that there had been nothing regular until Misty, so now what?

Would the potato-humper, budding businessman and Wimbledon-champion-to-be (a description firmly implanted in his own mind even if nowhere else) ever settle? He picked up the wine bottle again. Turning it upside-down, he waited for the last, moon-warmed drop to drip onto his parched tongue.

Then dozed off again to dream of fame.

***

Tennis was Bruce Saxon's burning passion. He adored the game. At twenty-six, some commentators suggested that he was now a bit too old to reach the very top, that his big chances had already passed him by.

But he, on the other hand, was as optimistic as ever.

After school, his parents anticipated that he would go to university after clocking up good results in maths and physics, but no, he shocked everyone by opting for a very different future: tennis.

School champion for four years running, Bruce was the top player in Ipswich by the time he was seventeen and carried off his first all-Suffolk championship the following year.

Throwing all advice aside, he decided to gamble on tennis and world fame, on Wimbledon and stardom, on the day when tv commentator Dan Maskell told viewers they had a home-grown men's champion on their hands.

As parents, it took some time for Joe and Hannah to accept the reality, but eventually they did and so as their son came through the door one evening, they called him and handed him an envelope.

"What is it?" he asked.

"Open it and see," said Hannah.

He looked at the envelope suspiciously. "Go on, open it."

He did and inside was a cheque for £9000.

"What's this?" he gasped.

He couldn't believe it because he knew his folks didn't have that kind of money to spare and three months later on he felt like crawling under the floorboards when he discovered how they had raised it: the first £3,500 was their entire life's savings, while the £5,500 balance came from a second mortgage on their home.

"I'll pay you back some day," he vowed. "Every last penny… and with interest."

"Don't worry about that," his father insisted. "Think of it as something to tide you over until your ship comes in."

With that settled all three of them laughed with nervous relief and to round things off, next morning Joe introduced his son to Frank Johnson, an old acquaintance. Before the day was out Bruce and Frank had formed a partnership.

Frank operated as a one-man band, delivering potatoes round the Ipswich shops from his one-and-only, down-at-heel van. But this development meant that things were about to change and two months later, the two-man band had leased a small warehouse at the end of Bramford Road and were running a pair of equally dubious vehicles.

Right from the start, Bruce liked his new way of life, there was plenty of fresh air and exercise during the day, and still with enough time left over to play tennis after that. He had no regrets at opting out of the academic world.

His tennis got better and better, though at a steady pace rather than anything flash. The East Anglian challenge trophy was presented to him in perpetuity after he'd monopolised it for years, and he became a major force in the annual South of England championships at Basingstoke.

With each passing year Bruce climbed a few more rungs on the ladder towards Wimbledon and stardom. He'd made it to the 'final 32' in two big tournaments and over the years, ignoring some notable hammerings, had registered a few important wins across on the Continent: against Mats Wilander and Thomas Muster, no less.

Now with a place in Britain's current Davis Cup team and a regular paring with Jeremy Bates in doubles matches, he felt that one more major success, one that would carry him into the big time, was getting closer and closer.

On the coaching side, all the while, he'd made solid headway and today was in big demand at Thurleston Tennis Centre, Ipswich's busy indoor complex.

When slipping into dreams of a night, he often heard rhythmic chanting: "Bruce, Bruce, Bruce" and saw a crowd that was up on its feet and in full voice. Yes, Wimbledon's Centre Court had erupted in a thunderous ovation as he stepped forward to hold the famous trophy aloft.

But it wasn't the roar of admiring fans that woke him from this snooze under the stars in a Suffolk cornfield.

CHAPTER 2

Quite the opposite in fact: his slumber was broken by angry shouting that was brutal and loud.

Recognising that it was time to get on the move, he hurriedly pulled his clothes on then stuffed his feet into socks and trainers. A clutter of startled pigeons rose noisily behind him as he looked at his wristwatch which told him it was an hour before sunrise. Still the voices kept coming. It wasn't a bad dream. No. This was real.

"There she goes, Rags, grab the bugger!"

"Damn, this stuff is legging me up."

"Don't let her get away!"

It was time to skedaddle quick, so grabbing the blanket from the floor, he ran to the Toyota, reached the driver's door and after a brief fumble with the keys, got in.

The voices kept coming closer.

"Baz, to the left, she's heading left."

One of the men got his legs tied up in the wheat plants and went down flat, falling on his face and cursing wildly.

"Rags, Rags, keep your torch on her!"

Bruce twigged that somebody was being hunted out there in the corn with a pair of chasers who were mighty cross. But it was a battle he didn't want to witness, so he released the handbrake and silently freewheeled down the gentle dip.

It levelled out in about 300 metres. Once he got there he would start up the engine and head back to the Gap.

But for the moment - no lights, no engine, no noise. That was the plan until suddenly something hit the side of his pick-up, a dull thud against the passenger door. He glimpsed a face and knew he couldn't scarper without doing something to help, so he yanked open the passenger door, shouting: "Get in, quick!"

It was woman or perhaps a girl from the size of her, panting and gabbling blindly as she jumped in. "Stop, you damn sod!" they yelled at Bruce as they got close. "This is none of your business, you dumb prick. Just get the hell out of here."

No time to lose.

Bruce turned the key and kicked the Toyota into life. The clapped-out silencer blasted away noisily as the well-worn truck shot over the stubble; the passenger door swung round and slammed shut of its own accord. The pick-up rattled through the corn like some crazy, carnival ride and reached the top of the rise where Bruce finally switched on the headlights and breathed a sigh of relief.

But two headlights appeared directly ahead, shining straight at him. More of them!

With the route to the Gap blocked, he swung the pick-up to the right, speeding hell-for-leather towards the less-than-obvious exit at the south end of the airfield. It was normally blocked by a padlocked gate. Dennis the farmer used this entrance as a short-cut onto what was once a Second World War airfield and where these days he grew wheat in the patches of soil between the strips of concrete.

There was the off-chance that Dennis might be busy with farrowing pigs at Climbing Tree Farm and might have forgotten to shut up shop.

Bruce bounced over the heaving and buckling track ways to make his get-away but then his mirror burst into light, the dazzling reflection announcing that his pursuers were still hunting after him. "Damn!" he swore as he saw that his escape route was shut off.

Urgently trying to figure out what to do next, he kept his right foot down hard. No point charging the gate: the sturdy metal barrier would slice through the Toyota's cab like a knife going through soft cheese. Going nowhere, fast...

He had no idea what was going on, but he knew he had to do one thing pretty quick and that was escape. Picking up speed, he raced on round the airfield's outer circular track.

Within this were three internal runways, two running parallel east-west, the third cutting across them at an angle of sixty degrees.

After a quarter of a circle and with both vehicles now in pursuit, Bruce knew his only hope was to get to the Gap first as there was no other exit. But things were not looking good as slowly but surely he was losing ground. His initial 300-yard head-start had already dipped to just 200 yards and would decrease further still as the Toyota just didn't have enough poke. That much was obvious: even with a backing wind, the crate wouldn't do more than 65 downhill.

He glanced back again to find that the nearest big bad wolf was no more than forty yards off. He'd never reach the Gap. Change of plan. "Hold on, this is going to be bumpy," he called out.

The pick-up slewed off onto the first of the two parallel tracks running across a part of the old aerodrome that had sunk over the years and now gathered standing water. In some places the pond was five feet deep; but the trick was to know your way through it.

Bruce steered a course down the middle of the runway, foot rock steady on the accelerator to stop water running up the submerged exhaust pipe and into the engine. After thirty yards he swung hard left. "There's a big drop in front there," he explained to himself as much as to anyone else. "Gobble 'em up, it will. Just watch."

Then, weaving a way steadily through the shallows, they made it to the other side… they still had six inches of cold water swirling about on the cab floor but they were on dry land again and still rolling.

Bruce looked in the mirror, waiting to see the rabble-pack plough straight forward and fall over the hidden cliff. But they didn't. They knew the trap: that meant that these were no strangers. The chase-cars all turned and high-tailed it back round the long way. The escape stunt hadn't worked.

He knew they would come at him again and if they spread out and circled in both directions they could nip him whichever way he turned. "We've got to break out this time," he said, again as much to himself as anyone.

Bruce rattled toward the Gap, a big circular area of concrete where once the wartime bombers had turned but where today, Dennis stored thousands of straw bales: by standing overwinter on a solid base, they kept dry underfoot.

Impossible to get through if you didn't know the way, but Bruce did. The Gap, leading through onto a quiet country road, was the last chance for freedom. Manoeuvring with care, he slowed down for the final acute right-hand twist, then out, free at last.

He spotted the set of field harrows mounted behind a John Deere tractor: the spikes were harmless while in the ground, but when the frames were lifted on high they became dangerous weapons.

He slammed on the brakes, flicking off the lights but leaving the engine ticking over, then bounded across to the tractor. He'd driven it a couple of times in the past when out at Climbing Tree for potatoes, and knew how to juggle the array of levers. It seemed like an eternity waiting for the diesel to warm up and for the engine to start.

"Come on, come on," Bruce urged, banging the instruments in desperation. It was going to be touch-and-go. Noises told him were almost here.

At last the green giant roared into life. He put the tractor into reverse, switched to four-wheel drive and ploughed backwards just as the front van emerged from between the bales and slap-bang into the rows of pointed teeth which sank into its bonnet, piercing radiator, grille and front tyres.

The tractor, still retreating, slide the first tin can van back into the oncoming vehicle right behind it. He flipped a stubby lever and leapt from the cab. Behind, a second set of metal teeth pivoted and fell, stabbing mercilessly through the van's roof.

As they pulled away, he took a look across at his passenger to find that there was blood everywhere; forehead, nose and cheeks. But a short while later when he gave her a second glance she was gone, her eyes had closed. Hopefully she was still breathing.

This wasn't over: they would come after him, sure as hell, he reckoned. Grundisburgh village was no more than a pin prick on the map, and nobody else living in Thomas Wall's Close had the words U-GOT-'EM splashed garishly across each side of their motor, so going home wasn't an option.

A groan told him that she was alive but she had started shaking. Given the quite nasty wounds and the need for medical attention, it was difficult to figure what to do "Ipswich Casualty's a long drive, and you're bleeding pretty badly," he muttered.

Rather than tangle with the NHS, he opted to play it safe for now and take her to Mary, a tennis player and friend who had been a doctor before her kids were born. So on to Osiers Corner, then a swing right four houses further on, before running the wheels down to a halt on gravel and stopping out of sight from the road.

He got out and pressed a front door bell. A light came on in an upstairs window, then went out again. After a couple more seconds, the window opened and a thin, bearded face appeared in the darkness.

"Who is it?"

"Bruce Saxon... and I'm in a big fix. I've got someone here who's bleeding quite a bit. I don't know who she is, but she needs help."

"Be right down," Ivor answered, ducking back inside.

Bruce brought her to the door, then passed her across to Ivor who carried her inside. He asked her: "Do you understand English?"

She nodded slowly but she didn't say anything.

"Where are you from?" Ivor asked.

No reply.

"What's your name?"

It looked like it hurt every time her head moved.

The door opened and Mary came out to help.

"Who is she?" she asked.

"No idea... ," Bruce panted. "She just appeared from nowhere with a bunch of thugs chasing after her, like she was escaping."

Mary looked a stern look. She was obviously confused.

"What are you talking about?"

"Sorry. Out at the old airfield," he continued. "I gave them the slip."

"Who?" Mary wanted to know. "Oh, never mind that now."

Then she took over and Bruce sighed with relief: once a doctor, always a doctor. "Shut the door. Get into the kitchen. There, on the table," she said, pointing.

"I don't want to get you in trouble," said Bruce.

Mary ignored him. "Pain is pain," she said, leaning over to get a closer look at the wounds.

"Those thugs weren't amateurs," Bruce said, "so I'll take her away if this gives you issues, like professional problems. Perhaps I could… "

Mary cut in saying: "Poor girl! She's been beaten for weeks. Old wounds all over her, old scabs freshly lifted... she must have been through hell."

Then she stood up straight. "Go on, you," she snapped, hands on hips. "Get out of here!"

Bruce wasn't sure who was being given their marching orders. "Leave her with me. I'll get her patched up. And I've something in the cupboard that will give her a good sleep.

"Just go. Leave her here, she's safe with us. Linda and Zoe are off visiting granny in Woking so there's plenty of room. And don't you worry that soft mushy thing you call a brain, we won't say a word to anyone."

Bruce breathed a sigh of relief.

"Go. Now. Get that noisy truck away from here quick," she ordered. "Go on! The longer you stay here, the more chance there is of someone spotting you."

Bruce shook his keys and said: "Thanks, Mary, I knew I could count on you."

"Oh, you did, did you?"

"I'll get off to the warehouse and kip down there."

"Right. Now go!"

Ivor held the door open.

"Give us a ring in the morning," Mary called out, "but you keep away for a while and concentrate on finding a way of us to talk to her."

Ivor gave Bruce a push and out he went.

He ran to his dirty yellow pick-up, the one with the bold lettering on the sides. "Yeah, we got 'em all right," he mused. After listening for any early morning traffic, he backed out onto an empty road and headed west towards Ipswich.

Bed that night was a pile of empty hessian potato sacks. Not silk, but safe.

***

Sunday morning dawned and Bruce was up and about in next to no time as the sack-cloth bedding had been more than a tad itchy. The result of that was that he found himself striding down Henniker Road well before seven, heading for Frank's house.

Because he needed a different set of wheels: Mary was right, his Toyota was a dead give-away.

The man was out in the garden weeding and, judging from the pile in the bucket, it looked like he had been at it for some time already.

"I'm in a pickle, Frank, and could do with your help," he said, opening the gate. "How about letting me have the Cavalier for the day?"

"What, and leave me stranded here all day?" Frank snorted, glancing guiltily over his shoulder.

The man was more than a little hen-pecked.

"Read my lips," Bruce said. "C-a-v-a-l-i-e-r."

"No way."

"Come on. I wouldn't be asking if I didn't need it."

"But I need wheels myself, for later."

"You can get away in the Toyota. It's round at the warehouse."

Frank conceded the point but it came at a price: he lifted a hosepipe, sending a fine spray of water over his partner. "Oh, you bloody pillock!" Bruce yelped, jumping away.

"You do realise what you're doing to me, don't you?" he moaned. "I'll be edging the sodding grass next, then moving the sprinkler every twenty minutes to make sure her roses keep growing."

"What are you two juvenile delinquents up to?" Bella roared as she appeared in the doorway. "Not thinking of sliding off to work, are you, Frank?"

"No, Bella, wouldn't dream of it, Bella," he replied.

Bruce made for the gleaming car and Bella's hand made for her husband's ear as he tried to follow suit and make off for the pick-up.

"FRANK!"

Bruce drove through the middle of town where the only sign of life was the early-morning queue of swimmers outside Crown Pools. A steady Ipswich start to Sunday.

***

13

"Mary Dunnett speaking."

"It's Bruce here."

"Hello, you're up early."

"How's the patient?"

"Fine, just fine. We've patched her up and now she's getting a well-earned sleep."

"I called at Withipoll Street on my way to Thurleston but my translator's out of town, and their shop round in Rope Walk doesn't open until Monday."

"Don't worry," she said, comfortingly. "The girl needs rest anyway."

"Has she said who she is?"

"Not a word," replied Mary. She stopped before continuing.

"Yes?"

"I found a bit of paper tucked away. You can make out the first half of someone's name, Kerry… and that's it, the rest is blotted out."

"Well at least that's a start."

"There's no rush, Bruce. You just stick with your routine. Bye-ee."

It was just turning nine o'clock when he arrived at the tennis centre and the car park was already heaving. As he stepped out someone hollered at him: "Come on, lazy bones, we're all waiting!"

It was Dorothy Jackson. She and her carload came down from Stowmarket every week: four of them in total. They were all devout. Dorothy herself was climbing through the ranks: she'd been to Peterborough twice for the East of England Championship, and last year had got herself into the semi-final.

Bruce's track suit top was already off.

"All warmed up, then?"

An affirmative chorus rang out.

He found coaching surprisingly satisfying. There was so much scope to pass on what he'd been told earlier on his own tennis journey, to work on people's weaknesses, to demonstrate, build up confidence, and improve their all-round game.

And today, on top of all that, it was also a good way to forget the problem that threw itself at him last night.

Dexy, on the other hand, said coaching was nothing more than an ego trip. Bruce didn't argue with that.

His favourites were the five youngsters who walked in from just down the road, rough and ready but keen as mustard and hard-working on court. They ran and ran, never giving up anything. Brandishing old racquets, they came in gear that some of the more moneyed players took exception to.

Of these, Luther was by far the most outstanding. Just 13-years-old and a couple of months, with thin legs and a dense mat of tight curly hair, the youngster looked more like a walking beanpole than a tennis player.

But looks were deceiving, for Luther was blessed with uncanny skills: his positioning was remarkable and he had a fantastic range of shots. After playing him in singles, Bruce already knew he'd got what it takes.

After putting in a gruelling morning session, lunch was welcome. Bruce looked round, wondering who to sit and talk to. There was a lone figure sitting outside on the steps so he joined him. Ogilvie was an odd-ball. He turned up week after week, coming all the way down from Peterborough yet said so little.

Bruce had worked on that and now had a sketchy picture of a lad living at home with a mum, or was it a step-mum, and working for British Sugar in its headquarters, mum doing the same, and with a budgie. That was it so far: it was work in progress.

So for better or worse, he decided to tell Ogilvie what had happened the night before, what with him being a complete outsider to Ipswich's various goings-on. Spelling it all out might just clear his thoughts.

Ogilvie sat there riveted, open-mouthed. Then Rex Tate muscled in and sat down, or squelched down, right between them. End of story.

Rex was an overweight 50-year-old with wobbly legs and on court he looked like a shaky, red jelly. Oblivious to any existing conversation, Mr Roly-Poly took a bite out of his salmon sandwich and asked: "Is there some particular reason for punishing us?"

"Punishing you?"

"This lark of covering the back of the court, hopping from one side to the other like a yo-yo. Sheer, bloody murder! It might help youngsters like Ogilvie here, but we're not all clockwork robots, you know."

He thumped his chest, then, spluttering as a result, wished he hadn't demonstrated so vigorously.

Bruce chuckled, then changed the subject.

"How's things then, Rex? I want to trade-in the pick-up. Ford offering any deals at the moment?"

Rex reeled off the price of half-a-dozen bargains; a chance like this was too good to miss, even on a Sunday. Bruce actually liked Flexy-Rexy, a local made good. Born at Earl Soham, the son of a farm labourer who didn't have a penny, Rex started out by dabbling in small-time car repairing.

Full of confidence, he then borrowed enough to set up a tiny garage at Sweffling, deep in the Suffolk backwaters. Before long a second garage, this time in Debenham. Now his name was splashed all over the county, from Bury St Edmunds to Saxmundham. He was currently turning over £15m a year and chalking up a healthy profit.

Bruce reckoned that if a trundle-trolley like Rex Tate could do it then so could he.

He stood up and shouted from the top of the steps: "Time up everyone, let's play some more tennis."

The afternoon session went smoothly.

The drive home was relaxing, a five-mile run along narrow road through villages: Tuddenham, Culpho and then Grundisburgh where Oakenfull's shop was doing a healthy trade in ice cream and Jimmy Foulger's cows were on the move after milking, moving slowly back to fresh grass and filling the road.

Just beyond the green, Bruce signalled right and cruised up to the top of Thomas Wall's Close, sliding to a halt outside No. 22, next to Dexy Fasbender's left-hand-drive Oldsmobile. The third resident was Bob Gatt and he spurned the idea of owning a car, as did his girlfriend Jean, who now shared his room. They got about on their bikes.

"It's only me," Bruce hollered, as he dropped his tennis bag behind the door. "What's the food scene?"

"Get your own," came an echoey boom from the bathroom. "I'm swanning off in ten minutes."

"You sound cheerful."

"I got a call from Diane."

"Diane?"

"Radio Orwell - that Diane," Dexy shouted against the noise of the shower. "You know."

"Do I?"

"Remember that night when we went to hear Mitzy and Meena at the

Fisherman's?"

"No!"

"Well that was Diane. So listen. Two singers who trade as Pinch Me I Must Be Dreaming asked her to do a video for them and she wants me to tell her what I think of it. So it's a meal in Ipswich at The White Horse, plus drinks. All on her bill. "

"You smooth-talking, jammy oaf."

Dexy appeared at the bathroom door. "By the way, the phone kept ringing all afternoon, but every time I picked it up it went dead. That said, the one call did connect. It was Fleur. She wants to talk to you, says needs some inspiration with a book."

Dexy roamed round in the nude, looking for his clothes, while his flat-mate foraged round the kitchen assembling a thick pile of lettuce, tongue and tomato for a sandwich.

"I know it's not my scene," he said, "but if Fleur gave me half a chance of inspiring her, I'd be on her doorstep in a flash... are you listening? This is good advice you're getting from ol' Dexy. You two click. It's so bloody obvious, 'cept you're too dim to see."

"Did she say anything else?"

"You've the option of doing the inspiring over the phone, or going down to Woodbridge before six o'clock."

"Thanks, I'll get to that next, but got to pop out first though, right now. Should only be twenty minutes or so. I'll be back, finish my tea, then ring her. Happy?"

"Suit yourself, you stubborn bucket of peelings. Seems to me you've got your priorities wrong... anyway that's me ready for the off, so I'll see you sometime, mate."

The whole village was on easy stations as Bruce walked round to Mary's place: Sarah Willetts was inside house No 4 practising the piano with the windows open while young Simon Connolly was out in the road leaping his BMX over a wooden ramp.

At Saddler's Cottage it wasn't the chattering of swallows that caught Bruce's attention but the smell of bacon ahead. Mary was cooking a late tea. "You in the market for a sandwich?" she called through the open kitchen window.

Bruce nodded adding: "Great, yes. Could you manage two?"

"Or three?" asked Ivor as he strolled around the corner and into sight, gardening gloves in one hand, pruning shears in the other.

"You take over in the kitchen," said Mary, beckoning her husband forward with her finger.

Ivor nodded. "Guess I'll have to if we're ever going to eat."

"Come see the patient," Mary urged, turning to Bruce.

"Lead on," he replied.

They went up the stairway. I was old like the rest of the house and its thick, medieval oak boards groaned beneath their padding feet. They stopped at the second door on the left, and Bruce leaned over Mary's shoulder, peering into the room.

The girl was awake. She looked across and faintly moved her bandaged hands.

Mary, trained doctor that she was, went around to the far side of the bed and leaned over the patient. "She's coming along fine," she said. "We've changed the bandages three times today. The scabs are nice and firm, and there are no infections underneath, so it's just a question of time."

She continued in a matter-of-fact voice: "She's had one hell of a time. Somebody's really been laying into her, not just once but over a long period. Her back is an absolute mess. I think she's had regular daily lashings."

Bruce winced. Mary reached forward, took the girl's left hand and, gingerly peeling back the bandage, revealed a second type of injury.

"Look, these wrists have been tied up."

"Then she must have been a prisoner, or a hostage, or something," Bruce said.

Mary just shrugged her shoulders. There was no need to say anything.

Bruce stepped up to the troubled patient: "Who are you?" he asked.

She tried to raise her head, nodding as if she wanted to say something ten reached for a glass of water.

"I can talk, yes, I have learnt from a friend. From Australia. I am Areej. Those men force me to come to England... to join Majid.

"Majid husband beat me... in Pakistan. He came England and Areej happy. Now they force me come. They will take Uzaif and Fal. I must see my children."

Her voice got weaker. Then she stopped and slipped away into sleep.

Mary broke the silence. "She's fine," she affirmed. "She's lost some blood and is still weak. But I can see a definite recovery so don't panic."

"That was a lot of names there," asked Bruce. "Let's get everything written down on paper while we remember what she said. And that name you had... Kerry? That feels like we've made a start."

"I like your use of the word 'we'," Mary mused. "You dug the hole, but I notice it's 'we' who have to get out of it."

"Aw, come on, Mary... if she'd gone down Heath Road there would have been police swarming all over her as soon as she got through the hospital doors and she'd likely be half-way back to wherever by now, cuts and all."

But Mary was in a different place, she was thinking ahead.

"Look," Bruce continued. "She ran and I happened to catch her. Fine. But I'm in it now, right to the end. It may all blow over, or it might get worse and worse. I just don't know."

Mary had gone quiet. That meant trouble.

So Bruce babbled on: "Look, I see your problem, Mary, because Ivor told me he wants her out right here and now, but can't we give it a couple of days?" There was no reply so he carried on: "If you feel you've already done too much, then I'll take her away right now. I could ask Norma Bye, she was a nurse once."

Mary had made her mind up and she spoke at last: "No. She stays here. In for a penny, in for a pound, as they say."

"I don't want you... "

A halting hand cut him short. "She stays here as long as she needs. Now, let's go down. I smell grub."

CHAPTER 3

Bruce had a restless night, his brain was harassed and bewildered, so he got up and wandered through to the back room and looked out to where, beyond the fence, the bowling green stood out in the moonlight

Its pavilion formed a shadowy outline. There were more shapes, all without colour and with little detail: Dr Odlum's house with a thatch, the black barn and then the metal owl perched up on the blacksmith's chimney pot.

Feeling a little better, he padded back through to the front window where he thought about the girl. She now had a name. Areej. Then Fleur came to mind as she was the one posing the more immediate puzzle because he had rung no end of times only to get the engaged bleeping sound, endlessly, which told him that she had taken the phone off the hook. On purpose.

It was a coded message saying 'don't ring me here' so he stopped toying with the idea of driving over.

The kids were growing up fast: Ysanne was 12 and in her second year at Kingston Middle School, while Louis, barely ten, was still at Kyson. As he didn't want to run into her man Jake, he worked out that appearing at the door of 8 Florida Way wasn't on.

The answer, then, was to pop down to Woodbridge first thing in the morning, wait in Beech Avenue and get a word with Ysanne on her way to school. Yes. Decision made. Realising that he wasn't going to get any more sleep that night, he donned on his tracksuit and trainers, and decided to take a run round Clopton.

After a shower and some breakfast, he scuttled over to Woodbridge to catch up with Ysanne and had barely stopped when she came pacing along up the pavement with two of her side-kicks, Rachel Nightingale and Vicky Jarrold. She saw him and squealed with delight.

"It's Bruce!" she yelled, beaming down at her friends as he spun her in the air and gave her a big kiss and in one breathless outburst she told him everything, or at least what seemed like close to everything.

"I'm going to camp in August, and I'm getting a rucksack... Mum's cut my hair, what do you think? I wash it myself now... we all saw you on TV... you were great... Louis wants to be a detective... I've got a clarinet from school and I'm going to be in Pinocchio next term... Mum's horrible: she says I can't have my ears pierced... when I'm sixteen she won't be able to stop me, will she? And I've got my name down for the school trip to Belgium... "

"Whoa, there, miss," Bruce gasped and lowered her to the ground, amazed at how heavy she had become.

Undimmed, she blasted on. "That's only the first bit," she said. "Come round on Sunday and take us to Shingle Street for a picnic, like when we were little? Louis's got a catapult! Come. Say you'll come?"

"How's your Mum?" Bruce asked, ducking the question.

"Bossy!"

"And how's Jake?"

"He's weird! Me and Louis... "

"Louis and I," Bruce corrected.

"That's what I said, Louis and me know a secret about him."

"And what's that?"

"Can't tell you."

"Oh, come on, I'm a big pal, aren't I? Well at least I was. What about those Funny Faces I bought."

"Oh, okay, then," Ysanne agreed, "but only if you promise you'll not tell anyone."

Bruce held up his hand in a Guide's-honour gesture.

"I promise," he said solemnly.

"Well," Ysanne confided, frowning, "Nellie reckons he's on drugs, and that we should be careful, especially when he's very happy."

"Doesn't sound good."

"Isn't!" Ysanne agreed. "Oh-oh, the bell!"

Bruce called her back.

"Hey, here's a note for your Mum."

"A note?"

"Yeah, don't forget to give it to her."

***

"Ah, so my yellow bird's back," Frank Johnson called out, as his young partner pushed open the office door. "Any springs left in the back seat?"

"A few."

Bruce gave a quick grin, then looked at the pile of post in order to ignore the tale of woe that he knew was coming… it was the same old story every Monday morning.

"Cecil Brazier called by last night," Frank said in order to open a conversation. "He's asking £110 a ton, and I reckon we could get him down to £105... yes?"

He got no reply as Bruce was reading the first of the letters. "Say, we've got a quote here from Bullivant's. They're offering two new Leyland 45s for a total of £44,000 and will take £9,500 each for our trade-ins."

But Frank wasn't interested, he wanted to air his thoughts on getting a divorce as, after all, it would trigger a big withdrawal of cash from the business. But Bruce ignored him since it was like this every Monday morning, a verbal hurdle he had to get through.

He scribbled out a note and then pushed it over to Frank saying: "You need to get in and make the first move, mate. Get out your wallet and go advertise."

"Saying what?"

"Shut up and read this."

The message:

LADY WANTED.
Company director, 46, with substantial financial assets, six-footer, bald but good looking, honest, seeks partner for immediate input of cash.
£75,000 secures offer of marriage. Box 253.

Frank was slightly skewered as it was both funny and serious. But it got him going regardless. "I'm totally changed from what I was back at the start when Joe came over and fixed the two of us up," he said. "It was Bella who pushed me along then, or held me back more like, but these days when I tell her what we're planning, she's the one who panics, not me. Amazing really how things change, go into reverse."

Bruce felt it was a good time to open up.

"Talking of changes, I reckon you get a raw deal from me these days," he said bluntly.

But Frank wasn't listening and cut him off.

"You don't know this, but Bella wants our partnership re-drafting," he revealed, "so your share of the profits varies according to the amount of time you spend here. I tell her to piss off every time she brings it up. Hell, left on my own, I'd have one hundred percent of £9,000 a year, which is sod all.

"With you as a partner I'm pulling in fifty percent of what... £48,000? I've a private office in a new warehouse now, eight wagons on the road and a full-time secretary. Even a swivel chair."

The words "full-time secretary" gave Bruce the opportunity he was looking for and he wasn't going to miss it.

"Can I throw in one more thing?"

"Sure, fire away."

"How about giving Kathy a better long-term role here? What about making her a third partner?"

Frank stared at him, numbly.

"She's more than just a secretary, isn't she? On those days when you and I are both out, she keeps the place running and running sweetly at that. The drivers all respect her because she's fair with them, and she's a wonder at coping with stupid wholesalers."

Frank nodded in silent agreement.

"Suppose she left tomorrow for another job," Bruce continued. "Sure we could get someone with fancy finger nails, but what if that someone turned out to be as thick as three closet doors?

"By my reckoning Kathy's a fair match for either of us in terms of what she contributes. She makes everything tick. So why not take on a young typist and let Kathy do more valuable jobs?"

"Never though of her like that," Frank mumbled.

He hadn't exploded, so Bruce jumped in once again.

"If we clinch that deal with Roy Palmer at Vandersteen and run 1500 tons a year into Covent Gardens, we'll definitely need another person in the office, well that's my opinion."

The ball was in Frank's court.

"Jesus, Bella'd go up the bloody wall."

"Well it's up to you."

Frank thought about it a while as the cost-benefit register rang in his head, then rang some more. He knew it was a big moment and that he had some serious thinking to do.

"Oh, sod it," he declared at last, holding out his right hand.

"You're right, it's good business… from now on, then, it's the three of us."

***

By the end of the day there was only one job still left to do: load five tons of potatoes into Transit 3 ready for the next morning. Driver George Tyler's first round on a Tuesday was to make drop-offs at the shops in Chantry, a suburb on the outskirts of town, then various village stores on the way to Needham Market.

Seeing as Trunk (their nickname for George) was off having a wisdom tooth out, Bruce decided he would load the van… but fork-lift had broken down. No matter. Manual loading was good exercise and he found it kept his mind uncluttered. By the time he had finished, sweat was pouring off him in torrents and he felt like a kettle on the boil.

Just then Fleur Hainault's Hillman Imp rattled into the yard and stopped. A collector's item, its original light blue body was now a patchwork of mis-matched colours, all connected by weld joints. She hopped out, shutting the driver's door carefully as the glass was prone to fall out of the window.

"Hi," he called, wiping his brow. "Nice to see you."

"I got your note," she said, giving him a warm smile, "and, yes, it was a better idea for me to pop around here, though it's not what the kids wanted."

"Where are they now?" he asked as he mopped up sweat with an old rag which happened to be handy.

"Round at Nellie's."

He shut the van doors.

"Jake's away, seeing some mates of his in Naverne Meadows."

She emerged from behind the Imp. Her dark brown curly hair was gathered into a bunch which cascaded down the left-hand side of her head, bubbling out from beneath a bright red beret which was perched at an angle.

She smiled. "Found the perfect girl yet?" she asked.

"Maybe I found her long ago but didn't know it."

"Easy. We're supposed to be platonic today. Wasn't that your deal?"

"I know," he said, "but Christ, you…."

He swallowed, then moved the conversation on. "Want to come up to Hedley's?"

"To eat?"

"Indeed," he said. "I'm starving."

The office door flew open and Kathy shot out.

"Bruce!" she hollered, waving furiously. "Walter's in trouble! He's in the Dartford Tunnel and the suspension's gone. Full load of Cyprus earlies on. Should he hire another truck or will you go down and off-load him?"

He motioned Fleur towards his pick-up.

"I'm not here, Kathy. You sort him out. Or ring Carrot-nose. He's the buyer so he might go for them himself if you knock £5 a ton off the price. There's no spare wheels here."

"You come and talk to him."

"Sorry. No. I've just left with an important customer. Be back in about two hours."

"Get in the Imp," Fleur said.

"I was going to take the truck."

"Love me, love my car," she said, her lips forming a pouting invitation.

She could always match him for cheek. "Don't all your important customers like to whisk you off in their fancy limousines?" she asked, gingerly opening her door with both hands.

At Hedley's they took a table with a red Formica top near the window. Bruce tucked into a plateful of chips, eggs, sausage and a double-ration of bacon, while Fleur had a tomato omelette.

"Still hungry?"

"Now that you ask... "

Halfway through ice-cream sundaes, they finally got down to business.

"I want to write a book."

"So Dexy said. Why?"

"Because I'm stuck. Having kids is like being in a trap where there's no way out. You saw that and quit pretty soon. You can do that if you're a man, but I can't. I need a way to let off steam or I'll burst. Will you help me?"

"Sure," he said.

They moved outside and settled in the shade of the tangerine-striped canopy. Rush-hour traffic in St Matthew's Street beyond them had ground to a complete stand-still. He was itching to work the conversation round to Areej but held his tongue.

Zell arrived with the coffee.

"Right," she said, settling down. "Here goes."

He listened to her tentative idea for a novel. He tried hard to concentrate but even so, from time to time, his mind ran off on its own, away on a tangent where there were questions like: how come I felt trapped with this woman? and: what exactly was it I feared?

She was about to delve further into more details of the main character when he made a contribution of his own. "Before you start writing," he said. "Consider this: there is something with me, right now, which might make for a second idea if you're after something dangerous and exciting," he said.

"Are you putting me on?"

"Listen, and this is for real, and I wish I wasn't involved in any of it... but got involved in a chase on Saturday night. Some guys in cars were after a runner, a captive who had escaped them. She appeared out of nowhere, right up in front of me and dived into my pick-up. We got away but that's not all. Now we're hiding her until she's recovered because she was badly beaten."

"You're working me!"

"No way. Her name is Areej."

"Show me."

"Alright. Could get you there in fifteen minutes."

"You're on."

She pushed back from the table.

"Ready when you are."

"In that case it's a good thing we didn't come in the pick-up."

"I don't follow?"

But then he remembered Mary's warning. "I'll tell you about it some time," he said vaguely. "Come on, let's go."

***

As they rolled towards Grundisburgh, Fleur decided she'd put her cards on the table first and tell him about the current man in her life... and also her thought about men in general.

"I'm getting to think it always goes wrong with guys and it's either because of me making bad decisions or I'm just some sort of magnet for weirdos," she said.

"Not sure where I fit in all that... perhaps I fit both boxes," he quipped. "But you should know that I've been de-magnetised recently, haven't you heard?"

She looked at him slyly and smiled to herself: maybe they hadn't closed the door all the way after all. She'd like to give it another try but not while he was hooked up with that silly cow Clarissa, and while she had Jake in tow.

It still hurt to think back to their parting as some bitter words were said. She realised he was waiting for her to speak so she started her story.

"Jake arrived three months ago, on an afternoon in March when... "

He braked hard and swerved into Humber Doucy Lane having almost missed the turn. "Sorry, sorry. Go on."

"Right then. Judith from across the way needed a break from her baby, it was teething, so I took him with me when I went to meet Louis and his pal, Edward Hanania, after school. Ysanne caught us up and they all wanted to stop off at Kingston playground before going on home. So I left them there and took the baby round to the Youth Club office to have a word with Maggie."

"Maggie?"

"Maggie Peel."

"Well...," she paused, searching for the best way to say the next bit. "Louis and Edward ganged up on Ysanne who went away in a huff to pick some flowers, leaving the boys to find someone else to pick on... well... despite everything I've told her about strangers, the

warnings, the fool got talking to a stranger, a man claiming to be a teacher who said he knew where she could find a lot of flowers.

"To cut a long story short, Bruce, he took her round behind the Canoe Club then suddenly pushed her to the ground and tried it on, but, as luck would have it, someone saved the day. The guy happened to be walking along the path and heard the scream and came over. It was Jake. He chased the creepy bastard off but couldn't catch him."

"Do they know who it was?"

"No."

"So, after that, Jake just sort of moved in?"

"Something like that," she replied. "I mean, I owed him a lot."

"Sure."

"The trouble is that he's a heroin addict. Hey, don't look at me like that. He is. It's bad. The veins in his arms are done, and his muscles are going the same way. He's had money off his mother and more off me, and I'm done, I can't give him any more, there is no more. I don't know what to do, Bruce. I can't just kick him out!"

It went quiet... there didn't seem to be anything more to say.

Maybe Areej and a new problem might give her different else to think about. They reached Grundisburgh. He tooted at Nicky Parker and her boyfriend.

"We're almost there," he announced. "Get ready for a surprise."

Mary's front door stood open as they drew to a halt, so he walked straight in.

"Hello," he yelled. "Anybody home?"

"Hello!" he called again. "Mary! Hello! It's Bruce with a visitor... come to see the mystery patient."

Still no reply. He looked at Fleur and shrugged his shoulders.

"They must be out in the garden somewhere," he said. "Let's have a quick peep upstairs, then go out and find Mary."

Still calling, they went up. On the wall a painting of Elmer Gozzeck and his wife, who built the place back in 1672. "You go in first...second door on the left," he instructed quietly as they reached the top.

She went ahead and stepped through the heavily panelled door which swung easily on well-oiled hinges.

"If this is a joke, Bruce, it's not very funny," she called.

"What do you mean?"

"There's no one here!"

"What?"

He pushed up close behind her and gazed in horror at the bed: it was empty. They heard a noise downstairs and Bruce put a finger to his lips.

"Who's there?" Mary shouted aggressively from below. "I'm calling the police!"

"Don't worry, Mary, it's Bruce. Your door was open so we came in."

"We?"

"Fleur Hainault," Bruce shouted.

"The door was open?" bellowed Mary, as she started upstairs at quite a pace. "Open?"

"Wide open," Bruce declared.

Mary burst into the bedroom and let out a scream when she saw the empty bed.

"Where is she?"

"That's what we were wondering," Bruce replied.

The two women exchanged brief greetings and then Mary went up to the bed for a closer look.

"Well, she was here when I left an hour ago to collect some more bandages from Woodbridge and I made sure everything was bolted and barred before I left."

"Could she have walked out on her own?"

"No way. I locked the door and she had no key."

"In that case someone came in."

Mary frowned.

"But the door hasn't been forced," she said. "It isn't even marked. But yes, it has to be what happened."

"And they took nothing at all apart from Areej, the one thing wanted."

They went downstairs and put the kettle on, then over mugs of tea, tried to figure out what might have happened.

"I reckon they've got her again."

"But who?" Fleur asked.

"The ones who were chasing her."

"Well how did they find her?"

"Through one of us," Mary said. "One of us has said something to the wrong person."

"Don't look at me," Bruce said defensively before adding: "Perhaps a phone tap then?"

"OK, yes, but not mine," answered Mary, "since they didn't even know Areej was here."

"That can only mean one thing: that someone got to his phone," Fleur said, pointing to Bruce. "Well it's not hard. Everyone knows that old pick-up of his and his phone number is plastered on the side, on both sides in fact."

He nodded. "Here's something else," he added. "I laughed when Dexy first said it, but he reckons someone's been in the house. He always keeps the airing cupboard closed, see, it's an absolute religion with him, but he found it half open one day last week. If it was somebody, what were they after?"

"Don't forget the U-GOT-'EM phone number points you to the warehouse," said Fleur

"What, the office as well?" Bruce said with dismay.

"Yes. Maybe they bugged both home and work."

They all went quiet, thinking.

"So, now what?" Mary asked.

"Ring the police?"

No-one fancied that so, drained of alternative ideas, they agreed to let things rest for twenty four hours.

Perhaps Areej would return on her own.

***

Bruce had a pile of paperwork to sort out on Tuesday morning but whenever he tried to come to grips with it, his mind wandered back to Areej. Where had she gone? Why? Who was she running from?

There was still no answer to the mystery, at least none that he could come up with.

Then he heard a banging and coughing outside that could mean only one thing: the impossible Imp! The roar was louder than the day before, suggesting that the silencer had finally dropped off. Fleur pressed her hands and face against the window, looked in briefly, then headed off round to the door.

"Come on, squire, get your coat and bring some money," she called, as she bounced into the office. "You're buying dinner for three and one's already started."

"What's the rush?"

"You coming or not?" she asked, grabbing his jacket off the wall peg and throwing it at him.

He hunted about for some money.

"Vite, vite," she urged, "there's no time to dilly-dally. Allez, vite."

"Abandon ship," Bruce shouted to Kathy as he rushed to catch up with Fleur. "If I'm not back by half past one, phone the police... and call out the breakdown truck."

Kathy chuckled to herself as they left.

The traffic warden outside Kesgrave High School halted progress, which gave Fleur the chance explained her mission. "I told Nellie about the Pakistani girl, and she's come up with a bright idea."

"For God's sake, Fleur!" he spluttered. "You told Nellie Raby?"

"I tell her everything," Fleur replied. "I trust her."

"Yeah, but... "

Fleur ignored him.

"Well, I told her, so shut up!"

At Woodbridge, the Hillman rasped noisily down the hill and then squeezed into a parking space outside the railway station. They walked briskly up Quay Street and found the Deben Tearoom.

"Long time since I last saw you, young man," said Nellie, smiling as they entered. The old lady kissed him on the cheek as he sat down next to her.

"The answer came to me in bed last night," explained Nellie. "When I lived in Wilderness Lane, during the war this is, there was a woman next door called Sticky Peg. She did abortions for girls who had got GI happy and who couldn't afford a posh London job."

Bruce wondered what this had to do with Areej.

"When Peg was on her little errands of mercy in Hasketon she got to know a lad called Boyza, a poacher. He too was after Yankee dollars, with freshly-caught rabbits and hares - as well as ducks and hens, anything he could get his hands on... "

Bruce made to interrupt but Fleur kicked him under the table.

"Well, now, this Boyza still lives in the same old shack. It's down past Kittle's Corner, just past Debach airfield, and according to Elsie, Boyza's still up to his old tricks. I go to Elsie's to play cribbage so we talk, before you ask."

Nellie stopped and saw that a light had been turned on somewhere inside Bruce's head.

"Debach airfield, did you say Debach airfield?"

"That's what she said," Fleur replied. "What it is to have good hearing, hey, squire?" She leaned across and slapped his cheeks in triumph… harder than he would have liked, so he winced.

"Now," Nellie continued, "I reckon if anyone knows anything about things that go bump in the night, then Boyza's your man. Elsie says if you take him goodies, and a sack of potatoes would do very nicely on that score, he'll talk to you all day."

"Nellie, you're a real brick," he declared.

"Is that a good lead or not?" asked Fleur.

"If I can give you anything back then just ask."

"Right then, tell you what I would like."

"Go on."

"The washer's gone on the cold water tap in the kitchen and these old hands can't squeeze the mole grips like they used to."

"Deal," said Bruce rising to his feet. "Let's be moving, let's get it done."

Nellie looked at Fleur then smiled to herself at the prospect of no more dripping tap.

***

It was heading up for eight o'clock on Wednesday night when Bruce finally got away to see Boyza, a day later than he had hoped. He was back at the wheel of his rather battered pick-up since with Areej now gone missing he was no longer afraid of his choice of vehicle carrying the risk of an attack.

He rattled on through Clopton and then past the entrance to Debach airfield.

The view over to the right looked so innocent: a straight, concrete road leading to some buildings at a distance, some of them new and in use, and others that were old and crumbling, windows blow in and now home for corn-loving pigeons. The old folk still talked about the crowds who came to a Vera Lynn concert here back in the summer of '45 when the war ended.

He spotted it and swung off at the next turn, left down Martin's Lane. There were a few houses but with no sign of life apart from a man in front of a garage, winching the engine out of an Allegro.

Beyond that the road then crumbled away as the tarmac split into cracks and potholes appeared. He pushed on, finding that things got steadily rougher as brambles closed in from each side and scraped across the windows as he passed. Finally, he pulled into a gateway and got out.

He saw the path, threw the sack of barter over his shoulders, and set out. It felt like entering the back of beyond. He pushed on until he found himself in a clearing, facing a ramshackle house with its end wall edging into some open-fronted outbuildings that were all full of junk.

An old lady sat on the steps, working at a peg rug and singing. Her song '*She moves through the Fair*' struck a chord: his grandmother used to sing it too.

Bruce stepped into view and she looked up though it was her three dogs who spotted him first. He noticed that they stayed silent: they didn't bark or move but simply pinned their eyes on him, watching motionless as he came closer.

"They be lurchers, bor," she said, looking up. "Bred to hunt in silence. No point 'em barking and warning they keepers."

"I'm here with questions for Boyza, if he's about, and hoping he might have answers to a puzzle."

"Don't get many visitors out here, us Tukes. You must've runned here for good reason, bor, an not just to mardle."

A man's rough voice came from inside the house:

"Let's be 'aving ee then. Come on in."

Bruce squeezed past the old lady.

The young age of their visitor told the couple they'd have to best speak in the Queen's English rather than rattle on in their normal Suffolk dialect, or at least do their best, otherwise there would be little or no useful conversation.

Boyza was fettling away on the kitchen table. "Know what these be, bor?" he asked.

"Snares?"

"You got it. Snares they be."

He looked at Bruce, and gave a grin.

"Making snares is an art," he said. "Spin these strands together and you gets a fine wire that's strong enough to hold a full-sized rabbit. And here, see, I spins an eyelet into the wire, so the loop comes round and runs back through itself, so it pulls tighter and tighter around a rabbit's neck every time he struggles."

Bruce gazed in fascination.

"Snare pins are cut from ash, while the set-pins come from hazel. No room for mistakes, lad, else they don't fire off when they should and you go hungry."

Bruce nodded. He understand the challenge.

"What brings you here?" Boyza asked.

"It's to do with Debach airfield and something you might have seen. It's about trucks moving in and out at night."

"Sit down, lad, sit down and sample a drop of Moll's ginger beer. Blow your mind, it will."

He filled two glasses, and handed one to Bruce. "Now then, start when you can," he said.

"Ever poach over there at night?"

Boyza grinned.

"Well for mercy, rabbits pour out from that wood over the far side. Great place, it is, for a man and his lurchers."

"Day or night?"

"Me? Just around dawn is best when I 'as young dogs running since they needs a teeny bit of light for to learn the trade. But wi' a good pair of old hounds working, then I'll go on a night-time, when the moon's up."

"So, you work over Debach airfield at all times of night, off and on?"

"Aye."

Bruce buzzed. There was hope.

"Are the old buildings ever lit up at night?"

"No," answered the old poacher, bluntly. "Except for harvest time when they work right round the clock, drying trailer-loads of corn."

"Otherwise there's nothing happening out there at night?"

Boyza nodded.

"You absolutely sure?" Bruce asked, holding up his empty glass.

Boyza read the message and poured out a foaming refill. Bruce smiled, for this well-timed interlude gave the old rascal more time to think and sure enough there was more.

"Sometimes a wagon do deliver during the night, 'bout once a month."

"What kind of wagon?"

"One o' them long, flat trailers with a big square container on it."

"Describe it."

"Well, there never be no lettering on the side. Always plain, always the same size."

"When did you last see it?" urged Bruce.

"Couple of days ago."

"And is it there every month on the same day?"

"Right as rain, always Saturday night. Reckon with Felixstowe having deep water they can unload whenever they want, no matter what the tide's like."

"What makes you think it comes from Felixstowe?"

"One o' me dogs went across once over and got on licking its tyres so I reckons they must have had salt on 'em."

"Does it unload?"

"Don't rightly know. Pulls up to some big doors, they slides open, in she goes and doors shut behind her. After about an hour, she comes out and drives off again. What they do in there I don't know."

Boyza paused and slurped at his clouded beer.

"But I'll tell you one thing," he continued. "Someone's in the building a'forehand, 'cos the doors slide open as the wagon comes running up the road - never has to stop, just drives straight in.

"One time I was rabbiting earlier than usual, before the lorry be coming. Well 'bout two hours before the big one shows up a white van pops along, and nips into the same building. It was a baker's van, you could catch the smell."

Bruce reckoned it was time to kick off himself.

"Right, I'd best tell you why I've come," he said. "It all started because I was out on the airfield last Saturday night with a woman, a lady friend."

Boyza hooted with delight.

36

"Was that you nannocking in the corn near on a pick-up and a prancy sports car?"

"What! You saw us?"

"Well, sir," Boyza said, grinning like a Cheshire cat, "I was heading out towards Playford, thinking as I might light on something tasty at the fish farm and I noticed two vehicles drives out 'cross the runway and stop."

"Anyway, later that night, after Misty left... "

"Misty?"

"Later... well, I must have gone to sleep. Anyway, I woke up to find she'd hived off so there was just me. Just when I'd got on the move, this girl comes running at me hell-for-leather chased by a load of angry blokes. She dived in and we escaped. Drove off. She was bleeding so I took her to... "

"Don't tell me - it was you as mangled those cars up back in the straw piles?"

Bruce nodded. "Right. Me. Yes."

Then moved the story on: "Well then, Mary, a doctor in the village, stitched up the girl's wounds and put her on the road to recovery, but then she just disappeared, kidnapped, taken from a locked house in the middle of a little village, snatched from right from under our noses."

"Well now," exclaimed Boyza.

"I'm looking for help, for ideas of what to do."

"Lor's a mercy. Me? What can ol' Boyza do?"

He poured another round of drinks.

"Listen," Bruce said. "Someone brings a container to Debach from somewhere, possibly Felixstowe docks, hides it out in the middle of nowhere for an hour or so, and then drives it off to some unknown destination. You say there's a pattern, so next time I want to be waiting."

"What you needs is an aeroplane," he declared. "People don't think of looking upwards."

Bruce's eyes lit up.

"A plane... to follow the container. That's great, though you can't catch 'em if you're stuck up there in a plane."

"You'd think of that next. Here now, have another drink."

He did, and another, then burst out laughing, throwing himself back in the chair, and spilling the home-made concoction all over the place.

He was getting well and truly garmelised.

CHAPTER 4

Next day Bruce's throat was like the Sahara Desert and on top of that his head throbbed, his eyes ached and his stomach felt like it was home to no end of runaway animals. A herd of stampeding camels most likely. Or flock. Or caravan. Or no matter. Or whatever. He leaped from his chair with a start and ran from the office, moaning: "I'll be right back."

"I wouldn't count on it," Frank laughed.

Between his trips to the loo, Kathy fed Bruce black coffee and a string of Diacalm tablets. She was sympathetic, in a limited way, while Frank, on the other hand, rather enjoyed seeing his young partner suffer.

"Coming for a pint later?" he chortled, as Bruce returned.

"What are you smirking about?" Bruce growled. "Have you no sympathy for the dying?"

"It's your own bloody fault," Frank replied. "Teach you to go mixing it in the backwoods on full-strength home-brew."

"I'll never ever drink again."

After another twenty minutes he still looked so miserable that even Frank felt sorry for him. "Go home, kid, and sleep it off. Kathy and I can manage."

"Frank's right," Kathy chipped in. "Away you go."

"No," Bruce said, weakly. "I don't want to die alone."

Somehow, he managed to get through the long morning and it was mid-afternoon when Mary rang to remind him of their meeting. The four of them. It was a relief to get out of the office early. Fleur was already at Sadler's Cottage with the other two, Mary and Ivor.

"What happened to you?" Fleur asked. "You look terrible!"

He sat down gingerly and was momentarily puzzled, wondering as to why exactly they were all there. Then he remembered Areej.

"Was Nellie's lead good?" asked Fleur.

"Yes... it was good, very good... and...," he said, holding his head, "... no, it was bad."

"Any bright ideas then?" Mary asked.

Bruce told them all he could remember. "Yes. We got to see that we must find a way to trail the next container," he said, "and there is a way, we can do it from the air."

"What?"

"Boyza's idea, not mine, but a good one."

Mary and Ivor looked at each other. They had been arguing and Ivor had said that he'd had more than enough of the fun and games. They both wanted out now. Well, at least he did.

Fleur's interest, on the other hand, was growing. "Sounds hairy but I'm all for carrying on," she said bluntly. "What do you have in mind?"

"Well," Bruce said, "we mark the container roof and then just... "

"How?"

"No idea as yet."

Fleur continued: "Plus a following vehicle and some way of communicating between plane to car. That the thinking?"

"Yes," said Bruce. "And before it's over, we'll need some muscle... "

"You've forgotten one other thing, squire."

"What's that?"

"Money!"

"Or someone rich and bored who'd help us for free because I'm skint right now."

"Doesn't your dear friend have a runway at Seckford Hall?" asked Fleur, sarcastically.

"My dear friend at Seckford Hall is not my dear friend, I'll have you know," replied Bruce, testily. "In fact she's now very much my ex-friend. But, yes you're right, they do have their own runway there, and a couple of private planes."

She noted the change.

"The hardest part will be marking the roof. I've been puzzling about it: how on earth can you jump on top of a well-guarded container unit, and spray it with red paint."

"Whoa there. Forget that, that's far too ambitious," Mary said, shaking her head.

"What if I jumped on while the wagon was still outside," Bruce suggested rather rashly. "Like from those piles of straw near the... "

"That's dafter still," said Mary.

Fleur snapped her fingers. "Hey!" she said. "That's it."

"What is?" the others chorused.

"Spray."

All eyes turned on her.

"Do you think," Fleur said slowly, still thinking it out, "we could fix up an automatic spray system to paint the roof of the container wagon as it passed below?"

"You mean...?"

"Yeah," said Bruce, nodding at the notion. "Look, if we rigged up a spray boom just above the door, we could mark the container as the lorry came out."

Ivor volunteered to provide a spray paint kit, nozzles, and a long length of cable... Mary stared at him in amazement... this was the husband who less than an hour ago had wanted out.

"Dangerous," Bruce said, "but it might work. It might just work."

"Ice-cream, anyone?"

"Not for Bruce," Fleur said, with a wink at Mary. "I'm offering him something else."

Bruce looked up expectantly.

"Fancy coming for a beer?"

Mary's hand shot to her mouth to cover a snigger.

***

With the plan of action decided, nothing much really happened that was different from normal for the best part of the following month; certainly nothing that would be of any help to Areej.

Days slipped by, and in no time July's greenery ripened into August and to signs of harvest-time… combines out at work setting up clouds of dust and leaving rows of yellow stubble in their wake.

The long suffering Ford Transit 1 died while on the London North Circular in busy rush-hour traffic and had to be towed back to Ipswich. It was traded for a brand new replacement, the bank manager agreeing to shell out a further £14,000 to finance the deal.

Frank persuaded two fish-and-chip shops on the sea front at Felixstowe to switch to U-GOT-'EM, while Kathy discovered that the vegetable buyer for Asda was wanting quotes for moving imported new potatoes during next year's March-May period and she set up a meeting with him.

And so it went on the Boss Hall Industrial Estate…

Mid-summer meant that Bruce was busy on the tennis scene and was away a lot.

He won the British Airways UK championship at Birmingham, beating Ulli Nganga in a gruelling five-setter semi-final, and was then handed the final as a walk-over when Nick Brown pulled out in the third set, injured.

A call came in from the Sarah Gomer camp, asking if he would enter the mixed doubles with her in next year's French Open. However he was already planning to make a similar approach to California-based Monique Javer.

Dexy, busy with a video project for Dire Straits at his nearby Akenham Studio, managed to keep the flat ticking over nicely, which was fortunate as Bruce just seemed to pass through the house like a ship in the night and their flat-mate Bob was away in Brittany with Jean, both of them savouring the excitement of the Tour de France.

But small things still happened: the toaster lost its automatic pop-up function; and the papyrus plant which was inside the front door but was outside of anyone's zone of responsibility, finally died of dehydration.

It was that kind of month.

CHAPTER 5

It was three in the morning and Debach village was sound asleep when two hangar doors quietly slid open. A couple of pugs poked their heads out and scanned from side to side, then the one wearing a black jacket turned and signalled to someone inside, the result being that a Mack tractor unit roared into life.

The big brute came snorting out of the hangar and made off down the tarmac with a fair degree of urgency... but only until a Hillman Imp appeared on the public highway, coming up from the south, which caused the driver of the container lorry hit the brakes and stop well short of the exit. Only when the Imp had safely passed did he engage gear to inch forward, then turn out onto the main road.

The plan had worked perfectly. Fleur's rust-rich skate fish had ensured that the Mack crept under the overhead gantry at the airfield exit at a mere snail's pace.

Ivor's paint-spraying rig was a success and the white top of the container was emblazoned with a distinctive red smear.

But the bigger gamble was still to come: the uncertainty of the route it would take. The best guess was that the lorry would use the A12 to cross towards Cambridge, then join the Al and go north. By then it would be dawn, and at last the red-roof splash would be visible from above.

It swung left and disappeared down the back-road to Coddenham where it roared over a narrow hump-back bridge, emerging onto the faster dual-carriageway beyond.

Cash, the driver, watched his mirror all the while to see if he was being followed until blowing the speedo round to 70 miles an hour, then tugged a CB from its socket and made his final call to the following car: "No sign of life here. You can go back."

"Fine," replied Rory McKnight from the back-up vehicle. "You know what to say if you're stopped: you're carrying Grade 190 Merino wool packed in 500 kilogram bales and you're delivering it to Hinchcliffe's mill. There's fake tickets in the docket if you need them."

"Cheers, Rory. Over and out," called Cash, pushing in a tape so that the sweet voice of Billie Jo Spears materialised and swamped the cab.

Bruce was high in the sky as dawn broke, a few miles south of Alconbury where the A12 joins the A1. With Pip at the controls, the Cessna 172 circled at 1500 feet. He sat beside the young pilot, peering through a set of binoculars but could see little in the early morning dimness.

Uncertainty ruled even though he accepted the reality of the situation which was that they could only cover one 'starting' point and this was it.

"Nothing we can do but wait, old boy," shouted the pilot, noticing his edginess.

"But we might have got it all wrong."

"Look," Pip said. "By starting from Debach it means they deliberately chose to bring the container into the country through Felixstowe. Right? Now then, there is only one route out of Suffolk: you go across to Cambridge. So shush, take it easy."

"I'll try," Bruce replied. "This is all so hairy."

The small plane seemed very flimsy, though he had to agree that the Cessna 172 was ideal for their purposes as they had uninterrupted views through the circle of cockpit windows. It grew lighter and he decided to use the binoculars again.

"Yes," he shouted. "We got 'em! Mega! We're in business. Well done, Pip!"

The pilot dipped the right wing and swung the plane round so he could see for himself, saying: "Want to tell Ossie the news?"

He pointed to the VHF communication set, and Bruce picked up the mouthpiece.

"Ossie, Bruce here... do you read me?"

"Loud and clear, man," replied Ossie, from the van below.

"We've spotted them. They're down there."

"Brill."

"Our red-painted friend has joined the A1. We'll talk you in from here on."

Ossie cruised on, waiting for the next message. It came two minutes later. "We're back. I think we're directly overhead. Are you tailing a coach with two yellow roof-lights?"

"Yeah," he answered.

Bruce switched off, turning to Pip.

"Yeah, that's them."

"Good," Pip said, nodding. "Say, what exactly happened last night?"

"Nothing," Bruce shouted above the din of the four-seater's engine. "Boyza insisted on keeping a look-out most of the night, near the hangar that is, but there was absolutely nothing to report."

"Well, I was standing by all the time, hoping the phone would ring, that you'd call to say all this had started. I had the plane fuelled up, ready to go."

"You must have lights on the airstrip then?"

"Rather," said Pip keenly, showing a lot of teeth. "You can land in the dark whenever you want."

As they talked, Bruce put the binoculars to his eyes at regular intervals. He pin-pointed the moving red dot again and put in another call.

"Ossie, do you read me?"

"Loud and clear."

"All good. Red Duster still flapping about half a mile in front of you."

Pip leaned over: "How are things below?"

"Fine."

"Coffee?"

"Great."

Bruce poured two cups and handed one to Pip, who drank eagerly and noisily, as one endowed with cast iron tubes. Bruce sipped more slowly but still burnt his tongue.

Then, for no reason, Pip's mood changed. "I'm a lost soul," he told his passenger. "I'm wandering, drifting. I should be happy: the eldest son of the

Duke and Duchess of Waveney, living in luxury, just waiting for the day when I'll inherit a golden crust and a cellarful of loot."

Bruce didn't know whether to laugh or cry.

"I just just hang around and play games… this plane is a game and the expensive cars are just a game. There must be something I can do in life."

"Well, you could build me an international tennis centre," Bruce said, in mock seriousness.

"Yes. Splendid. That would suit me fine," agreed Pip, nodding. He was on the pint of getting heavy about what was intended to be just a joke so Bruce changed the subject. "Shame we couldn't have persuaded Boyza to take the empty seat."

"Where is the old rascal?"

"Back at the airfield," Bruce replied. "Said he was going to wait until the coast was clear and have a look around, hopefully find something he could slip under his coat."

Pip laughed but then went silent and concentrated on flying: billowing clouds were building up in front of them.

***

Ossie held a steady position about half a mile behind the container where he was just nicely out of sight. He was at the wheel of U-GOT-'EM's new Transit van. In the back the group of Ipswich muscle was divided, one line sitting along the left-hand-side seating and another bunch facing them on the right.

Peffpeff was cracking his fingers while Laughing Boy and Half-Breed took occasional turns with a grip-squeeze. Regulars at Thurleston Boxing Club, both were fighting fit and the first to sign up to today's anticipated action.

In the back corner, Floyd, otherwise know as The Gripper, sat staring out of the back window and said nothing. He had a curious addiction which was crushing the uncrushable: metal pipes and unopened beer cans, while his most endearing art form, that is if you would believe his mates, was radiator origami.

Three more boxing club regulars were on board: Phantom, Jimmy Lens and Vassaboy, all happy to sign up for this, the chance of an 'up-north' dust-up as Laughing boy had presented it to them. Adding their weight to the group were Jocky and Hal Halford, known to all as 'jobbers' which seemed to be a loose term for almost anything.

"You played them Bruno videos?"

Peffpeff nodded. "He still caught a few from Tyson, mind."

While his men chatted, Ossie drove with reduced attention, forgetting all about the speedo.

"Ease back a bit, old son," Bruce suddenly called over the VHF. "She's lost speed for some reason, and you're closing up on her a bit too much."

"Message received," Ossie replied. "Will do. How're things up there?"

"We can see the Lincolnshire coast way over at Boston," Bruce said. "On the other side there's a grey sprawl that must be Newark. And we can still see you OK."

Bruce switched off the Com Set and turned to Pip run through, in a bit more detail, exactly why they were out on this Sunday adventure.

"Because Lord Jim rang from Rio de Janeiro and put me on to you," Bruce replied, grinning.

"Pardon?"

"Misty's brother. I thought he might enjoy a lark like this, but Gloria something-or-other at Seckford Hall informed me, quite blandly, that he was in Brazil and put the phone down right away. Anyway, She-Glorious must have thought it over and decided to get James to give me a ring. Which he did."

"Ah, I see," said Pip. Then he chuckled: "Yes, dear Gloria. That girl is some p.a. No one really knows where she came from. Probably America. Got some job or other with Lady Seckford and then worked her way up."

"You didn't tell her about the lorry?"

"Who?"

"Gloria."

"You must be joking," Bruce replied. "I said I was hoping the intrepid James could fly me over to Antwerp for a tennis match. Listen, Pip, it's really good of you to help like this... and not even charge."

"No bother, old chum. I'm enjoying every minute of it." Cocking his head and looking

a tad mysterious, he asked: "Tell me, anything you've rumbled as regards the Seckfords, the parents that is?"

Horace Seckford inherited the family fortune after his father, the ninth Duke, was killed in the Second World War. He had done the rounds of Eton and Cambridge, then married Vivienne Holmsby, Deb of the Year.

He thought Pip must also know, him being a regular guest at Lady Seckford's annual Save the World's Children mid-summer ball, that besides Clarissa there were three other Seckford siblings.

"Why do you ask?" he replied in an aimless fashion.

"There's just something that doesn't click," Pip said. "Mother won't have anything to do with Her Ladyship… 'that scheming slut' to use her precise words."

He waited for Pip to continue.

"Mother could be wrong," he said. "After all, it was the rather glamorous Vivienne who pushed her out of the way when she and Horace were rather sweet on each other. Even so, there's more there than meets the eye.

"Mama's heard that the Seckford fortune crashed to zero, Horace took out big loans and that vanished too, the man being as thick as a plank and a total mug. But ten years on and it's all change and they are stinking rich again and that has to be thanks to her ladyship. She's up to something for sure."

"I see Lady Seckford when she comes to Thurleston, but that's rather on and off," said Bruce, continuing the idle theme. "But only at a distance, mind you, as they all come off the courts after their booking finishes at five and we get to go on for the evening training. Gloria fixes it all up, so I'm told, she books a party of them in for a whole day."

Then it was back to business.

The red-marking-on-the-roof target down below took the M18 and found Sheffield, then rolled on to Leeds where it turned left, rattling through various West Riding towns until it reached Huddersfield and left the motorway at long last.

It dropped into busy suburbs. It was time for action.

The Cessna circled like a hawk as the meal continued to move forwards but now at a slower pace.

"Ease back, Ossie," Bruce barked. "He's stuck at some lights. There's been a crash. Stop, Ossie. Stop! You're just 200 yards from him and he's still stuck. You should be able to see him."

The van found a gap in a row of cars parked outside the Lockwood

Laundrette. Traffic lights blipped red to green, then from red to green. Cash had been here before and knew how to play it smart. Biding his time he slowly moved himself right up to the front of the queue and then stopped. Counting down the seconds on green to close on zero, the mighty Mack surged forwards leaving a plume of black smoke soaring behind and the lights on red.

Ossie switched his engine back on and inched out into the queue. He was in fourth place and anonymous. He didn't want to lose the moving mountain as it climbed the short hill in front, but he had to wait. His caution paid off as after only 150 yards, the truck braked and turned down a cobbled side-road.

Floyd came alive.

"What now, Bruce?" Ossie called.

"Looks like the end of the ride, guys. He's dropping down a track that leads to a brewery. Good place to unload... but wait a minute! He's gone past and under a railway viaduct. He's on the far side of it now. There's just a cricket pitch and big old mill. It's a dead end!

Ossie moved forward to the spot where the container had left the main road, then waiting for instructions.

They weren't long in coming.

"He's backed the truck up to the mill and driven it in. They've shut the doors behind them. You've got them cornered now."

"Shall we come?"

"Yes!" shouted Bruce. "No! Wait. Can anybody drive a Drott?"

"Jocky can."

"Drop him off then. Tell him he'll see a Drott – he can use it to push rubble across the lane to block off their escape. Then drive further forward up the road, pull in next to a red phone box and drop four of them off. Send them to go down through the trees to the back of the mill."

More instructions followed which Ossie passed on. This was it. They knew the challenge. Find Areej.

With that the van doors burst open.

It was game-on.

CHAPTER 6

Laughing Boy and Phantom were the first to reach the back door of the ramshackle mill. The roof of the nine-storey building had fallen in, the windows were broken and tall weeds sprouted from blocked gutters.

Jimmy and Vassaboy arrived next and the foursome pushed open a door to find themselves inside on the third floor. It was empty so Jimmy went over to a flight of steps and cautiously went part-way down until he could see that the second floor was equally bare.

Then he lay down and snaked down the upper portion of next flight of stairs and gave another all-clear. Once on the first floor, he pointed to the final part and lizard-crawled to within a few feet of its handrail. He took one look down and then came back.

"Two guards at the bottom," he whispered.

Laughing Boy and Phantom volunteered to go first while the other two followed. Laughing Boy laid one out with a left hook, while Phantom's uppercut took care of the other: he crumbled like a soft coat slipping from its peg on the wall.

The container unit they had followed from Debach stood in the middle of the floor, surrounded by numerous cars, all with their doors wide-open and taking on passengers. Thirty or more of the human cargo had emerged and walked over to where glasses of water and food stood waiting on a make-shift table.

As they fed and talked quietly, priority was being given to the unloading of packages labelled up as being 10 kg packs of Winalot dog biscuits but most likely something else.

Pandemonium broke out when a couple of uninvited ferrets dropped into the rabbit warren. Shafiq Raja, the leader, took control. Barking out orders, he grouped his six best men in a solid line. They advanced towards the bottom of the stairs. Vassaboy and Jimmy bounced off the stairway, doubling the headache that they faced.

The six had the advantage in numbers, and, for a while, held their own but the Thurleston team battled furiously and the attackers steadily gained the upper hand.

Seeing he was in trouble, Shafiq started to clear the deck while his defensive barrier still held and in next to no time the immigrants were all herded into cars, the dope was loaded, car boots slammed shut and the outer doors opened. All eight cars streamed out away from the mill and down the lane.

Back inside, Shafiq marshalled his remaining gang into a battle formation, pulling his best men out of the fray and sending the pack of them tearing off across the cricket pitch while the invaders were temporarily held up by a wall of flailing second-rate feeblies.

The chasers broke through their ranks in next to no time and gave chase up through the wood. Beyond the trees, Ossie, Floyd and Half-Breed stood and waited. Shafiq saw the problem. He turned and pointed, already running towards the viaduct.

"This way," he shouted. "Keep close together."

The viaduct was an 800-yard skyway with a deep drop down to a valley below.

Halfway across and things looked good, but then the exit at the far end was blocked by three new faces. Jocky, Hal and Peffpeff had arrived. Having halted the get-away cars by jamming the Drott across the lane, they were now in the hunt for the bigger fish.

Shafiq saw that he had problems. The priority was for him, as leader, to escape at all costs so he gave the order to attack.

Jocky and Peffpeff were flattened by punches from Shahid and Rehan, the two strongest of the Huddersfield group, and their handiwork created the necessary gap for Shafiq to spring forward, give Hal the knee, then head off down the track.

In front of him, Bruce and Pip appeared but they were no match for the slippery customer who ran straight at Pip, bowling him over on the railway lines, while a stiff blow sent Bruce reeling.

Not much time lost there, but even so it was enough for Floyd to close the gap and take a flying leap which brought Shafiq down. "Who the hell are you?" he asked from down on the floor.

"We're Ipswich, and we want the girl," said Bruce. No reply.

"Where is she? Areej?" he demanded.

Shafiq's mouth stayed shut. Remembering how Atta Qureshi, his boss, had punished informers apart in the past, he knew that nothing these surprise intruders might do would match Atta's fury.

Floyd stepped forward. "Mind if I try?"

"Be my guest."

Putting one of his hands on Shafiq's hair and smoothing it gently, the giant whispered: "My friends call me The Gripper and I'll tell you why. I can hold a 50 kg weight, arm straight, for ninety seconds. So… what's your weight, scumbag?"

No reply.

He grabbed Shafiq's shirt with his right hand and thrust his left hand into the man's groin. Hoisting the hapless victim high in the air, he strode to the side of the viaduct and dangled him over the edge, then removed his hand-hold on the shirt.

As a result, Shafiq was hanging by his balls.

"You know the question, man, now talk!"

The Lockwood railway viaduct is a mighty structure, standing high in the air with a 300-foot drop straight down onto a river and a cricket field.

There was silence.

"Reckons I can manage one minute more," Floyd announced. "One minute."

"Trouble is, see," The Gripper confided to his parcel of weight, "my grip will just fade away, gentle like, and you'll slip free before I's realised you gone. You up shit creek without a paddle, man."

Shafiq screamed with the pain.

"Just talk, and you can come in," Gripper said, encouragingly. "Oops, almost dropped you there."

The man screamed again.

Peffpeff gave a peff, followed by another, making it a double.

Laughing Boy laughed.

"Grip's going now," Gripper hissed.

"Okay," Shafiq groaned. "Okay, you win. Let me up quick!"

Floyd eased the human payload in to the wall, close enough for Shafiq to grab the top, and Bruce stepped in. "Where's Areej?" he demanded.

"I don't know... you gotta believe me. She was locked up in Atta Qureshi's cellar then moved on. That's all I know!"

"You know where she is, man," insisted Gripper.

"No, only Atta knows that."

"Who's this bloody Atta?" Ossie snarled.

"Boss... "

"What?"

"My boss, organises everything here in Yorkshire."

Gripper never eased, still waiting for a nod from Bruce.

"Who does this Atta Qureshi answer to?" Bruce asked. "Those people in the lorry came half way round the world. Who's the big fish?"

Shafiq groaned every time he felt Gripper twitch. Paralysed with fear, he readily spilled the beans. "Atta says the one right at the very top is known as MC or Cloud," he screamed.

"What about the container? Where'd it come from?"

"It came from F-Division."

"F-Division?"

"Felixstowe."

Enough information to call it a day. Gripper hauled Shafiq in as if he was a spent salmon. Once safely landed and unhooked, he crawled away groaning and clutching his bits.

CHAPTER 7

Once they were all back home in Ipswich again, everyone wanted to hear the story, even Frank's beloved Bella was silent as Bruce described the flight in the plane and the scuffle up on the viaduct.

Those two episodes complete, the next one involved the tracking down of Atta Qureshi. Their guide for this was barely fit for sitting on anything, but under duress he guided them across to the posh side of Huddersfield.

Their social call caught Atta by surprise: he was in a huge, heart shaped bath with a friend. "What the fuck's going on?" he shouted, jumping from the water as Half-breed and Peffpeff pinned him to a chair for a chat that brought results.

"We made a switch and then we were rolling again," Bruce told them. "So Raja went into the warm bath with his nuts while we took his boss along with us."

On the journey, Atta had found himself squeezed between Half-breed and The Gripper. He had sat glowering silently as they drove through Bradford city centre, then another two miles out the far side. Ossie thought the place was a real grot hole and said so.

"At last we get to Areej's house," Bruce told them. "The place was packed: in a single terraced house there was a whole heaving community living there. Men presumably off at work, but four women or wives and around a dozen children. There were nippers everywhere… kids' bunks squeezed in four-high in a makeshift corridor."

"Was this Areej woman there?" Bella asked.

"Yes. She was in a mess though, worse than before. The window in the room was boarded up; there was just a mattress on the floor and a bag of all her things on the side. Gripper was the one who found her. He picked her up, along with her stuff, and carried her down the stairs and out to the van. The husband showed up and she spat in his face."

***

At Sadler's Cottage, Mary and Ivor had three big questions: they wanted to know where Areej was "right at this moment"? and was she safe? Plus what about her new injuries?

What they learnt was that she was in safe hands in a house in an un-named place a hundred miles away from Suffolk, that the fictitious names of the people were Billy and Pearl, while the fictitious name of Pearl's friend who was a qualified nurse, was Gladys.

"The less you know the better," reckoned Bruce.

"Agreed on that," said Mary. "Anything more about her life?"

Bruce nodded.

"She was never keen to marry this Majid in the first place, but the parents forced the marriage on her because she was getting on too well with an Australian engineer who was working out there. So they assembled a big dowry and had no difficulty in finding a taker.

"Majid beat her right from the word go. He resented views she'd picked up, women's rights in particular. He reckoned she had none because he owned her."

"Go on."

"A friend of Majid's uncle is foreman in a factory over here that makes blouses. Majid coughs up money and gets shipped in through this pipeline. Joins this uncle in Bradford. Moves in with relatives."

"Then sends for her." Mary anticipated.

"Yes. He left her behind with a baby boy called Uzaif and another on the way, a girl they later called Fal. But the husband sent for Areej to join him.

Just her. Not the children. She knew two other girls who had been shipped over and they had never seen their babies again because the families sold them for adoption to cover the cost of passage.

"She was afraid the same thing would happen to Uzaif and Fal, so she resisted. But she didn't stand a chance."

Mary turned to Ivor: "Those twin girls that Sally and Paul adopted, weren't they from somewhere out East?"

"Thailand," he said. "And that malarkey sure cost them plenty."

"This Islam," said Mary, "it's just a man's club masquerading as a religion. It's not a religion at all, it's excuse for men to own women just like they own dogs!"

Bruce finished off by telling them a bit more about what he'd learnt: that the network they and Areej had become caught up in had a local base in Felixstowe and also that its main-man hereabouts went by the name of Sykehouse.

Having taken all that in, Mary reckoned they all needed to stay well under the radar from now on.

"Let's hope they do nothing," she said. "Just accept their small loss and let things heal."

***

Scene: birthday party at Rollerbury for Louis with Fleur, Ysanne and Bruce making up numbers. They were all in a good mood. Everyone was happy.

"Wish I'd been up there in that plane," said Louis, "I'd have zapped them, and set everyone free."

Ysanne poked her brother in the ribs and told him not to be so stupid.

He slurped noisily through his fat drinking-straw, even though there was no lemonade left in his glass. Bruce fell for it and ordered some more. Ysanne nudged her brother and gave him a secret grin. Louis grinned back and then, still bubbling with enthusiasm, looked seriously at Bruce.

"How did you land, I bet it was on the motorway."

"No. Pip had a little book in his plane called Pooley's Guide. It lists all runways, every single one, so we looked in it and found the one nearest to Huddersfield."

"Then what did you do?" enquired Louis.

"I called Huddersfield Radio... "

"And?"

"A woman answered. Pat Whitham... "

"And?" Louis urged.

"She said it was all right to come in and land. It's their own airfield and as well as the runway they also have a hangar big enough for fourteen planes in it."

"Was one a Concorde?" asked Louis.

"No," Bruce said. "These were all small jobs."

"How small?"

"Really small. One, a tiny one, a man had built all by himself."

Louis turned to his mother. "When I get bigger, I'm going to build an aeroplane," he said.

Right then, as if out of nowhere, five red-faced boys thumped into the side of the skating rink, demanding attention. One of them, his mate Edward Hanania, leaned over the rail, puffing and grinning. "Come on, Louis," he called. Then, skating off, urged the rest of them on with: "Let's go, you guys!"

Louis leapt to his feet and joined the madness.

Ysanne seized the opportunity to get a word in. "He's been nattering ever since Easter to come to Rollerbury for his birthday treat. Keeps pinching my roller skates to practise." Then added, with a pout: "She lets him. It's not fair!"

Fleur chuckled, watching the birthday boy disappear into the whirling madness, typical of Saturday morning sessions for under-13s. Young splots and splats having a glorious time.

"I've asked the DJ to announce his birthday," whispered Ysanne. "Louis doesn't know."

With that, big sister was off, blending into the waving gallery of windmill arms and bee-busy legs.

There had been a hint, but nothing more, that Jake wasn't about, so Bruce laid on a bit of over-the-top charm. "So how about a break in some far-off place that's hot and romantic?" he asked, but with a give-away grin to show it wasn't exactly serious.

Matching him for cheek she came back boldly with: "Or a dirty weekend in Clacton."

That shook him. Was it serious? He didn't dare to ask. He took a deep breath and conceded defeat: she'd beaten him at his own game.

The jolly voice of the Rollerbury disc jockey boomed over the loud-speaker, wishing Louis a happy birthday.

Hours later, picking out clothes and packing his bags ready for the off the following morning, Bruce was still feeling good about everything.

CHAPTER 8

Cyrano Zafros gazed out of the plane's window as he soared up high in space, flying over the Andes and thinking of its mountains of gold.

Money thoughts brought warmth.

On the seat opposite, Ettrick was less comfortable as he felt an unease whenever he was anywhere in, on or over South America, hence he was mighty relieved that their business was done and they were flying back.

Ettrick argued that his fears were confirmed by the very fact that Cyrano's team of body-guards doubled whenever the pair of them ventured into this part of his boss's empire.

Across from him, Cyrano relaxed, satisfied that it had been a most useful trip.

They had called in at three factories, all sizeable ones, involved in manufacturing and packaging well-known products, but fakes, all of them, but good ones: they boasted exactly the same quality and the same ingredients as the originals, namely Chanel No. 5 perfume, Night Nurse medicine and BASF tapes.

Perfect look-alike substitutes with no marketing costs, so producing extremely healthy profits.

"It gets to me, the poverty down there in Antofagasta," said Ettrick, still feeling on edge.

"Don't knock it," replied Cyrano. "The world is far from an even place and the bits that are lawless and unregulated, well the upside for us is that they are loaded with opportunity."

He presented himself as a benefactor rather than as a greedy bastard who made money by walking over others. His factories provided work and dignity, he argued and he had even met economists who agreed.

The door opened for the in-flight service, coffee and a selection of drinks. Both opted for the former.

"I have vision and do many others: most go for the grot end while a few aim for quality and that's where you find me. If our quality matches Chanel's quality then we're more than laughing because we pass all their checks…. and make fat profits, even fatter than theirs."

Ettrick just nodded. He was the one who did the books and knew all too well the cost of the 'security' that they employed to keep things ticking smoothly.

"The drugs business got too dangerous," Cyrano continued. "New York is full of flash arse-holes, Miami's stacked high with pimps and Aspen has more snorters than skiers.

"Five years ago, 90% of my business was drugs but give me another six months, no more than that, and I'll be out of it completely. Off on a new front instead. Pioneering a new space where a whole new world beckons."

He was feeling quite satisfied.

"And no one is going to trip me up," he declared.

Ettrick agreed with that: an employee suspected of running his own little scam had been bundled away and shot only three hours earlier.

At numerous times during the past couple of years Cyrano had told bankers: "I took Ettrick on to keep me spotlessly clean". In that respect he had done well and his salary had climbed from an initial £500,000 to £4 million. The trick, if that is the right word, was to put Zafros's profits into "legitimate reinvestments" that would stand up to financial scrutiny.

The reality, like it or not, was that the man sat across from him was worth billions.

"It beats shooting turkeys when you have eight governments clamouring for me to go ahead with new investments, as they are right now. And you know what? Not a bribe anywhere," said Cyrano with a chuckle. "Only yesterday you yourself heard the man from Mexico pleading with me to build a factory in his country to manufacture hair driers."

Ettrick laughed out loud saying: "Yes... and what brand? We said Clairol 1200 if I recall and that was it: no questions asked, no confirmation needed from Clairol head office back in the States to check us out, more a case of 'just you bring employment and we'll turn a blind eye to your little game'."

Cyrano smiled, then gave a sign for Heidi to go to the door and call Haas in. She did so and then left.

"You did well in Iquique, Haas," said Cyrano. "I think we should see output rise now with Jorge Munoz in charge of production. It had to be Espinosa who was double-crossing us. I will not have fiddlers running petty rackets."

Haas nodded, it was a job well done. Cyrano moved on: "Where are you at with Qureshi?"

Haas reported on his next assignment just as the plane left the jungles of Venezuela and the blue sheen of the Caribbean came into sight as.

They both snoozed after he left until Heidi returned with a tray of food. Ettrick chose the moment to ask a question that had puzzled him since his last visit to the accountants. "Garabed Hovagemian. Can I ask? Why does his name appear in the first document? Where did he go?"

The questions were met with nothing but silence and Ettrick quickly realised that this territory was probably beyond his pay grade.

The silence continued until Cyrano finally threw his head back and gave out a huge sigh.

"Who was Garabed indeed... was, was, was... and why is he named in the formation of TopCo? Well now, it might surprise you to know that he didn't vanish at all, in fact it's the very opposite because you are looking at him right now."

Ettrick's eyes widened.

"Because that's the name I was given at birth. I loved it and was happy with it until I got to school and then discovered that everyone mocked me for it. This was a spot called Snohomish, tucked away up in the top left-hand corner of America. We'd migrated there from the far end of Europe.

"I reckoned I was stuck with it until I discovered it could change. A man called Jim Connally lived three houses up. Irish you'd guess from his name. They give you jobs with that sort of name.

"But surprise, he wasn't Irish, he was Chickasaw tribe and at birth Jim was given the name Two Tall Pines. He had a friend called Moving Cloud at birth who sold me a car."

Ettrick was getting more than he'd bargained for, much more.

"Why not me, I thought when it all clicked," continued Cyrano. "I was mocked in America by ignorant people. They don't know that over a million of us were slaughtered in Europe's first genocide. The Turks want you to forget they did that.

"Dzia, my grandmother, got lucky. She was in a prison camp being starved, then one day a guard picked her out to sell to an Arab Bedouin. But she slit both men's throats and made it to Azerbaijan, then a long trek halfway round the world to end up in Washington State.

Ettrick nodded as he pictured Cyrano being stirred by this piece of his family history, emboldened by it even.

"I wanted a smart, new name so I chose Cyrano. But having a battle name is also good. I use Moving Cloud for that, to link me to something in my past."

Ettrick said nothing, but was thinking: "If your grandmother could slit throats, it's no surprise that you do the same."

He wondered exactly how many people Cyrano had killed in total as his threshold for murder seemed to fall year on year... indeed, the evidence against Espinosa was close to none-existent and that made him wonder if early retirement might be a good idea, a thought he'd never had before.

The conversation over, they settled back in their seats and took another snooze.

Ettrick dreamed of having a battle name.

***

It was four in the morning, all quiet and dark, when Atta Qureshi awoke to find a band of cold steel pressed across his throat. He opened his mouth to speak, but no words came.

"Get up and get dressed. No noise!" As the knife was taken from his throat, he leapt out of bed only to find himself gazing into a Magnum .45.

"What do you want?" he squeaked, spreading his arms, emphasizing his naked helplessness. "Just put your clothes on," one of the two intruders snarled. "You're off to the seaside."

He wasted no time getting dressed. Followed closely by Mr .45, he then went downstairs. Arms above his head as instructed, he staggered forward through the dark. Entering the kitchen, he stumbled. "Take it easy, sunshine," said a new voice, one without sympathy.

The third man was sat at the kitchen table.

"Let's go," said Gronigen, the man with the gun. He was Dutch and did work for Haas. Gronigen had driven off the ferry at Hull, booked in at the Best Western, then gone to the bar to meet the other two, Robert Coney and Digger McShand.

"Where are we going?" Atta asked, breaking a long silence. No reply. He knew he was caged.

It was seven o'clock when they swung into the Humber Bridge car park and stopped.

Gronigen pointed to the steps leading up to the mighty span. "Up there," he ordered. Atta obeyed. "No fancy tricks. Robert will go in front, Digger behind... so be a good lad and someone will meet you all on the other side."

They couldn't afford spectators. He was still trying to decide how to move a family along, when the two kids solved the problem for him by racing each other down the steep steps.

That left no-one apart from a woman walked towards the group of three men from the Lincolnshire side.

"Okay," Coney said to Qureshi. "We stop here."

"Now what?"

"We wait and enjoy the view."

Since there was nothing else he could do, Atta leaned on the side and waited. He little realised that the woman approaching was a professional wrestler.

She was also the surprise assassin. As she passed Atta she suddenly bent down, grabbed him by the ankles and tossed him over the side, comfortably, then continued along the walk-way, as if nothing unusual had happened.

Gronigen drove to a lay-by and waited for her green Alpine to draw up beside him. "Thank you, that was fine," he told the woman at the wheel as she wound down her window. "Here's the other £500 we agreed. Have a safe trip back to Chesterfield."

***

Bruce was only half-dressed when the doorbell rang, but since he was alone in the house he had to answer it, only to find Ogilvie standing there with surprise news. "We are in love!" he blurted, stepping in without waiting to be asked.

Words came pouring out. He couldn't stop.

"Areej is so nice," he gasped with a beaming face. "She talks and smiles and I told her I loved her before I even realised what I was saying. And she does too. Then we even had a kiss. It's fantastic."

Bruce opened the back door and pointed to the garden as it was obvious Ogilvie needed cooling down. They made across to two of four white chairs that circled a plastic table.

It was just a case of sitting and listening.

"Her children are back in Pakistan," Ogilvie said. "She's already married, perhaps you knew that anyway. Although she's here illegally she has a plan. Listen.

"We go back to Rawalpindi and she collects her dead sister's birth certificate. Then we go to Lahore, a city where no-one knows her, and we get married. Next, we find Uzaif and Fal and all fly back here and live in Peterborough as a family, a new family."

Bruce didn't quite know how to respond. The plan was a bit bizarre to say the least. And it had several holes.

Like how could Areej, an illegal immigrant, get back to Pakistan, to start with? Then, how could she get her family to part with her sister's birth certificate? And how could tongue-tied Ogilvie tell endless lies, especially to the sort of officials who would give him a grilling at the passport office?

But he swept such worries away, adding that his step-mother, Sadaf, would help as she had relatives in Pakistan, though he did concede: "The children will be the trickiest part."

Bruce was thinking "what if… what if" to no end of stuff. Like what if the false papers didn't work? or what if some vengeful relative of Majid scuppered his plans? or what if Areej's children weren't there as they had already been sold?

It was all very hairy.

But what the hell. He told himself to keep his mouth shut. Ogilvie had led such a miserable existence until now, so why should anyone clip his wings?

And on top of that, he knew that his management of his own emotions weas far from perfect so who was he to judge anyone else.

"She tried to escape while coming here," Ogilvie said.

Bruce looked up. This was news.

"It was when they were half-way here. They anchored and everyone was sent ashore. The place was a cross between a hospital and a hotel and they were expected as a meal was ready: lamb curry and chapattis and stuff."

"And where was this?"

Ogilvie shook his head.

"They sailed from Karachi and came to Rotterdam. Then the container got switched onto another boat to come across to Felixstowe. The place on the island was about halfway here, she reckons."

Bruce said nothing and let Ogilvie carry on.

"The problem was that it was only a small place so they caught her even though she had a great place to hide. Thankfully all this stuff is in the past now."

Bruce smiled.

"Indeed," he replied even though he knew it was highly questionable… and that was because the name Sykehouse had just popped to mind.

A detail he kept to himself.

CHAPTER 9

After Amsterdam, it was good to be back in Ipswich for the simple reason that the place was home.

The town was bustling on a Monday morning as Bruce swung the wheel and rounded the corner into Boss Hall Lane, his own back yard where three Transit vans stood in a row almost ready to go and with a fourth one already brim full.

The hustle and bustle took his mind off a problem. It was quite a big problem, namely that Fleur was off on the train to London to meet Terry Clackett who he knew was intent on sweet talking her over to Las Vegas for a second time in the space of two months.

Terry and Bruce had been pals for years and it was something of an irony that it was he, Bruce, who in fact introduced the pair of them, but such is life. Before that all started, he had described Terry to her as being a smooth-talking lookalike for the lead singer guy in the 10CC pop group... haircut, clothes, face and all.

Terry was doing rather well. Three years earlier, he'd left plant hire group Ashtead to branch out on his own, then persuaded some of their clients to jump ship. Right now he was pushing bigtime to establish a foothold in America.

What was working a treat was to invite big potential clients to Las

Vegas, then treat them to a big-name show, along with their wives or partners, that being followed by food and drink, all on the house. For that he needed a woman and Fleur had proved perfect on the earlier trip over when the group saw Van Halen on stage.

The choice for the upcoming junket had been narrowed down to Tom Jones… Bruce knew that the prospect of seeing the Welsh heart-throb live would be more than enough to get Fleur back into Terry's clutches.

Kathy spotted him immediately, threw open the office door and came racing across. "Congratulations, you really did it," she yelled, then threw herself at him in exactly the same way his mother had done when he dropped back in at home yesterday. "We're so proud of you!"

Frank was equally overjoyed. "You had the world on a knife-edge, you did," he declared. "I bet you enjoyed yourself when it was all over."

Bruce managed a wide grin at the very thought as memories of the night of celebration in Amsterdam with his big gang of travellers came tumbling back. "Yes, we did our fair share of that."

Nobody did any work as the festivities rolled on all morning, with old friends and complete strangers alike streaming in for a handshake and a word. After an hour of doing bugger-all, Bruce popped round to Debbie's shop in need of more top-up items… three big bottles of fizzy orangeade and one of her biggest cream cakes.

In just a few minutes the cake had vanished as had the orangeade, so it became a regular run up the lane then round the corner and into Debbie's for further supplies, then back to base. Once her stock of orangeade had been drunk dry, they switched to bottles of lemonade and then with that exhausted, to limeade. Finally, the only thing left on the shelf was raspberryade.

"No, no, you can't fob me off with that stuff, it's baboon piss," Bruce muttered.

"What did you just say?" Debbie snapped from close behind him, feigning part-anger.

"Slip of the tongue, Debbie, honest."

"Bruce Saxon," she declared loudly. "You're not too famous to feel the back of my hand."

Bruce ducked.

"I'll take three bottles of the red stuff then," he said. "And thank you Debbie."

Chapter 9

The clock reached two in the afternoon and he realised that he had a formal proposal to make to Kathy and Frank… but it was one that would have to wait until tomorrow as today was carnival time and it was all too good to spoil.

***

Next morning things inched back a little bit closer to normal, though before getting down to work proper, Kathy set about sticking all the loose newspaper clippings into a scrapbook along with photographs and mementos like the plane ticket and the receipt for the hotel room… she noticed that there was quite a surcharge to cover the cost of sorting out all the mess they left in their wake.

After that a semblance of normality was restored as they tackled the post. Bruce waded through his share which included a quote for two new vans; and a couple of overdue cheques, one from Fred's Plaice and the other from Sea Suppers.

Then more again: £680 for repair work on Transit 3 and news that Harry Booth wanted an extra two tons of Maris Piper delivered any time between now and Saturday.

Frank had said next to nothing all morning and was building up a head of steam as he felt that the moment had been reached for the parting of the ways.

"You don't need me to say this Bruce but I will anyway: you're there at last, you've made it so don't feel tied to me or U-GOT-'EM anymore, just go," he said as he rose to his feet, "because there's more in you than potatoes. We've all seen that. It's served its purpose so go, feel free to move on."

Bruce leaned back. He had a proposal to make, the question was, how would it go down.

"Here we are then," he said, indicating for Frank to sit back down and listen.

"I've worked away at tennis for the best part of ten years and now I've had my biggest win, so where am I? Good question. In my first years I averaged less than £2,000 a year from tennis: in other words I lived off potatoes, then, as in right now, I have a good spell and make a stack in just a few months."

71

Both Kathy and Frank were wondering what would be coming next.

"You're right in a way, Frank," he continued. "Hit the trail, go for the big income, tuck away £50,000 a year or even more... the sky's the limit. Dream come true. Sure, I want money, lots of money, but on the other hand I seem to have a problem, which is that I need to show someone I have roots."

"And that someone is... me?" Frank ventured. "Well thank you Bruce."

"No, not you, you great pratt," said Bruce, shaking his head. "That someone is female. I've got to get my house in order and see if I can sort it out though it might be too late already but who knows?"

He left them in limbo as he hived off into the kitchen, coming back with three brews. The one with no milk was handed over to Kathy.

"I'm leaving it until next Wimbledon," he then told them. "The decision, that is. If I can put two more big results behind me, then it's all systems go.

"But as of right now, well I'd like to put last weekend's winnings into the business, that is to say £70,000, the whole shebang. Use it to expand and move to a bigger base, perhaps one of those double units around the corner; have a couple of London-based drivers; take a look at importing, maybe?"

Kathy chipped in with more of the same: "Even frozen foods? What do you say Frank?"

"If you do that then my cash and your cash won't match up any more. I can't come up with £70,000," he said.

They then sat in silence as Frank was thinking and he was finding it difficult to take everything in, particularly the fact that Kathy seemed to be already on board with this sea-change that was being aired.

The proposal on the table was for Bruce to commit the cash investment on a long-term basis to a major expansion of the business and if he did leave for the world professional circuit in nine months then, even so, the money would stay; he'd not pull any of his capital out.

Also, should such a situation happen, then he'd leave the pair of them in charge of everything... the only condition being that Kathy would not only be a board member, but would also have joint control.

That came as a shock: the idea would not go down at all well with Bella.

But recognising that it was the future he said: "Come on, I'm in for that so give me a pen quick and let me sign."

Kathy sat there smiling. The plan had been put to her earlier and she'd said yes to being a director without a moment's hesitation, knowing that just as soon as there was something in writing she'd be off to show it to her daughter and they'd both do a dance of delight.

Frank stood up and headed for the door, saying: "Must be off. Felixstowe beckons."

Bruce stood up but then hovered. He was deliberating over how much, or little, to tell Kathy of the development in his love-life. "Out with it," she said, reading his thoughts. "Sit down. Is it Fleur?"

He nodded as she'd hit the nail right on the head.

He opened up. It was a long conversation.

***

It was a warm evening and muted mumblings from bowls match gently wafted over the hedge and into Thomas Wall's Close, when Bruce relaxed. He was sat on a little brick wall watching polish being applied to a 1968 Ford Zephyr, Dexy's famous rolling hallmark. The car was a gleaming rock-'n-roll heirloom.

He rested the remaining contents of a can of Guinness on his knee and watched: it was vigorous work but his housemate seemed to enjoy it. Finally, Dexy stepped back and made the grand gesture of a bow, first to the car and then to the audience.

"Behold!" he said. "A Ford Zephyr à la Waxbender."

"It's big, brash and buggered," Bruce said.

"Yes, something like that," Dexy agreed. "It's also showy and unique."

He tossed his shammy into the bucket and sat down, leaned against the car's shiny grill, then said: "I think someone's been in the house again."

"You're imagining things," replied Bruce, trying to seem unconcerned.

"Listen, while you, Bob and our Bob's lovely lady Jean were all away I put some plasticene under the carpet on the top two steps before I went out and when I got back there were footprints. Someone had gone up and someone had come back down.

"On top of that, I can tell you that whoever it was wasn't interested in money because the ninety quid I'd left beside the toaster wasn't touched, so whoever it was, or is, I don't like it… and you need to think."

They decided that another two cans of Guinness would help them think better or differently… and it did just that because Dexy had more.

"I also need to tell you that Ysanne phoned twice, very upset, crazy upset," he revealed. "What have you done or said to that brood? Is there something I'm missing? Whatever it was it was quite the trigger because she rang Terry Clackett and told him 'yes' to something he'd been suggesting for weeks."

Bruce winced.

"Plus, there's more if you haven't heard. Jake's skedaddled: gone to live in Amsterdam with his pals."

"About time."

"Past time, as far as you're concerned, old son."

Bruce knew what Dexy meant but didn't say anything.

"You can't get it into your thick skull, can you, that the woman is good for you. Or was."

"You say she left with Terry?"

"Yeah."

Bruce was struggling so Dexy changed the subject.

"What was that letter about that came yesterday morning, the one with Seckford Hall embossed on the back, if it's not being too nosey."

Bruce crushed his empty can. "Ha! Good question, I'm as intrigued as you."

CHAPTER 10

Seckford Hall, its aged brickwork bedecked in ivy, shouted of the Middle Ages. Bruce had visions of Roundheads and Cavaliers as he drove down the long driveway with pea-sized pebbles popping in protest as his tyres pummelled over them.

Still not at all sure why he had been invited to come, his eye caught the line of cars parked in front of the Elizabethan knot garden with its clipped dwarf hedges and small formal beds.

They were all very expensive. A dark blue Jensen, a red open-top Bentley and an Alfa Romeo. A Lancia and a Volvo with foreign plates. Numerous ferry stickers on display, pointing to inward travel from places overseas.

An attendant waved him into a space next to a white Cadillac.

Ushered through a timbered hall, he walked out onto a raised veranda at the back where a crowd of people had already gathered, taking in the view across open fields to the slow-moving River Deben where leisure craft with white sails were sliding silently up and down the central waterway.

With the outdoor reception over, the party moved back inside, grateful to escape from the heat. Lady Seckford was in the hostess's chair, wearing a pink jogging suit by Asconali and a pink, white and silver headband.

Bruce scanned the selection of chilled fruit juices and plumped for a pineapple and mango mix. He recognised one face immediately: it was Jürgen Hingsen, Germany's top decathlon star and the man famously voted as having the most perfect body in the world. Then he tried to recognise some of the others.

Lady Seckford was talking earnestly with the man on her right. It seemed very private and involved a lot of head-nodding. He paid little attention until he distinctly caught the words 'Saxon' and 'results' which made him smile. It told him that they were talking about his recent performances on the tennis court.

But they weren't and wasn't supposed to be listening. Gloria spotted his attempt at eves-dropping and struck up a conversation in a loud voice with athlete sat immediately to his right, so the rest was blotted out.

"We have the results back," said Vivienne to the man. "Ruby here has brought the information."

"He will be a splendid sire to add to our stud," said Dr Stones and reading out from the document in her hand, she reported: "Sperm quality is excellent with 80% showing motility Grade A and the other 20% Grade B. That means they'll virtually all get through the challenge of the cervical mucus barrier and give us fertilised eggs.

"Morphology shows close to zero abnormalities in sperm shape, just a few with pyriform heads but they are under 0.1% of the total and so are totally ignorable."

The man sounded pleased and chipped in with his verdict: "He'll make Class 1 Supersire if we establish that his IQ is up to mark. And that comes next, I take it."

Dr Ruby Stones had further details to offer: "The laboratory verdict is that we can dilute at the top rate, which is to say 20-to-1. There was six millilitres in that first ejaculation and it had 150 million sperm per millilitre."

"So we are laughing all the way to the bank," said Vivienne.

Bruce wanted to burst in. Did they say semen? If they did then he suddenly had a horrible thought.

But he couldn't hear the words properly. Gloria was playing him and they both just knew it.

"Did he produce!" Lady Seckford exclaimed with eagerness, but out of his earshot.

"Just that one night and there is enough for more than four hundred straws already. Can we do it again without suspicion? Yes, I would say so.

"Gloria tipped off his girl-friend and, wonderfully for us, that seems to have thrown a spanner in the works as the two of them are now pretty unsettled. Astra is good for a second set-up. Says that he enjoyed the last extraction process It didn't cost much at all to set up."

Dr Stones left.

Cyrano turned to Vivienne. "I took your advice on the man Atta Qureshi," he told her in a discrete whisper.

She never flinched. "Haas in charge?"

"Yes."

"It just had to be done Cyrano," she said.

A gavel pounded the table, silencing further chitchat. The man who rose to his feet wore a blue jacket draped over a light purple shirt. "I'm Femi Ogunyemi," he announced, "and on behalf of Global Enterprises, I welcome you all."

Saxon, along with Hingsen and several others, all looked at each other with question-mark eyes.

"In case anyone doesn't recognise the line-up, we have six famous names, each from a different sport," Femi said in a loud, clear voice.

"On the right is Jürgen Hingsen, twice world record-holder in the decathlon; then we have Bruce Saxon, the recent tennis match winner over Ivan Lendl in Amsterdam; next to him is the charming Chris Dean, of the Torvill and Dean ice skating partnership.

"Moving further along we have Jahangir Khan, world squash champion; Bernhard Langer, the brilliant golfer from Germany; and at the far end is Ayrton Senna from Brazil, the world's leading Formula One racing driver."

Lady Seckford stood up and led the applause.

"The objective today," continued Femi, "is to establish an IQ figure for each of you. Don't worry, this is not a comparative test, rather a basic fact-finding mission.

"Global has been working on a concept project, an idea for a future television series. You might call it a Superman competition for the brain. We believe that there is the potential for profits of many, many millions. During the session today, we will show you how we propose to share that between you all."

Bruce whistled at the sums being thrown about: a basic fee of £2,000 for coming today with a further £2,000 bonus per test for anyone who decides to stay on and take some or all of the tests. Five tests in all.

"In other words it is possible, if you decide to join in, for each of you to earn a total of £12,000 before you leave," said Femi. "I will now hand you over to Professor Volkov who will explain today's routine in greater detail."

Volkov rambled on but Bruce switched off and drooled over the £12,000 fee, wondering what Global Enterprises had in mind with their test. He noticed that not one of the six contestants got up and walked away.

While the celebrity brainboxes all had their heads down, Vivienne chatted to Cyrano as she escorted him away, down the pathway and towards his private plane. It had been re-fuelled after its flight in from Dusseldorf and was ready for take off.

"The six in there would all be welcome additions to the SuperSires catalogue," said Cyrano. "Five have been on our 'desired names' list for two years and you were right to see the potential in that new guy Saxon."

Vivienne smiled. "After his win in Amsterdam, Jackie had sixty enquiries for him in less than an hour, and two hundred within the week."

"Wow!"

She continued: "I thought it wonderful the way all six of them inside were totally duped by the bullshit that Femi gave them about a Superman series when all we're after is a credible IQ figure. It's the second of the five tests: the other four are just camouflage… complete flannel.

"The statistics show that buyers, the vast majority of them, are willing to pay more for sires if we can offer an intelligence figure and pay still more again if that figure is top-of-the-range. For myself, I think it's pure hokum, but hey, if the Wechsler Scale has traction, has strong credibility and makes us money, then junkets like this with Femi calling it, are winners all the way."

Cyrano's thinking went back a step and he asked how many of today's six stars would be in their next catalogue. She told him that he should see two of them as certs because there was semen already in the pipeline, while third was being targeted in a sting operation and was to feature in Astra's next under-the-sheets offensive.

End of questions.

They were done.

In a blink he was on board and away.

CHAPTER 11

Back on the Boss Hall Industrial Estate it was all go as this was moving day.

"When I started delivering potatoes twenty years ago, I never dreamed of anything like this," said Frank, beaming with pride. "All I ever wanted then was to own a brand-new van, all shiny and straight out from the factory."

"Sad to leave the old place behind, then?" Kathy asked.

"In some ways, yes," Frank replied. "After all, we've spent a lot of time here, you and I."

"I remember you ramming a potato up the exhaust pipe of that miserable rating officer's car while I kept him talking," Kathy said with a laugh, "and when he started it up, the spud shot across the road and broke the paint shop's glass door across the road."

A heavily laden van trundled out through the gate and as he came alongside, the driver wound down his window. "That's it, then," he shouted. "Anyone want a lift?"

"No, thanks," she answered. "I'd like to walk round."

The big day was set for Friday: the formal opening of their new headquarters.

"It's smashing!" replied Kathy. "I'm getting a car - a Metro, a light blue one. Fancy me having a car. So what about you, Frank? You planning anything rash?"

"I think I'll just float gently into town straight from here, get a bite at Hedley's, move on to the Great White Horse and drink the night away. Want to come as well?"

"To the cafe or the Great White Horse?"

"Well, either," answered Frank suddenly feeling rather giddy. "Or both!"

Kathy hesitated a moment, then answered Frank's impromptu invitation.

"Right, you're on - after all, someone's got to look after you."

They turned the corner. Pointing forwards, he said: "Look, isn't that fantastic?"

"Our new home," said Kathy, excitedly. "Our very own. And a new name to go with it *Hotpolarity*. I'm not quite sure I like that yet."

Frank wasn't quite on-board with the name either but he took a deep breath and thought of the positives: "New lorries... new main depot... leases in motion for two smaller units... we're in the big league at last."

Next news they were having a hug.

Lor, whatever next.

***

Dexy cycled from Grundisburgh across to the next village every Thursday night to play badminton, his only weekly exercise apart from polishing the car.

It was three miles along a narrow lane with high earth banks that rose on each side and then folded back over, pouring their overspill out into the farmland, made up of huge corn fields. A plantation of poplars announced the arrival in Great Bealings.

Its village hall was sunk into a sandy hillside and had just enough room for one badminton court so that on busy nights, the numbers were such that players got one game on and then stuck their names at the bottom of the waiting list. They were all friends and the next chance for action would come soon enough.

Dexy turned up spasmodically; his badminton was poor but his banter was good. Fleur made it on a fairly consistent, but intermittent basis, while

Bruce's father was a stalwart, except that tonight, surprisingly, he was missing.

Joe was supposed to be reporting back on his progress in acquiring photocopies of certain documents from the office at Felixstowe docks, discretely acquired, hopefully, while tending to its wonderfully maintained Xerox machine.

No news meant that this was still work in progress.

Fleur finished a game and sat down.

Dexy nodded and told her: "Joe's plan was to go down there late Friday morning, when someone called Paula's sure to be alone in the office. He said he'd tell her the whole truth. Reckons she'll help."

Fleur snapped her fingers, pointed to her bag, and said: "I've got something for you to take back, but be discrete. It's for Bruce. Not from me, from Ysanne. She bought a blank tape out of her savings, then recorded some Planxty music onto it."

"You could come and hand it over yourself? Why me?"

That met with no reply and Dexy suspected that he already had the answer to that. Did it suggest that some unravelling was in progress here? If so he'd take the tape even though he wasn't a fan of Irish music.

Fleur bit her tongue. She wanted to tell someone all the details of what was happening to her but couldn't say the words so she changed the subject. "I bet you're happy about this new company… Hotpolarity. What a name. Did that come from you? Because it has Dexy written all over it."

"You are way, way too insightful."

"Well now," Fleur told him. "You might be surprised to know that I'm coming to the big do, to the opening ceremony, but don't let on, promise you'll not tell Bruce that I'm coming, I want it to be a surprise."

"Well OK. Deal."

But then that something else that she had to tell someone just burst out. "Listen, but it's got to be a secret, OK?"

"Right, go on."

"Promise?"

"Promise."

"Well, I've put some money into the new company," Fleur said. "Thirty thousand pounds. You're not to breathe a word of this to anyone, mind, especially Bruce. Let's just see how things go on Friday at the opening.

"But for you to know and no-one else, mind, they granted Kathy her shares for free, but she has no money, so since she needs money right now she sold them to me. I bought them, every one. And at face value, no more and no less."

Surprise. Surprise. He sure hadn't seen that one coming.

"Thirty thousand!" he gasped. "Jesus! Who is this? Raising two small kids all on her own. Penniless and abandoned. Now this!"

"I know," signed Fleur. "But penniless breeds desperation and desperation can bring results."

"So, how come the big change?" he asked in a quiet voice and leaning in.

But she shook her head and made no reply, after all she'd only had the solicitor's letter three days ago and no one else knew yet.

Players bounced back from the main hall so that would do for now.

"Dexy, don't you even dare so much as tell Bruce that you've even seen me here tonight.

"I want him to stew a bit longer, think I'm away in Las Vegas for the week. So give me that tape back, on reflection, or keep it in your bag until Saturday morning… no passing it on before Friday's do," she said.

Four names were read from the top of the board and the two of them found themselves both back on court but on opposite sides of the net as it was Jane who had made the pick: she thought Dexy was better as a doubles partner because Tom was inclined to fart when he lunged for low shots at the net to keep them off the floor and Fleur was welcome to savour that.

By the last game of the night, the letter was still on her mind and she told Dexy the news after all.

On his way back to Grundisburgh he wondered if it was full moon.

CHAPTER 12

In Areej's case there was no moon at all as things got darker and darker. She was living in turmoil and desperately in need of good news.

She had written to Rabab, her friend back in Pakistan, and after a long wait, she had received word back that Uzaif and Fal were missing. In a second letter came news gathered from Areej's grandmother informing that the children were in Hyderabad, at the home of their uncle Rizwan.

The letters were not addressed to where she was living, a house in Isham Road, Peterborough but sent anonymously to PO Box 450, Leicester, and picked out by Max. His mother also lived in Isham Road and was a neighbour but Max had been promoted to the main Leicester Post Office. He was happy to be given the hush-hush task of delivering incoming post and sending fresh replies back.

Follow-up news, in a third letter, was that the children were no longer with their uncle. Rabab hadn't been able to get Areej's grandmother to say another word about them. She had totally clammed up so she had contacted Dennis, their Australian friend and he agreed to pay the uncle a surprise visit.

Dennis reported that the uncle opened his door and listened and in an attempt to prove his words invited Dennis in to see for himself. Dennis walked round quite freely and found that there was nothing, no trace of children at all: no cot, no clothes, no toys, no nothing.

A fortnight later a fourth delivery arrived by way of Max and Areej opened his large envelope, then recognized Rabab's familiar handwriting on the smaller one inside that. But this time there was more as there was an additional note which was brief and to the point.

IF YOU WANT TO KNOW MORE ABOUT YOUR CHILDREN PHONE 071-772-9831

"Ogilvie!" she screamed. "They've been sold and I'll never see them again. This is all Majid's doing, I know it." Then she broke down and cried, her whole body shaking.

He helped her through into the living room, where she collapsed on the sofa. He sat down beside her, holding her as she sobbed. Eventually she said she wanted to go for a walk with him to clear her thoughts.

By the time they'd walked a while and then found somewhere to sit near the river Nene, she was much better and she confided: "I have something that will get my children back."

"What do you mean?" he asked.

"I was in panic," she replied, but answering his question, "but now I see clearly. They have sold them. My father and his brother Rizwan would not miss the chance of money."

Areej sat and thought for a couple of minutes, then became quite resolute and tapped Ogilvie's hand saying: "They are alive, even though I don't know where. But they can't frighten me now. They don't know my secret, do they? Not the ones we've met so far.

"But for the man who sent that note with that phone number, then he must know I have something that they need get back. He knows he has to make a deal."

"Can you tell me what it is?"

"No," she said.

Ogilvie blinked as he stroked her thumb.

"I know things I shouldn't," she volunteered. "Dangerous things and they are all written down. Things I've never told anyone about, not even you, because then you'd be in danger too."

"What?" he asked.

She shook her head, then changed the subject. "Look, it's after one already. I'm better now, really I am, so you go in to work from here and I'll walk back home."

They kissed, not knowing it was their last.

Four hours later, when he got home for tea, Ogilvie found the house empty.

He went through the rooms calling. "Areej!" No answer. "Areej!" Silence again. He hurried through to the kitchen. "Anybody home?" He opened the oven and saw a neat array of food: the tea was all in perfect order but where was Areej?

He returned to the dining room and, taking a closer look, he noticed that the table was only set for two... it should have been three as Sadaf, his step-mother, was due in from work in fifteen minutes. It was only after he had stared hard at the table for a while longer that he noticed the note, slipped in-between the salt and pepper pots. He made a grab for it and tore it open.

Ogilvie,

I have gone to London and will be back tomorrow or Friday. Don't worry, I'll ring you at work tomorrow afternoon to let you know what has happened.

Please do not try to follow!

I don't know where Uzaif and Fal are yet, but they now know what I will do to find them. They know I have information and pictures and things.

I do love you, Ogilvie, and we will see the owls again.

Areej

He shot upstairs and dived headlong under the bed where his worst fears were confirmed: their one-and-only case, a battered grey one with one catch that didn't work properly, was missing.

Flinging open the wardrobe doors he checked Areej's clothing, but then realised that he didn't know how much stuff she had anyway, so that proved nothing. In the bathroom, however, he discovered that her toothbrush, hair brush and clips were away. And his step-mother's blue, flowery toilet bag had also gone.

Hearing a noise at the garden gate, he rushed back downstairs and, sensing movement outside the door, he flung it open only to see Sadaf standing there looking for her keys.

"Areej's gone!" he shouted. "This is not good."

***

Areej spent the night in a cheap hotel near King's Cross in a fourth-floor room which had cracked window panes, the tap dripped and the pipe under the sink gurgled every time the man in the next room flushed his loo. Despite all this, she'd paid for two nights in case she had to stay a day longer.

She sat up late into the night writing her insurance policy against disaster should her plans collapse. It was very quiet, none of the rooms having televisions, so she worked without distraction until, finished at last, she addressed an envelope, sealed the document inside and placed it on the dresser where she wouldn't miss it the next day. It was after twelve when she finally turned off the light.

Inside the envelope was a letter together with the black book she'd left behind on that night when she escaped from Debach airfield. But her friend Mizha saved the day as she spotted her Areej's suitcase when they unloaded everyone later up in Bradford and claimed it as her own, then passed it back when her friend was frog-marched back a few days later.

By the time she was freed and driven away from Yorkshire by the men who brought her back to Peterborough, the valuable black book was hidden among her clothes, down at the bottom of her suitcase.

It had been slipped into her hand during the journey from Pakistan, at the mid-way point of the long sea transit across the world, when everyone came onshore to a small island in the Red Sea to recover a little.

There was a building with lots and lots of empty rooms where they all slept and washed and ate before moving back on-board two days later. Not everyone enjoyed full freedom during that time, however, as the group of ten women who were each being forced to come to England against their will, were kept under guard, all of them sleeping together in a large, single room.

Quite early on, though, they all managed to escape only to be tracked down, one by one, until Areej was the only one evading capture.

A young woman in a white coat who had helped her find a good hiding spot, listened to Areej's story and decided to help. She took her to a further room and went across to a desk with many drawers, then got out a key and unlocked the one with no markings. She came back with something in her hand which she handed it over.

"You deserve better," she said. "Here, take this but keep it well hidden, I think it's worth a fortune. My boss Ruby guards it with her life. She keeps it in a locked place and never lets anyone see it.

"I saw her tuck the key away one day and I've already had a peep. The man who sometimes comes, the top man, says it's their deepest secret and must be guarded at all costs."

Leaving the hotel in King's Cross next morning, with the letter and black book already popped into the post as her insurance cover, Areej felt relieved and with oceans of time to spare, she walked to Piccadilly Circus in one direction and then back the opposite way as far as the oval building with the BBC branding.

With the walk over, she entered Garfunkel's restaurant. She was still early. She had bought a paper but didn't read it, it was just something to hold in her hands while she sat and waited.

At 10 o'clock on the dot a car pulled up outside and Areej watched the occupant get out. He came in and looked round, then sat down at a distant table, looking across at her. It was only when he gave a nod in her general direction that she realised that someone else had sat down next to her.

He was cleaner and dressed in a suit. "Are you Areej?" he asked.

"Yes," she replied firmly.

"I am Wraxall. You keep writing to Pakistan for news about your two children."

"How do you know that?"

"It doesn't matter."

He ordered two coffees without so much as asking Areej if she wanted one, then handed the waiter a tenner, telling him to keep the change.

"I want Uzaif and Fal," she demanded. "Don't tell me they are dead because I won't believe you."

The man looked at her. His eyes were cold when he spoke: "They are gone. Forget them. Your sweet life in Peterborough will come to a sudden end if you don't do what we tell you. So listen…"

"My life in Peterborough?" she said, cutting in.

"Yes, in Isham Road with Ogilvie."

"But I live in Manchester," she protested, bluffing.

Wraxall sneered in disdain, then took a long sip of coffee. "Don't waste my time; consider yourself lucky to be alive."

She stood her ground saying: "And I have something the world would like to see. I'm here to trade it for Uzaif and Fal."

"It is too late," Wraxall said, still nonchalant and unruffled. "The girl is in Chicago. A couple who have their own bakery business bought her. They call her Pauline. The boy is in Aspen, with some very rich people who call him John."

Areej could take no more.

"Get them back," she screamed.

Everyone in the restaurant stopped talking and turned round to see the cause of this commotion, but Areej continued, oblivious to the stares: "I want them here, or I'll bring you down."

Wraxall didn't like the attention and grabbed her wrist painfully.

"Now listen, woman," he hissed. "Listen this one last time. Yes, a book has gone missing, a very important one. And my boss doesn't like it, not one little bit."

He paused to let his words sink in and then, loosening his grip, he continued.

"The question is have you got the lost book. It is very valuable. It is so valuable that he is offering £250,000 to whoever who finds it for him and I want that money, so I have searched every house known to you… your little nest in Peterborough, the house near Ipswich where Bruce Saxon lives, his depot, the vans, the lot.

"And you know what? There's nothing, absolutely nothing. So that means that so you are no threat because the truth is you don't have the book."

Areej wasn't done and free from Wraxall's grip, she dipped into her bag and pulled out a note with the words she had copied from the first page of a book.

Chapter 12

Dr Ruby Stones
Confidential – not to be shared
CD Project

Wraxall took a hold, turning it slowly in his hand. It met with his brief. He knew immediately that she had what he was hunting for.

Areej noticed a change. "You believe me now?" she asked.

"Where did you get this?" he asked, trying hard to conceal his curiosity. It was now Areej's turn to appear indifferent.

"The book then. You have it?"

"Yes."

Wraxall's face brightened.

"You are in business then," he conceded. "But where is the book? Is it with you?"

"No, it is not here," she replied.

"So what do we do next?" he asked.

"I want my children," replied Areej "For that you can have the book and keep your £250,000 reward."

"Right," he said. There was no pause, no hesitation and Areej sighed with relief.

"You have a deal. You will get your children back but it will take a week or two to get them because it's no easy job snatching children in America."

Areej said nothing.

"I will telephone the house where you are living, you will come to London again, we will meet here and you will only hand over the book when I produce your two children."

Wraxall opened his briefcase and lifted out a red radio phone, then spoke into it. "She has the CD Project data so we have a deal. She gets her two children back and we get the book."

Returning the Vodafone to the briefcase, he announced: "I am leaving, if that is all our business done for today. Before you go back for your train, however, you should know that we have photographs of your children in America, proof that they are alive and well."

"What? You've got photographs?" yelled Areej eagerly, "I want to see them!"

"If you wish. The other car will take you to the studio then."

Wraxall left Garfunkel's and stepped into a dark green car which slipped away effortlessly.

Areej followed, full of excitement at the prospect of what she would discover at the studio, and eagerly accepted a lift with Haas.

***

All three cars rolled into the Wildlife Safari Park at Petersfield as a group, the first driver having paid for the lot. The woman inside the ticket office was happy as groups made for less work.

None of them warranted a second glance and anyway it was almost closing time and she was tired.

They had specially chosen a time of day when the number of visitors would be down to a bare minimum in order to ensure as much privacy as possible.

Pon, driving the leading vehicle, was to go ahead to the far end of the first zone, the one which held lions and little else, and send a message back once he got there. The second car would then move off. If the third car remained motionless, blocking off any further progress from the ticket office, then the middle car would soon be out of sight and no-one would see it veer off and become lost from sight in the trees.

Baz, the driver of the third vehicle raised his car's bonnet, then strolled back to the car behind. "Sorry, I've flooded the carburetor," he explained apologetically. "You need to get past. I'll ask the gatekeeper to come out and help push us out of the way to make room."

"Oh, we're in no hurry," came the answer, "I've done the same thing more than once myself."

Up ahead, the middle car of the trio headed towards a pride of lions, sheltering from the heat under a tree. A man in the back wound his window down and threw out a rabbit and a quick-witted young male lion ran and grabbed it, swallowing it whole before the rest pounced.

Tony offered them a second mouthful which was enough to get all the lions on high alert. The car speeded up and the hunger-aroused pack galloped after them. There was a commotion in the back of the car where two men and their female prisoner sat all squeezed in. She had been gagged and bound up until then, but she was now cut loose and pushed out of the open door.

The car roared off with the third car coming up hard on its heels. Next minute they were gone.

Back at the ticket office, the woman at the desk realised things were on the move again because there was now a minibus standing outside and the driver was asking for nineteen tickets. She set to work to calculate the price.

***

The phone on the desk in the hallway rang and Ogilvie sprang to his feet as Areej was long overdue. He had already decided that if there was no word from her by ten o'clock, he'd go to the police and tell them everything, difficult as that might be. The clock on the wall said five minutes to ten.

"Hello," he said, hopefully.

"I need to speak to Sadaf. Is she there?"

Ogilvie handed over the phone.

"Yes," she answered, "This is Sadaf."

"If the person who handed you the phone was Ogilvie, tell him to sit down right now."

Sadaf repeated the man's words and Ogilvie sat down.

"Were you watching the news tonight?"

"Yes."

"The bit about someone being killed by lions in a safari park?"

"Yes," said Sadaf, "we saw that."

"That was your girl."

The phone went dead.

All they had left were Areej's bunch of everlasting flowers.

***

"Sir Michael, I'd like to introduce you to Lorraine Chase," said Frank who found himself relishing his role at the formal opening, of being dressed up all smart and playing the perfect host.

"Aha, the lovely lady herself," said the media heavyweight with much money and a grand mansion standing directly across the Thames from Ham Polo Club. He kissed the proffered hand. "So pleased to meet you, my dear."

She smiled for the bevy of cameramen who were gathered in a circle then stepped away smartly before the renowned groper got his hands-on act in play.

It was the big day for Hotpolarity and everyone was in high spirits. The new office was decked out with balloons and fancy trimmings and lights and shiny things. Winnie and the new lad Steven were busily letting off indoor fireworks and showering streamers on everyone.

The crowd was a mix of drivers, workers, bosses and council dignitaries. The press were out in force, chasing quotes and setting up groups for happy snaps. Frank, Kathy and Bruce saw to it that people kept circulating.

Waitresses fluttered here and there, first with fizzing champagne in big bullet-shaped glasses, then with trays of both red and white plonk. A chef topped up plates, carving slices of beef, pork and turkey on demand.

The editor of Travel and Food agreed with the general sentiment that the TV star's speech had been great, packed as it was with witty anecdotes and colourful Cockney slang.

Then, with the formalities over, people started to settle into clumps, with like talking to like, which allowed the three Hotpolarity directors to step back: they'd done their task and could now mingle and relax.

The hubbub went on and on with no-one seeming to be the least bit interested in leaving for home. As a result, waiters continued to dip into a veritable bucket-like bowl of fresh strawberries and waitresses were kept busy topping up glasses.

"A success," Bruce declared. "Wouldn't you say?"

"Yes indeed," replied both Frank and Kathy together.

All three raised their glasses and clinked them together by way of a toast.

They had done it.

Bruce was glad to find that the pair of them were happy with the way the old company had evolved and so he was left with his final task of the day which was to track down Fleur and hopefully talk. The fact that she was here at all and not in America with Terry was a puzzle as he'd not expected her to surface today of all days.

But here she was and out on the dance-floor with the band in full swing. Just the place to find out, he though. "I thought I saw Fleur earlier," he said, trying to sound casual.

"Yeah," Frank offered. "She's around somewhere."

Chapter 12

"Oh, Bruce!" Kathy cried, grabbing his elbow and pointing. "Look! There she is!"

"Where?" asked Bruce.

"There."

Bruce found a waitress, relieved her of a bottle of bubbly, and made off in a bee-line for the dance-floor.

"I always thought he had it all," said Frank.

"And now?"

"Now I think he's the one with problems."

Kathy smiled. "Does that mean you're happy, Frank?" she asked.

"It does."

Squeezing his way through the guests while absorbing bumps and slaps on his back, he got closer to Fleur who was talking with someone he had met earlier. She was a senior purchasing officer for P+O European Ferries called Teri Bolt. Realising that their verbals were heavy stuff, he ducked out and waited a while longer.

Teri was having a problem with her marriage and her in-and-out-of-work husband and she was pleased to have found someone she could confide in.

As a result, she was telling it all.

The husband was pushing her to get pregnant and start a family as he badly wanted a child. Teri argued that they couldn't afford for her to turn down the offer of a better job, even though she wanted an offspring just as much as he did. The offer had come from British Airways where the pay would be a jump to £26,000-a-year plus there would be a car. Moving to Staines wasn't the problem - motherhood was.

"I let on about all this to one of the girls at aerobics," explained Teri, "and, blow me, five days later we got this phone call out of the blue from a woman who wanted us to think about buying a baby."

"And did you?" asked Fleur.

"Pete and I had this long conversation and we decided we'd like to know more, so we asked her round. She asked us precisely why we wanted a child and was either of us sterile. Then she asked what we knew about artificial insemination and embryo transfer."

"Heavens, what is this? It sounds more like science fiction," said Fleur.

"That's exactly what we thought. But no, it did seem to be a way

93

forward: the full package they offer amounts to someone else having my baby inside them for nine months while I keep a career and a job."

"No way!"

"She said four couples in Colchester alone have already had babies this way: two were infertile and two were like me - busy."

"Did you get as far as asking a price?"

"Yes," replied Teri.

At that moment the conversation turned on its head with Teri asking Fleur: "Have you any children?"

For some reason Fleur felt rather guilty. "Yes," she mumbled, "Two: a girl, Ysanne, twelve and a boy Louis, who's nine, well almost ten."

"Good grief," Teri stared incredulously, you can't be more than twenty four or five."

"I'm twenty-eight," Fleur said. "Ysanne was born five months after my sixteenth birthday, if you see what I mean. Seems like my problem's the exact opposite of yours: I got the kids, but no man. Well, not the one I really want. Or wanted.

"It's a juggling act at the moment and there's two of them in the frame: one's rich and getting richer but wants us to move out to America and settle there. He's not the one I really want in my heart though. If I'm honest, I've been using him to try to catch the other, or get him to sort his mixed-up views on… well on everything."

"And who's the other guy then?" asked Teri.

"This one," replied Fleur as she stretched out a hand to take a glass from the figure who had squeezed in next to her and nodding her head at him to indicate that she meant Bruce.

"Hello again," he said, looking at Teri.

"Hi", he said to Fleur.

Teri was wearing a two-piece suit, blue high-heeled shoes, a white blouse and a thin silver-black bootlace tie made from velvet. She looked smart and professional.

"We were having a heart-to-heart about men and the problems they cause," said Fleur, "and we'd just got to you."

"Aah, yes... this I must hear," Bruce declared. "Fire away."

"I was into athletics at school and twice I was the under-15 girls' 400 metres champion for all Suffolk, no less," said Fleur. "Bruce did hurdles, but only so he could come and watch me. My legs, see. He says they drove him wild.

"But then bang, bang, it's winter and there's no running and I don't see him and suddenly here I am pregnant by this other lad. By the time I was eighteen I'd had Louis, my second, as well and the father was gone: it was good riddance.

"That was when Bruce sort of moved in. We were alright until I mentioned marriage. Then, before I knew it, he'd moved out."

Bruce gave a nervous smile.

"I couldn't handle it," he admitted. "I really did like being with her, especially her lovely legs, but being responsible for somebody with two young kids when you've not even a steady job, when you're wanting to go out there and risk all on an uncertain voyage in your own life. I couldn't cope."

He looked at the floor, then at Fleur. "Now, I feel like I let her down."

"No," interrupted Fleur. "It wouldn't have worked: you'd soon have hated me for holding you back."

Just then Harvey and the Wallbangers announced that this was their last number. It was a waltz. Bruce looked at Fleur and cautiously took her hand. He hardly dared ask if she wanted to dance. Teri read the moment and took their two glasses and with a forgiving smile, Fleur stepped into his arms.

Bruce pressed her shoulders lightly and she came closer. Readily. Her warm body pressed against his chest. Jesus, she felt good.

"I'm such a mess," he said softly.

"I already know that," she replied.

"A bigger mess than you can imagine."

"Yes. But sometimes a mess can be fun," she told him. "I like fun."

Fleur ran her hands up his back, exploring: it had been so long but still there was that heat between them. Slowly, hesitantly, they kissed, gently, at first, then, although the waltz continued, they stopped dancing and stood in the centre of the floor. Surrounded by other dancers, they were in another world.

"Take me home, Bruce."

Bruce looked into the blue depth of her eyes.

"I want you to stay."

"I don't deserve you."

"Let's give it a try."

They kissed.

No-one noticed them leave except Kathy.

"Hey," she whispered to Frank. "Looks like they're back together."

CHAPTER 13

Fleur and Bruce lay in bed with their fingers mingled together, their bodies motionless, still breathing heavily, a couple savouring and prolonging the warm after-glow after mating.

It was only seven o'clock and still early evening,

But Ysanne was away on a trip with the Guides and Louis was at his pal Simon's for tea, so, taking full advantage of this quiet interlude, they had undressed each other on the sofa, then chased eager flesh up the stairs before making love in the bedroom.

Bruce got up and headed off downstairs, returning with two cups of coffee. "My legs are still wobbly," he confessed, settling back down.

Fleur put her drink down at the side, moved across and spread herself out on top of him, lying there quite still. "But your coffee's great and so are you," she said, kissing his ear. "I'm glad we're back together and doing this. Oh, Lord, I'm running. I'm leaking all over the place and it's all on you."

"I don't care."

"But you're getting all wet."

"I know. It's lovely."

Bruce rolled her over and kissed her breasts in gratitude for what had been, then mumbled: "Paradise is… a warm bedroom in Woodbridge."

She squeezed him.

He tried again. "Paradise is... a warm woman in a warm bedroom in Woodbridge."

She laid her head on his chest, running her hands over him.

"I'm glad I can make you happy," Fleur sighed. "I'm not fighting your tennis. I'm with it, supporting it."

Bruce nodded his head up and down showing agreement. "Mmm, I can believe that now," he replied as he wriggled down until his face nestled between her thighs and his voice faded as she cuddled him with them.

Contentedly, she rubbed the back of his neck. "You're good, Bruce, really good. Just stick by me."

"I will."

It sounded like a promise.

It was.

It was only later, though, that he'd realise the size of it.

***

Half-past eight and Louis clattered noisily through the door right on cue, breathless and bellowing.

"I beat Simon's big sister at table tennis," he yelled, "and she's twelve. She's hopeless. Mum, when can I have a snooker table? Can Simon come round after school sometime, Mum?"

"Later," Fleur protested. "Right now it's time to get Ysanne."

"Are we going past the playing field?" enquired the young lad, hopefully. "Can I bring my boomerang?"

"Yes. But we'll not be staying long mind, she's due back at quarter-too."

In fact the bus was twenty minutes late as they'd had to stop three times while Katey was sick. Louis didn't mind the delay: there was good fun to be had chasing other youngsters round the square as everyone waited.

Ysanne was bushed when she stumbled off the bus. She was happy to see Bruce and couldn't decide if she was now too old to have a piggy-back ride. So she waited until they'd walked past Notcutt's Nursery and were out of sight of everyone else, then had a carry up the last part of the hill. The steepest bit.

"You big lump," said Fleur as her daughter struggled onto Bruce's back.

"It's alright," Bruce insisted. "Humping sacks of potatoes is good for training."

He waited for the biff from his passenger. It wasn't long coming.

Louis chipped in: his sister was getting too much attention.

"Have you decided about the tent yet?" he asked, bobbing up and down, tugging at his mother's arm.

"Mmm, yes. We're going to go," she replied.

"Oh, yippee. Hear that Ysanne? When can we go Mum? Mum, when can we go?"

"When Bruce gets back from Italy we'll all go to the Isle of Wight together."

They rounded the corner. Home was in sight.

"Quick supper and then off to bed you two," Fleur declared. "You can both have cereals because there's plenty of milk."

"Bags the good spoon," snapped Ysanne, quick as a flash.

Louis groaned, caught off guard once again.

"And you hang your uniform up properly, young girl. It's not to be left in a crumpled heap on the floor."

Bruce stopped at the front gate.

"I'm no good at parting scenes," he said, turning to Fleur.

"Me neither, just go."

After a quick kiss they split. "I'll ring you as soon as I get there," he shouted as he got into the van. "Look after yourself," came the reply.

No sooner had he turned the corner than Nellie shot out from next door, but too late to catch the person she was after. "Fleur, Fleur," she called. "Come in here. Someone wants to see you."

"Who is it?" asked Fleur as she came round.

"Best brace yourself. It's bad news," warned the old lady as Fleur reached her neighbour's door. "Areej's dead," she whispered. "He says she was killed."

It was Ogilvie. He had called at Thomas Wall's Close first, apparently, but the house was empty and no one answered the door so he went to the tennis centre but Bruce wasn't there either.

Young Luther found him meandering aimlessly. Hearing the tale of woe, he called for help and Dorothy came over. Together they then brought the lad across to Woodbridge. Ogilvie was shot, completely spent.

Nellie had managed to get him to drink some hot milk with sleeping pills dissolved into it and once all that hit him, he went out like a light. "Leave him there," she whispered. "I'll find some blankets."

Fleur said nothing but she was frightened.

Dexy had told her that he could swear someone still keeps searching the house in Grundisburgh. And who is it that could send a message to Areej in letter because they knew she was living at Ogilvie's? Who?

"We're still in the thick of it," she said. "We should all be on our toes for anything odd."

***

Next morning at the crack of dawn Ogilvie insisted on getting off back to Peterborough as he'd decided that it was time to tell the police everything. Some while after he left, the kids went off to school as usual. Fleur put a load of washing on, then left the house also as she had shopping to do in Ipswich: sheet music to buy for Ysanne's Grade Four piano exam and new shoes for the boy.

Nellie's morning routine was less eventful: after tiding up the living room she sat peacefully at the window reading a Zane Grey novel.

All in all, it started off as an ordinary kind of day.

But that was to change dramatically.

At tea-time, the five o'clock chimes found Fleur in the kitchen watching over a big panful of chips; the peas were on the boil, while an army of sausages spluttered noisily under the grill.

"Tea's ready. Someone fetch Nellie," she shouted, pushing the kitchen window further open to get rid of the billowing steam.

Neither Ysanne nor Louis moved: both were watching Sesame Street.

"I went last time."

"No you didn't. I did."

"Don't lie."

"I'm not lying, you fat pig."

Fleur burst through the door into the sitting room.

"Right, you two," she screamed. "That's enough. Louis, get round there for Nellie this minute, and you, m'lady, you can tidy up. This place is a tip. Turn that television off, and it stays off until everything's put away. And I

100

mean everything."

Louis scrambled away without a murmur and Ysanne grumpily began the sort-out. Fleur, still furious, returned to the kitchen.

A few minutes later Louis returned. His mother was busy setting the table; she didn't even look up as the boy walked through the door, open-mouthed and trembling, and then stop, standing on the spot in frozen silence. Nellie followed and there was not a word from her either.

"That bacon I got you alright, Nellie?" shouted Fleur. "They only had middle back so I got three packets of that." She threw a brief glance in the general direction of the table but immediately returned her attention to the chip pan. The chips looked ready so she slid the pan off the hot ring.

That's when the man behind Louis and Nellie moved. There was a gun in his right hand. Fleur still hadn't noticed.

"Enough for seven?" he asked snappily, startling her.

She looked up and froze.

"You got visitors missus," the man growled.

There was a roll of thunder and Ysanne came pounding down the stairs, arriving at a breathless gallop. "I've tidied everything except your big scissors and........"

Two men caught her from behind, stopping her in mid-sentence.

The kitchen started to look very crowded.

"Don't move. None of you," snapped the gunman. "No funny tricks or we shoot."

The other two unbuttoned their jackets, revealing more weapons, holsters and guns.

"Who we got here, hey?" asked the first intruder.

"We got Nellie Raby from next door at Number Ten," he said, answering his own question. "We got Fleur Hainault doing the cooking; and the two brats, Ysanne and Louis. So all that's missing is the tennis racket, Mr Bruce Saxon, and he's nicely out the way... we know that."

"I don't like kids," said the second man.

"Get on with the tea, woman," barked the first mouth. "We don't want cold chips. Put it all on three plates, and bring us some vinegar. You four are dieting so get over there in the corner kids. And you too, old woman."

Louis's eyes were transfixed on the man's gun.

"Listen Hainault," their leader rasped, walking towards her and waving his gun about, "we want the little item that Areej girl has, or should I say had. The black book. We know she has it because she babbled before we got through with her. Only it seems that she passed it on to… guess who? None other than our dear friend Mr Saxon."

Fleur just stared at them all. She didn't know what to say. "Cat got your tongue, sweetheart?" sneered the man doing all the talking. "You know, the book - the little black book. We been through Saxon's place but it's as clean as a whistle. So, seeing as how close you two are, it narrows things down to you-know-who."

Still sneering, he went to Louis, waving the gun slowly and menacingly under his nose. The boy was rigid with fear.

"Talk woman," he snarled at Fleur, "or he gets it."

There was a deadly silence. Both Louis and his mother were paralysed.

At last Fleur opened her mouth, trying to remain calm for Louis' sake. "Bruce has never, never ever mentioned either a package or a book," she said. "Ogilvie was here last night but he didn't make much sense. The fact is that nobody here knows what's going on."

She then stepped forward bravely. "If you must threaten someone then please pick on me instead of him," she said. "If I had your precious book I'd give it to you. But I don't have it, and I don't believe Bruce has it either."

The gunman didn't move. No-one moved. Louis stood helpless, frail and frightened. The rest watched and waited. Then at long last the man lowered his gun and the hostages sighed with relief.

"She sends a package to Bruce Saxon and ten days later he still hasn't got it. You saying that?"

"Oy! You saying that?" echoed the second thug.

"Easy, Mealer."

"We got these four, so what we doing now, then?"

"What we goin' to do?" repeated the one who was doing most of the talking. "Well I'll tell you what we goin' to do, we goin' to sit here and wait."

He herded the hostages together.

"Now you all listen to this," he said. "You got us for the next few days, see. We're gonna sit right here and wait for Mr Tennis Star, 'til he gets back from Rome. If anyone bolts for it, we'll kill the rest then disappear. So don't do it. See?"

"That quite clear, you old bat?" the second man barked in Nellie's ear.

No-one moved as the third man ripped the phone out. "Right woman, we want feeding. Go get some food," snarled the pack leader. "I'll be right behind you, so no tricks."

Nellie and the Hainaults were forced to watch as the three men scoffed the lot - sausages, chips, peas and a sponge cake as well. They knew how to shovel it away. It was a regular pig-out.

After dark, two of them slipped round to Nellie's and did a search there but found no black book. They did return with spoils for the coming siege though: mattresses and blankets, soup, beans and fruit. They'd also pocketed £300 in notes that Nellie kept hidden away in a stocking at the back of a drawer. Not a bad bonus for a brief sponsored walk.

**

The four captives found themselves penned in the back bedroom day and night. There was no privacy, the door having been taken off its hinges. They had given two of the men nicknames, Mealyface and Creep, and it was this pair who took turns at keeping watch round the clock.

They felt cramped, threatened and numbed. The only time they were allowed out was to use the toilet at the end of the landing. Creep took the door off that as well, checking also that the window was too small for Louis to fit through.

Fleur, singled out and pushed downstairs to do all the cooking, decided to serve big portions, it might help build a rapport with the captors, soften whatever was in store for them. Not that anything showed.

Digger Turnbull, who seemed to be their leader, troughed each and every morsel put in front of him, then let off wind. Mealyface had a big thing for chips, rhubarb crumble and ice-cream, so he was no problem. It was Creep who was the bad news.

The thin man from Hackney didn't eat much at all. Each day he just picked at his food and licked his pencil lips as it became clear that he was more than interested in the cook. "I'll have you when we're done," he told Fleur. "Probably we all will."

She was furious but knew she had to let things like this flow over her and stay calm. On the third night, as they lay cramped and sleepless on their mattresses, Nellie reached across and touched Fleur. "What time does Bruce get back?" she whispered.

"He lands at two o'clock tomorrow afternoon. He should be back here six-ish."

"If he's got the package they're after and he's already opened it they'll kill him. Listen, Fleur, you've just got to escape and warn him."

"I can't go on my own. We've all got to get out together. But how?"

They both puzzled for a while.

"Found out anything more about this fourth man?" asked Nellie.

"Yes. In the kitchen tonight I heard them call him Coney," whispered Fleur. "He's watching Bruce's house. When Digger goes out the back they meet up somewhere and talk. The other thing is he's using the phone in your house to report to somebody called Haas."

Nellie's voice went even quieter than before and Fleur had to ask her to repeat what she had just said. "I do have one idea that might work," she hissed.

Fleur listened and her eyes brightened: it was a good idea, so they built on it until at last they had a plan. Ysanne and Louis, scarcely breathing as they listened in, were excited to find that there may be a way out after all.

All Mealyface could hear, sitting in the open doorway, was noise from the television downstairs. They had boxing on and it was beating their boredom no end. He had no inkling of the plot being hatched within the bedroom.

***

By now, a breakfast time routine had been established which was cooked breakfasts for the three men, cereals for the kids, with toast to follow for all and sundry. Today it was different, however, as there was an extra frying pan on the go because everyone would be getting a fried egg along with their bacon, even Ysanne.

As a result the kitchen was the busiest it had been, with hot fat crackling away, a pot of tea mashing and a back-up kettle already on the boil. Smelling good, toast popped up like it was launch day at Cape Canaveral.

While laying the cloth on the table, Fleur checked that the keys to the gunmen's car were in the usual place just to the right of the television, next to Digger's customary seat. He'd thrown the keys to her car out with the rubbish,

104

a move that assured him that the four captives were stuck inside.

Digger's new rule was that they all ate together. After the first two days he had decided it was easier to watch his victims if they came down and ate in the dining room rather than have their meals upstairs, sitting on their matrasses.

Fleur became tense, knowing that the moment was fast approaching.

Creep had been on guard duty upstairs all night and he followed his charges down, his gun trained on their backs. Then he put it away, sat down and rubbed his weary eyes. It was Mealyface's shift now.

"What's this?" he cried, noticing the extra knives and forks placed all round the table. "Hungry are you? At last? Hey, come here you - the pretty girl sits next to me this morning." He looked at Ysanne and gave her a knowing smile but she didn't move. Instead she remained stood where she was, next to Louis, waiting for Digger's instructions since it was he who normally told them where to sit.

"There and there," he snapped, pointing to the same places as usual.

Creep glowered as Louis took the chair next to him.

This was countdown.

"Tea's ready," shouted Fleur. "Can someone carry it through?"

Mealyface looked at Nellie.

"Go get it," he ordered.

The old lady brought two pots through, one in each hand. Catching the guard's eye, she used visual contact to establish whether she should sit on the green chair on the far side of Creep. He nodded and so she sat down.

Then Mealyface took his seat. His place was some distance from the rest since he was on duty: his gun lay on the table and he ate with one hand.

Ysanne and Louis were nervous, itching in their chairs. Everyone waited for Digger to move, but he didn't budge. Everything depended on him choosing this moment to go upstairs for a piss just like he always did.

He had to go, he just had to... but he showed no sign of moving, no, he just flicked over to the next page of the magazine he was reading, totally oblivious to the fact that their secret breakfast manoeuvre was on hold all because he wouldn't...

The escape committee started to panic. Something had to be done so Fleur picked up an empty milk bottle, took it to the sink and washed it out. She let the tap run. Water splashed everywhere noisily, very noisily.

Although Digger wasn't listening, he suddenly sprang to his feet as his sub-conscience got the better of his conscious brain. This was a man on automatic pilot.

"Put mine out with the rest," he ordered as he shot off upstairs. "I won't be a minute."

The ploy had worked and Digger was now away for his customary, but overdue, tramp to the upstairs bog. The four hostages listened to the heavy kluds as he climbed the stairs, followed by a lighter padding as he crossed the landing, then the customary pause while he fiddled about with bits of clothing to create an opening at the front, then at long last... the sound of a pouring torrent.

You could almost hear Digger sigh as the discharge shot forth.

And that was Fleur's cue: her part of the programme got under way the very instant Digger's pissing started. She emerged from the kitchen carrying a frying pan, while Nellie, grumbling about weak tea, lifted the lid off the nearest pot and stirred vigorously.

"I thought it would be quicker if I brought the bacon in still in the p....." she started to explain, but stopped mid-sentence as she moved towards Mealyface, giving him a brief smile.

He was the breakfast guard so she had to serve him first and he was drooling at the prospect of the hot, crispy bacon.

Fleur had other plans, however, and gripping the long pan handle with both hands, she threw the entire contents at him as hard as she could. Everything. Bacon, eggs, hot fat and went straight in his face. He screamed in agony as his flesh scalded. He was in utter pain.

His screech was matched by a second agonised roar, for Nellie had launched an attack on the second front, upping the teapot on Creep. Its boiling stream ran all down his front, swamping his stomach and legs.

The kids immediately did their parts: Ysanne was up and running, off to unlock the front door, while Louis snatched Digger's car keys.

"Get going Nellie," yelled Fleur, grabbing Mealyface's gun. "There's no time to lose."

"The door's open," Ysanne shouted from the hall.

"Get outside then and shout when the key's in the ignition. Hurry!"

Although Digger hadn't finished upstairs at the toilet, he grabbed his gun and ran to the top of the stairs. Having added Creep's gun to her armament, Fleur was walking backwards, SAS-style, ushering Nellie towards the front door while guarding against an attack from the rear.

Although she had never held a gun before in her life, the moment Digger appeared at the top of the stairs, she pulled the trigger and fired. He ducked as he shot back, aiming blindly, splattering bullets everywhere. Even at full speed, Nellie wasn't going fast enough, so Fleur was forced to return more fire.

The car horn sounded outside at long last. But then disaster struck.

In her haste to get through the front door, Nellie missed her footing, slipped off the top step, and went sprawling. Her old bones were brittle and weak and there was a loud crack as she hit the flags.

Knowing his neck was on the line, Digger raced downstairs. Firing repeatedly, he forced Fleur to back off and take cover just outside the door, next to Nellie. He might yet salvage the situation, he decided.

After all, the kids couldn't drive and the old woman was finished, that left just Fleur and she was obviously out of her depth. Digger was sure she'd be watching the door: so if he jumped straight through the front room window, he'd surprise her by arriving from behind her back.

It was hard to think straight while his men were still screaming, but two shots rang out and the cries then stopped. Digger had killed the pair of them.

Fleur shuddered.

As Ysanne backed the gunmen's car up the road, she blessed the times she had taken them both out to Parham airfield to practise driving, despite their young age. Louis had proved to be still too small at the time, but Ysanne had mastered the art of starting, steering, clutching and gear-changing.

The gears crunched uncomfortably. Fleur turned, waving madly. "No. No closer," she screamed. "Stay there!"

Digger seized his chance to fling himself across the gap where she could easily have shot him if only she'd been on full alert, but he hadn't reckoned on the mirror behind him on the far wall and when Fleur turned back she saw, thanks to its reflection, that he was heading straight towards the front window, the one right behind her.

She spun round just as the former paratrooper came crashing through the glass, knees tucked up and arms wrapped protectively round his body.

She fired, pumping bullets into her would-be assassin who went down and stayed down. It was then she felt pain searing through her arm and realised that at some point she'd been shot herself. Nevertheless, she got to her feet, gun still at the ready.

Taking no chances, she trained her aim on Digger as she moved slowly towards him. Cautiously she kicked his gun away, stepping back with a start as he twitched and his arms began to slowly brace, like a crocodile waking up after a sleep.

Nellie, lying on the flags next to the dustbin, groaned, taking Fleur's attention away from the wounded man behind her.

"I reckon my leg's broken and this arm's gone snap as well," she moaned. "You best go love in case that fourth man comes back: he could still turn up and finish the lot of us off."

"I'm not leaving you here!"

"You must, you three go. Don't worry, dear, someone will look after me."

True: doors were opening and neighbours were peeping out of windows, not sure if it was all over yet. Someone found a phone and rang 999.

"Look after yourself and the kids," Nellie ordered. "Find Bruce, but leave me a gun - I might need it."

Fleur passed her Digger's gun, kissed her faithful old friend, and as Ysanne honked the horn once again, she ran.

With the car gone and fighting back against unconsciousness, Nellie kept an eye on Digger who had started wriggling slowly across the lawn towards her. She groaned but couldn't move, the pain was awful and she knew she might never walk again, but still she hung on. The hit-man slithered closer then reached down and flicked out the blade of a long knife from somewhere.

As he stretched his hand towards her, the one holding the knife, she closed her eyes and pulled the trigger. One shot was enough.

They found her passed out but triumphant.

CHAPTER 14

Heathrow was hectic, with incoming flights swooping nose-to-tail and landing one every ninety seconds. It meant that the array of arrival boards was busy with non-stop flashing figures that continually flickered and re-adjusted.

Air Italia was on time and Bruce touched down at exactly two in the afternoon with the sun shining. There was a bounce in his stride because he still felt pretty good at having reached the semi-final and collected a prize of £9000, taking Miloslav Mecir to five sets before going under. In the final, the six-foot-three-inch Czech went on to wipe out Stefan Edberg 7-6, 7-6, 6-4.

Bruce was lucky; his bags were among the first cluster of clutter to emerge from the hole in the floor.

He had barely stepped through customs, though, before everything changed.

Fleur came racing up to him, alarmed and flustered, kicking off with a high-speed summary of a string of events that covering gunmen, shooting and escaping. She paused to catch her breath and then told him about Areej and the black book... and explained that this was the thing they were killing for... and that they had worked out that either Bruce already had it... or it was on its way to him.

When she had run out of breath and finished her story, he hugged her and asked: "Where are the kids? Are they here?"

Then added: "I can tell you no, I don't have it, that book."

Fleur pointed and said: "The kids are there. Look, next to those airport security blokes."

He waved but noticed that they didn't wave back.

"You haven't heard the worst of it yet," she continued. "We're being watched right now. See those four over at the British Midland counter. See? They followed us here.

"We escaped from Woodbridge leaving three guys dead, the three who had taken us prisoner. Shot dead in my house. That should have been the end but it isn't. It's a nightmare and it just goes on and on."

Although he was totally stuck for what to do next, he picked his bags up off the floor saying: "Come on, let's go sit in the VIP lounge while we think of something." She waved the kids across and they all had a big hug.

Not having a business class ticket to show at the VIP lounge door, it took some slick talking to get inside but eventually the security man remembering where he'd seen Bruce and stood aside allowing them all to enter the reserved zone.

The guys outside knew they must come out sooner or later so they just hung about and waited some more.

Bruce was in a tizz. To buy time to think, he made a tour of the counters and came back with cups of tea and a couple of glasses of Pepsi, then sat down.

Louis chirped up saying: "Mum thought we'd sneak round London on the North Circ... "

"Circular," said Ysanne.

"Yes, that what I mean, the North Circular. We got right to the end of it, right to the junction with the M4, and we were going round this big roundabout, right underneath the motorway, just behind a bus, when it came out."

"Then it followed us," Fleur said. "All the time it stayed three cars back and watched. I thought if they were using us to get to you then we'd be OK until we got here."

She went quiet after that as the bullet wound in her right arm, which she'd pushed into the background while driving, was hurting more than it had been earlier.

"Come on," he said, sounding falsely cheerful. "You'll not be in a flash place like this again for a while, so make the most of it." He leaned over and said: "There's two tennis faces you might recognise: Zina Garrison and Mary Joe Fernandez."

Next, he went over to the phone and all three of them wondered who he was talking to because whoever it was was about to find himself on the brink of a sudden storm.

Two men at the next table had overheard Bruce pointing out celebrities, so one of them leaned over saying: "We're with someone famous, do you know his name? He's over there, the one pouring three shots of tequila. Wait until he turns and you see his face."

But they all shook their heads even after he turned to look straight at them. "You've heard of Courtney Pine?"

"Yes," said Ysanne, "I've taped him on my tape recorder." Fleur shook her head a little... this was not information she'd expected to hear from her twelve-year-old in a VIP lounge at Heathrow.

Then it all went silent for quite a long time until Bruce finally put the phone down and walked back. "Well?" they all asked.

"There is a plan," announced Bruce. "That was Vernon Bosanquet: he's a millionaire, a stockbroker who lives out in the countryside, about 80 miles west of here and he's been a vice-president at Wimbledon for three years. I know him because he's chairman of the finance committee that covers our costs when we play abroad as a team."

Then he added: "He says to sit tight and he'll ring us back."

They all stayed sat down and waited. The kids tried to pass the time by making a list of aeroplanes that landed and the different airlines they belonged to. But their hearts weren't in it, and pretty soon they gave up.

A voice boomed over the tannoy. "Call for Mr Saxon. Please come to the reception desk."

When Bruce returned he was all smiles, saying that Vernon had come up with the answer and they had an escape plan.

"Let's move," he said.

Outside Heathrow's Terminal Two building they faced a stream of airport traffic and stood waiting on the pavement. When Louis spotted a gap, they scurried over to the multi-story car park at Terminal Three while their followers tagged on at a distance.

Once at the foot of the zig-zag flights of steps, Bruce bounded ahead with Ysanne while Fleur and Louis dropped behind, talking loud enough to be heard and trying to act natural.

The front two reached the third level and Ysanne pointed out the car they were driving as well as the black Mercedes saloon belonging to their followers.

"OK, then," Bruce said. "Away you go."

She shot across to the Mercedes, hurriedly stuffing matchsticks into the lock on its driver's door and then breaking them off flush with the outer surface. As soon as that lock was jammed full she ran round to the front passenger's door and did the same again.

Bruce arrived in the red get-away car. "Jump in!" he shouted.

Fleur and Louis arrived, ran across from the top of the stairs and piled in too. It all caught the men following on the hop a little, for by maintaining their discrete, wait-for-the-right-time distance, they'd not realised that two of four had run ahead to play tricks.

"Jesus H Christ," roared Roberts, the driver, as he fumbled with the door. "The fucking key won't go in!" Bounding around to the other side, he tried again. "Shit and derision, this one's the same."

Lignin, his passenger, smashed a window and unlocked the car from the inside.

"Get in. After them, and fast."

The delay gave them something of a head-start and as they disappeared into the airport tunnel, Louis, his face pressed against the rear window, reported that the Mercedes was nowhere in sight. They might escape.

The string of orange lights along the tunnel roof flashed past and a trembling roar told them that a jet was taking off right above them.

But Bruce's mind was on the road ahead. "Oh hell," he yelled. "There's a bloody jam. That's all we need. We're going to get stuck unless... hang on." He swung the car over into the inside lane, where a gap produced a free run right up to the lights. Although they were on red, he saw that there was no traffic crossing and went through regardless.

It meant that they were free.

They sped towards the M4, the plan being to turn left and use the motorway to carry them into the depths of Hampshire.

As they got closer to the motorway there were three cars that had been close behind them for a while, but Ysanne, from the back, said that she couldn't tell if all or none of the three were actually following them.

"Right then let's find out," Bruce said as they reached the roundabout. "I'm going full circle, right the whole way round and then keep on some more, so we'll only take the road marked M4 (West) at the second time of passing, not the first. That way we'll see if any of those cars tailing us are on back-up duty. Keep a close watch, you two."

First exit: no change. All three cars followed.

Second exit: action. Two cars winked and heading north for Watford.

"The Rover's still coming," reported Ysanne as they drove on.

As the third exit came up, it should have gone left but it didn't. Worse still, the Rover was still there even after they completed a full circle.

"He's still following," moaned Ysanne. "That means he must be one of them."

Now on their second lap, they headed off down the slip-road marked M4 (West) and the Rover followed suit. It confirmed that the chase was still on.

Fleur looked horrified.

"Don't worry, it doesn't spoilt the plan but it will make thing tighter when we get there," said Bruce, reaching over to catch her hand. "We got rid of the black car back at the airport which was something. At least they can't come up, one each side, now and nip us in the middle."

He put his foot down, gobbling up the motorway. For mile after mile, they tore along as if the speed limit was for others, with the Rover stuck to their tail like glue.

Thirty miles behind them now and tension mounted with everyone counting junction numbers as they sped past. They all knew the plan.

"Junction Ten," announced Fleur. Then, two miles further on: "Here comes Junction Eleven."

This was it. All eyes were on full-ahead, scouring the horizon, with Louis first to spot the advance marker for Junction 12 which was the baseline for Vernon's lifeline.

Ysanne turned, looked out of the back window, and said nothing. The car was there.

They left the busy Thames Valley far behind as Junction 12, together with the bright lights of Reading, faded to the rear. Darkness might be coming in but they could nevertheless see that they were now in countryside and climbing steadily, past corn fields with stubble and then into woodland and trees.

Three anxious miles after Junction 12 they saw what they were looking for: ahead in the distance was the first of three overhead bridges where minor village-to-village roads passed straight over the top, offering no access. Two miles further on and they zoomed beneath the second such over-bridge.

This was it. Vernon had picked the third overhead crossing point as their meeting spot because it was exactly halfway between Junction 12 and Junction 13. With no access, no slip roads, no nothing, it just existed in splendid isolation.

"Look! There it is!" yelled Ysanne, pointing forward past the side of her mother's head.

"Yes! I can see the three big trees on the left," Louis yelped. "Just like the man said."

Bruce leaned forward and spotted tell-tail pricks of distant light. "And there they are. Waiting," he said with a sigh. "Excellent." As the third overpass got closer, he took a deep breath as this was the tricky bit.

He pulled into the slow lane, dropping speed drastically and hoped that the copycat car behind would do exactly the same. It did. Relief. This was the weak spot in the plan. The Rover might have decided to pounce but thankfully it didn't, instead it was mirrored them, holding steady behind at a gap of fifty yards.

An articulated lorry that both cars recently passed came shuddering through in the middle lane like a moving mountain.

It was level for quite a while until eventually it was ahead. Instantly, Bruce was hard on the accelerator and pulled back out into the middle lane, onto the lorry's tail. The Rover did the same. Then the front car jumped into the fast lane and the second car mirrored that move also.

Bruce came level with the lumbering rhino's front wheels and paused, waiting his moment, until suddenly, accelerating once again, he shot across in front of the lorry in the middle land, then across more again until the car was back in the slow lane once more.

Braking hard, he took the car off slow lane altogether and onto the gravel track beyond reserved for breakdowns and emergencies.

With only 30 yards to play with, the car lost some grip and skidded because he was braking too hard. It was going to be touch-and-go because the make-shift, would-be car-carrier ahead loomed up fast.

It was exactly where Vernon had said it would be. "Hang on," Bruce yelled as they hit the flat steel platform, the front wheels bouncing madly onto its two guide tracks.

He brought the car to rest midway between four steel chains that ran upwards, one from each corner. They all linked to a crane overhead, where a driver waited briefly until they were locked on. The platform rocked forwards and backwards as it climbed until they were safe.

They made it. They were up and over. "Well, we're in Vernon's hands now," Bruce announced.

Fleur was still on edge. She checked inside her bag to make sure the gun was close at hand, then grimaced as the move caused her arm to twinge once again.

The first part of Vernon's plan had gone well and they were now in no-man's land, somewhere near an isolated settlement called Burnt Hill, deep in quiet countryside. "Why here?" asked Fleur, as they touched down.

He repeated what Vernon had told him earlier: "Because it's the safest place to make an exit like this and that's because the distance between Junction 12 and Junction 13 is twenty miles. That's the biggest gap with no access along the whole of the motorway anywhere between London and Wales. It'll take that lot ages to get back round to here."

A clanking sound told them that the wheels were unlocked, so they rolled forwards and off the platform. The crane driver and his two guides set off walking away, then dived into the back of a Rolls Royce that was waiting for them.

Vernon, as its driver, leaned out and waved, signalled for them to follow, saying that somebody would come back in the morning to clear the crane away. The little convoy slipped through Stanford Dingley, the first hamlet, then headed south.

Back on the motorway the pursuers were fuming.

That great wedging wagon in the middle lane had completely blocked them. By the time the first man scrambled up to the top of the bank and leapt over the bridge rail, all he saw was an owl settling on the top of the crane's jib.

***

Vernon lived in unbridled opulence, his luxurious mansion at Preston Candover, a much sought-after village in the heart of Hampshire, nestling comfortably in a prime rural setting.

"Your plan worked," Bruce said, shaking Vernon's hand.

"I thought it might."

As the new arrivals followed him in through the front door, he explained: "They call this the Golden Valley and that's because there are more millionaires per square mile round Preston Candover than anywhere in Britain."

"Sure is plush," the visitors all thought as they gazed round the magnificent room.

First off, Louis and Ysanne were settled with food: a plate of Penguin biscuits to eat and flavoured milk to drink. Vernon's wife Betty then washed the wound on Fleur's arm and applied clean bandages. After all that, they sat down and listening to her story as she repeated all that had happened since the moment Bruce left for Rome.

"You wouldn't be safe here, much as we'd like you to stay," declared Vernon after listening with interest. "You need to vanish; buy some time. Don't panic and don't do anything rash. Just call me once a week, or more if necessary, but not here, as they will probably bug the phone here – I would.

"So call the switchboard at Wimbledon, call yourself Ralph, and ask for Jill. Say you're due to play doubles at 11am. Don't use my name. There is no-one called Jill but I can explain all that to the team in reception.

"These men are professionals and way out of our league. The Beresford-Pierces, neighbours who live just over the hill, hired such people to get their daughter back from the Moonies. They're impossible to trace."

Not what they wanted to hear, but someone had to spell it out.

Vernon went on: "Today they've had a set-back, but they won't give up. Oh, no.

"If I was them, I'd work on what I know. There's a number plate on the vehicle we left on the bridge. They'll kick off tomorrow morning. First, using access to the police computer in Swansea, they'll trace the owner in 90 seconds flat. I know that as I've done the same myself.

"That done, they'll be round at Ravenslaw Plant Hire within an hour, playing it casual and throwing easy money about. Someone would happily talk and by half-ten they'll be here, guns a-waving, to drag the four of you off."

Talk about newly-won feelings of security slipping away fast.

There was silence until Vernon continued: ""So this is the plan. When they arrive tomorrow morning at half-ten... "

"Surely not," interrupted Fleur.

"Oh, they'll be here all right," Vernon told her. "Of that there is no question. But when they get here we'll all have left: Audrey, our maid, will have gone off for the day, for safety, and the front door will be wide open, so they don't need to smash it down. There will be a note on the table, one that might just throw them off the track."

Everyone listened. The man had a combination of authority and vision.

He went on to say that he was going to drive them to Southampton straight away, suggesting they book in at a hotel under an assumed name. Tomorrow morning they should buy a second-hand car for ready cash and go. Vamoose. Get out... as far away as possible, and then hole up for a few days somewhere on the coast.

"Here's three thousand pounds in cash," he said, in conclusion. "Go on, take it, man, you can pay me back later. What you need is plenty readies… draw a couple of cheques from the same bank and they'll be onto you in a flash."

He stuffed a fat wadge of twenty-pound notes into Bruce's hand.

"Well, OK then, but…" he protested, "you'll get it back, every last penny."

Vernon waved his hand. He didn't really care one way or the other.

"Right, we must move, let's get rolling," he said. "And don't be afraid to shout if and when you need more dosh to stay off their radar. The priority right now is to buy you some time."

***

One of the passengers in a taxi driving towards the Red Funnel Ferries terminal on the Southampton sea-front in a taxi, chatted to the driver, letting him know that his name was Max Renglstetter and that they were coming for a stay at his mother's house at Norton Green across on the Isle of Wight.

Once the cab drove off and had turned the corner, the four doubled back and hailed a different taxi. The message to this second driver was that they'd just arrived from Cowes, after crossing the Solent on the hydrofoil.

They finally tucked in for the night at the Haverstock Lodge, a neat little hotel nestled on the edge of a nearby country town. Next morning Bruce bought a second-hand Citroen, a 2CV model priced at £700 and paid for it in notes.

They piled in and drove north, non-stop, up through the Midlands and then past Manchester, before arriving at their final destination which was the windswept outpost of Lytham St Annes.

A brash hotel on the seafront suited their needs just fine: its outside facade glittered and hinted at class but the illusion quickly faded when you stepped the front door. It was wonderfully cheap, meaning that the money would last longer.

It was also anonymous. The car park had room for ninety cars, but there were only twelve in tonight. Management was hesitant about them all sleeping in one room, but when Bruce suggested that if that was a problem then they should perhaps try somewhere else, the deal was quickly agreed.

Once settled behind a locked door, and with the two kids into bed and immediately asleep, the other two sprawled across the big double bed with their clothes still on and Bruce nodded off in a flash.

With the kids slumbering, Fleur quietly called to him from the bathroom, saying: "Come look at this."

She'd taken her bandage off and had been bathing the wound on her arm. "It still hurts," she said.

"I'll bet. It looks worse than earlier when Betty dressed it for you."

"Reckon it needs looking at?"

"Yes, I'd say you need a doctor."

"I agree. So I'm going right now."

"What, on your own?"

"Yes."

"But... "

"No buts," she said. "Someone has to stay with Ysanne and Louis."

She gave him a peck and a brief smile and with that she was off out the door leaving him to watch over the children. There was no-one at reception so she knocked at the door to the kitchen. A waitress popped out and yes, she knew where to find the hospital and she gave directions.

The hospital doctor put fifteen stitches into the wound and handed her a big shaker-full of antibiotic powder. Next, a nurse told her to register with a local doctor as a temporary visitor because she would still need follow-up attention.

By the Monday morning, in Doctor Lucy Rawson's sea-view surgery, the wound was dressed for the third and final time and Fleur was given the all-clear.

"I think you'll live, young lady," she said, bidding her goodbye. "Take care."

***

The 2CV stopped under an oak tree and the driver got out and stood watching for a long, long time without moving. He was checking, making sure that there was no-one lurking about near the grand, wide-open gates ahead. Satisfied, he then got back in, repeatedly drove up and down the road, passing the entrance twice more and only after that, at the third time of passing, did he turn in.

The car rolled along the crunchy splatter of private gravel, making no end of noise.

The reason they were here was because Bruce had rung Thurleston Tennis Centre the day before, as anonymously as possible, so from one of the cluster of phone boxes along the seafront at Blackpool. Recognising his voice right away, Tracy had read him a message which the receptionist who had been on duty at the time had written down. It said:

Lady Seckford came in to say that she has received a package with instructions that it must be handed to Bruce Saxon personally. It says on the back that the sender's name is Areej.

They knew it was risky to return to Suffolk from their perfect hideaway, but the message had proved irresistible given that it seemed to have the answer to their problems. As a result they found themselves entering Seckford Hall and coming face to face with Gloria.

"Bruce Saxon," she said. "Nice to see you. Please do come in."

They followed her across the entrance hall and on past the library until finally they reached the expansive lounge with so many chairs that they felt spoilt for choice. "You didn't say when you'd be here," said Gloria, indicating for them all to take a seat.

"I know."

"Coffee, then, or juice for the children?"

"Two for coffee, please, and two for orange juice," Fleur answered for everyone.

Gloria continued her the chit-chat.

"You're in luck. Lady Seckford is due back any moment. Her private plane left Eindhoven at half past two, so she should be landing about now. The children might like to go out and watch. She's off again tomorrow, it's a ten-day tour of Japan and the Far East, fund raising for Save the World's Children. You could so easily have missed her."

Saunders arrived carrying a glass tray with silver edgings and carefully handed out the cups and glasses, then left an array of biscuits for them to pick from.

"You sounded miles away on the phone," Gloria said casually.

"We were in Lancashire."

"Oh gosh, Lancashire," echoed Gloria, playing her card as instructed which was to keep them entertained whether they want it or not. "My. I must say I phoned your house no end of times, and Hotpolarity as well, but never got you at either so I left messages all over the place.

"Vivian suggested leaving one with the receptionist at Thurleston. Wasn't that good thinking? I think I know that Tracy girl there - doesn't she come from Dallinghoo? I'm sure we met once."

"Where's the package?" asked Fleur, finding herself uncomfortable with all the small-talk.

"In the safe of course."

"I don't like this waiting. Can we go and get it now?"

Bruce looked at Fleur. The welcoming tray of biscuits and the drinks had dampened his worries a little, but suddenly they returned.

"Well...err...yes, of course. You just sit there."

"Hang on, I'm coming with you."

"All right then, come this way."

First, though, Gloria reached over and took off with a couple of wafer biscuits, a move that rather threw all Louis's calculations regarding who might get to scoff the odd ones that looked like they might be left over. Bruce poured himself some more coffee and took a gulp, Louis munched away, while Ysanne's eager eyes explored the room.

Fleur pressed forward as Gloria swung the door of the safe open, only to find that it seemed to be empty. As she bent further forwards to take a closer look, she felt a stab of pain as someone pressed a gun into her side.

Her heart sank because when she turned to look she saw a familiar face. It was all a trick and they had been found.

He motioned with his head and sneered.

As they re-appeared, Louis tugged at Bruce in alarm and whispered: "He's one of them.
Remember at the airport?"

A noise from behind told them that any retreat had been blocked off.

"Gloria is gone. She's scarpered," Fleur replied. "Must have been in on it from the word go."

Roberts cut her short with a punch that split her lip and sent her crashing to the floor, then felled Bruce with a similar blow. Then he stood back, handing over to his leader as Haas was here to over-see things in person. He smiled as he had all four of them at long last.

He moved across to the table by the window and helped himself to half a dozen cherries from the bowl, then stepped forward to stand over Fleur. "That's for Digger," he hissed as he kicked her in the stomach: it was a vicious blow and she screamed before curling up and starting to vomit.

Bruce struggled to get back onto his feet only to flattened by a hit from somewhere behind.

Having worked off his pent-up anger, Haas switched back to his professional self and nodded for two of his men to help Fleur into one of the lounge chairs near Ysanne and Louis.

"Curious as to how we found you, are you?" he asked, in a triumphant voice. "You all tucked away and hidden so perfectly, weren't you? Sampling life on the Lancashire coastline until one of you went to see a doctor by the name of Lucy Rawson in Lytham St Annes about your right arm no less, would that be right?"

"Oh, God!" moaned Fleur.

"Yes, we found you ourselves by radar even though you were well hidden. But then, getting a little bored perhaps, you come home all by yourselves, tempted by a little bait. As a result, you saved us making a trip up north, so thank you for coming back. It means we can now start to make a little progress."

Haas nodded and Lignin stepped forward. He leaned over the sofa, grabbing Ysanne by the hair and dragged her screaming across the room to a pillar next to the fireplace. Gun-blocked and helpless, they could only watch as the man wrapped a fine wire round her neck. "He likes to garrotte people," explained Haas.

With Lignin on hold, he continued: "To business then: unless you tell us where the black book is, he will finish off the Inca princess here. If he pulls slowly he'll block her windpipe and she'll go blue in the face, if he pulls harder the wire will slice right through her neck."

"Jesus, man, WE DON'T HAVE THE BLOODY THING," screamed Bruce, desperate to help. "I mean, would we have come here if we'd already got it? Hell's teeth man, we're not that thick."

They could see that despite all, Lignin was still pulling and the wire digging in, bit by bit.

Haas still seemed locked in his own thoughts. He just wasn't listening.

But then he suddenly he smiled to let them know he was relaxed about everything. "There, there," he said. "No need to get yourself so worked up. I do believe you, yes, but we had to be sure."

"But she's my daughter!" Fleur screamed.

"Now, now. You can relax on that score, she's good, she'll be all right," said Haas. "No. It's you that's got the problem, dear, because you're coming with us so we've got something to exchange when Saxon finally gets in touch to say he's got the missing item."

He nodded for the wire to be loosened and Ysanne immediately took a hold with both hands, pulling it away from her throat while gulping and gasping for air.

As they pounced on Fleur, stuffing a gag into her mouth and tying her arms, Bruce jumped up to help but was knocked out cold with fierce punch to his jaw. He fell face-down in a ragged heap as they left, dragging the kicking-and-still-struggling Fleur along with them.

Louis first pulled his sister to a safe distance away from the pillar, then came and whispered in Bruce's ear, imploring him to move, to show signs of still being alive.

When he came to his senses, he crawled across to Ysanne and Louis. They were on the sofa, crying.

He joined them and did the same.

CHAPTER 15

Christina was the first to arrive, jetting into Miami well ahead of everyone else. She called a taxi and made straight for the hotel to check that everything was in order and sure enough, yes it was. The New York-based boss discovered that Betty-Lou had done a first-class job.

"Well done," she said with a rewarding smile.

Two hours later the rest of the troop started rolling in. A Tristar brought Jackie over from London. On board with her had been Dietrich from Bonn and Maria from Rome, the three of them having all met up at Gatwick before crossing the Atlantic in adjoining seats and making merry. Next came Antoinette from Paris who was on the following flight.

Zee had a shorter hop from Montreal, while Jolene flew in from Los Angeles to the west. By the time they all took their places round the boardroom table, the head-count came to nineteen.

Jackie glanced at her watch and saw that was ten o'clock and with the introductions over, the coffee trolley cleared away, they settled down to business.

"You will each find in front of you a copy of the new SuperSires catalogue," Christina announced from the front, looking resplendent in a cream trouser suit with sign-silver fittings. "You also each have a set of annual accounts and the latest promotional back-up packs, again one each."

Papers rustled, pens tapped and the meeting began.

"My message today is that you should all feel proud to be part of the world's leading commercial breeding company. We insist on the highest standards and we give the widest choice: the result of that is that no-one can touch us in our particular market.

"Last year, SuperSires broke all records, with a total of 400,000 inseminations with semen from our bulls, that's a rise of 21%. Cow analysis shows that 80% of our females held to their first service, with only one in five needing a repeat insemination."

Heads nodded with approval all around the boardroom table. Jolene raised her hand, her question producing a reminder of the procedure to be followed when the repeat insemination also fails.

"Thank you for raising that, Jolene," remarked Christina. "Our new practice is that any cow who fails to hold after three straws is offered a full medical check. With our wide range of services, even women who are totally barren can still have a child from SuperSires' sister company, Stork Delivery, of which much more tomorrow.

"Our main rival regarding semen, namely Bullpower of Detroit, continues to focus on low-cost, do-it-yourself packs. They beat us on cost, obviously, but they are now acquiring a reputation for poor successful pregnancy rates. It is important that SuperSires distances itself from their mediocre performance.

"And we will - you'll see that our new brochure devotes two full pages to each Top Ten sire. These bulls are our big earners. I can't tell you often enough that these lists are highly confidential - many of the bulls was have in stock don't even know they are being used."

The sales team looked at each other, laughed and made the usual range of suggestive comments, before moving down the morning's agenda.

Christina turned to individual bulls and swings in popularity.

"Your pack gives you a comparison between today's SuperSires stud list and the average of ten recent polls where women ranked individual bulls, that is to say men, who they deem to be the world's most desirable. For us here, I think a better way of expressing that is to call these guys 'the most desirable semen sources' or even 'the most profitable semen sources'... take your pick.

"After collating the findings of the ten polls, the overall result sees Tom Cruise at the top for the third year running, though he is now being challenged closely by both Michael Douglas, second, and Mel Gibson, third.

"Things to note, ladies, is the progress made by Ayrton Senna now at No 7, and by Seve Ballesteros who's climbed fifteen places to take the No 10 slot.

"The table on the next page takes us to national preferences based on further polls conducted within each country. You can see that it shows UK voters go strongly for Steve Backley and Neil Webb, both new entries in the Top 20, while Americans are rooting for Jim McMahon and Michael Baryshnikov. France is very hot on Rudi Gillett.

"On the down side, you'll note that Magic Johnson is right out, while Robert De Niro is as steady as ever.

"Next page again now, and here you see a comparison between the World's Top 100 desirable men with our 'available semen' list where the good news is that twenty nine of the world's Top 100 men are available through SuperSires, a record we are proud of… for comparison, three years ago that figure as just twenty one.

"Moving on again. This shows you that the semen supply for our leading ten bulls is variable: three of them - that's Bull Three, Four, and Seven - are in healthy supply, with over 10,000 straws in the main store in Toronto, but a surge in demand for Bull Six has taken his reserve down to just 400 doses."

"Can I volunteer to get some more?" Zee asked having looked to see who Bull Six was.

Christina let the girls laugh knowing asides such as this always lightened the atmosphere and, sure enough, a string of bawdy remarks rang out next.

"We should all pull together," quipped Jackie.

"You can't beat hands-on experience," added Betty-Lou.

She paused before bringing the meeting back to order.

"Behind the scenes," she explained, "we have been evaluating contenders for the next crop of young bulls, the plan being for the best of them to appear in next year's catalogue and Astra is working on the practicalities of collecting semen. Company policy continues to swing further towards sportsman: punters see them as being clean-living and honest, not that it's the reality in many cases, but then who cares about reality.

"Returning to the current stud, you'll note that we have expanded over the latest 12-month period from 90 to 105 bulls.

"The good news is that the total of those getting paid for contributing semen has remained unchanged at just 15. Yes, these 15 guys produce for us knowingly and willingly and for money. Last year, total payments amounted to £300,000.

"At the other end of the scale are those who offer us free donations, though as you well know, in many cases we have to resort to blackmail to achieve this.

"That said, one of the bulls in this group actually volunteers free semen without any pressure from us at all. He's Rick Garner, the Australian surf-rider and champion diver. Seen as the epitome of cool, it would seem. Rick is nuts, thankfully for us, and he regards fathering children to be his destiny."

Christina lowered her notes to take a sip of iced water before moving on.

"The next item on the agenda then, is the SuperSires market: turn over, it's on the next page, Maria. Analysis shows that 70% of our buyers are white, 15% are black, and 15% are Asian. Looking at these figures on a more detailed, country-by-country basis, we can see that America is still our biggest market, accounting for 45% of all semen sold, though Europe now comes close, taking a challenging 41% of total sales, with Britain and Germany proving to be strong growth areas at the moment.

"I must make special reference to Japan, however, where SuperSires is catching on in a big way. We see a lot of further potential there, and three new staff appointments will be announced for Japan in the next few weeks."

Christina continued for another 30 minutes with more facts and figures, and then it was question time. Zee's grumble was that videos of newer bulls weren't getting to her quickly enough, while SuperSires' chief executive for Australia, Marie-Jo, pointed out that she'd had to reject 500 straws because the liquid nitrogen coolant hadn't been connected properly. After nine more queries had been aired and answered, Christina called time and the meeting closed at noon.

The company booked the entire top floor of the Miami International annually for this gathering and so by mid-day it meant a lot of strong, incoming sunlight. But with the first morning's business session over, executives left behind their briefcases and worries and, after a quick freshen up, gathered in the foyer downstairs.

Ahead of them, an afternoon trip in a ninety-foot luxury yacht where sun cream, bikinis and dark glasses would surface as the temperature rose further still. Although Christina and Jackie would have liked to join them, they were due an afternoon session with the boss who arrive sometime soon.

Half an hour later, they were nicely freshened up and fully recovered when a wind-ruffling whirring started up. The noise grew louder, little by little, heralding his arrival up on the heliport roof immediately overhead. He was here.

"You'll see that we have ten items on the agenda," said Christina, handing him a copy of the Specials List. She and Jackie already had their own copies.

"Thank you. I'm ready to start whenever you are," Cyrano instructed. "The list is fine, apart from the first item, but go on."

"Item One is Charles and Diana," said Christina, now changed into cool white trousers, fine-strapped high heels and a turquoise towelling top.

"No. We think he should be listed," Jackie told him, "because there is a specialist demand for royalty."

Cyrano shook his head. "You made the same point in Cairo six months ago and the answer is still no."

"But that's mad, the inventory list shows that we have 500 straws of his semen," protested Christina. "Some has been there for the past seven years, doing nothing."

They were stonewalled as usual. "Oh, you two do go on about this. Now listen, I'll have to let you know, I can see, it was collected by Lady Seckford and Daphne Bletchingley, better known to her friends as Crumbs. The two worked in collaboration. At the time it was a private project.

"And don't look so surprised: someone had to help him into manhood, someone both experienced and discrete. We are fortunate that Vivienne was one of the two involved.

"The result of them assisting him through his apprenticeship, that is to say in providing him with a stream of willing participants, was that he went on to great things. Look at his successes: Lucia Santa Cruz, Amanda Knatchbull and others."

"Yes, yes, but none of that answers the question: why the block?" Jackie persisted. "Some of the offers we get are incredible. A quarter of a million dollars, for instance, from the young wife of a coffee plantation owner in Brazil who is mega-rich but he sterile so she knows she has to look somewhere for an answer. You want to hear more?"

Cyrano raising his hand for silence.

"Prince Charles will not be used," he insisted, politely but firmly.

Jackie from London, however, was determined to have her say. "But 50 straws were used some time years ago. The records show that."

"No, that is wrong. Computer error," snapped Cyrano. "There have never been any commercial transactions involving Prince Charles."

For some reason Christina's brain homed in on the use of the word 'commercial', it seemed somehow unnecessary and that made it odd. She was tempted to point out that she had seen the records herself, with her own eyes. She was also tempted to add they were in fact hand-written documents: that they were written on paper and far as she knew there was nothing at all about Charles on any computer anywhere.

But she bit her tongue and let Cyrano spin that one because she wanted to push him on the second part of the same, forbidden subject. She took a breath and then dived in:

"Stork Delivery has unfertilised eggs from Princess Diana. They are in perfect condition, yet we don't use them. Why?"

She expected anger and so was surprised when he broke into a big smile. Her comments had brought back memories of the time he gave the go-ahead for an overnight break-in. Or was it two? Or was it three? Whatever, it was a clinic halfway along Harley Street, in central London.

A modest place from the outside, but extremely classy within. Because it had nothing of particular value, so to speak, it had scant protection, just so-easy-to-pick codes, straightforward locks and no added security in the shape of cameras or guards.

What a wheeze it was, the switch of non-fertilised eggs, the smile on the little team's faces on exit, the excitement of 'job well done' soon afterwards as they speedily handed the plunder over to Ruby for vitrification.

He had Lady Seckford to thank for alerting him to such possibilities. She had realised that in this day and age, royals would most probably subject all the various females who Charles talked up as potential brides-to-be to a

130

fertility check, indeed to several fertility checks, and in the process of that, unfertilised ova would be collected, stored and analysed.

.… and would also be thievable.

Later, thanks to test-tube fertilisation using semen from Charles, the future king, Ruby's skill in this new technology had resulted in a fertilised ova, in other words an embryo.

Ruby also dipped her toe into something more and quite advanced, namely cloning, done by use of a process called somatic cell nuclear transfer.

In fact it was Hana, deputy to Dr Ruby Stones, who removed the nucleus of an egg cell and replaced with the nucleus from another cell, effectively creating a genetically identical copy of the original egg. Although it was highly complex, the team had 40 clones from that first egg. The tally doubled when they did the same with a second fertilised egg.

But Cyrano had no intention of revealing these deeper secrets of The CD Project.

Even so, after a long silence, he melted a little and told them that Hana was actually here today and, while she had separate meetings herself, he could ask her to come through so that they could quiz her, if they wished, on the technicalities that were restricting further progress.

"Shall I call her in?"

"Yes please."

Hana arrived and took a seat. Cyrano spoke first, setting out what were his limits: "Between us, we can tell you a little, perhaps enough to put your questions on hold."

Hana took over and followed his brief: "We want to be right at the forefront when the technique of embryo splitting arrives, which I think will start to happen five years from now. We are ready but everything is on hold because at this moment, we lose embryos too frequently every time we try. In other words for a company, the commercial risk is too high.

They both listened, hoping for more.

"In humans and in all primates for that matter," Hana told them, "as Ruby herself has explained to Cyrano when he quizzed us just like you are doing, progress is fraught for the reason that the two proteins that are essential in cell division, known as spindle proteins, these two proteins are located very close to the chromosomes.

"We can't as yet remove one cell's chromosomes without taking these adjacent spindle protein out at the same time. People in labs round the world are trying. Work in Japan looks promising. Ruby and I have visited Russia twice now to talk to a team there who have made a step forward but working on monkeys."

That should have been enough to satisfy their curiosity but it wasn't because today they felt somehow emboldened.

"I've seen it documented, written down on paper that is, that we've released 12 embryos, presumably from cloned eggs from what you've just said, already… but there is no trace of who received them," said Jackie. "Where have they gone?"

Cyrano glowered but said nothing and it was Hana who spoke next:

"I'm not in marketing like you two are, but I think the company should get 400 of the 500 straws of Charles sold as quickly as possible. He's just not sexy like our other sires."

"On the other hand I can see a massive demand for unfertilised eggs from Diana. She is close to winning the status of being the most beautiful woman in the world. That will mean, for a company like us, couples willing to pay good money to match the husband's semen with Diana's egg in the hope of getting a pretty baby as a result."

Jackie looked at Christina, then said outright exactly what she was thinking: "I think you're spot on."

"How many?" asked Christina, "as a ball-park figure?"

"Five thousand," replied Hana.

Cloud raised his eyebrows and the other two nodded vigorously, showing that they were on-board with that.

Hana left and they moved onto Item Two which was bonuses."

This was a subject that always brought a smile to both their faces, though this time Cyrano held up his hand saying: "Give it a week. The financial package still needs to be signed off, but you will be pleasantly surprised I promise you.

"So can we move to Item Three?"

"That is John Kilner, the man most likely to become America's next Vice-President. Formerly an actor, he is still very good-looking and thanks to blackmail we have a healthy amount of semen already. But we hear that Bullpower is shaping up to muscle in and should it do that, it would suck out a lot of our potential profit."

"Is it indeed," said Cyrano. "Right then, thank you very much for the information, Christina. We'll see what we can do about that. We're not sharing Kilner with anyone."

He called for the next item and so they moved on, steadily working down the agenda, ironing out thorny questions, settling problems.

The sort-out took close on two hours. After they were done, Cyrano's private helicopter flew to two of them out to sea to join the rest, homing in on the now-stationary yacht out on the water, then hovering obligingly above the gentle waves while they dived in. The short swim through the azure water, clear, warm and deep, was refreshing.

That afternoon was a haze of Bucks Fizz and cooled champagne, fresh crab sandwiches, slices of chilled melon and sunbathing.

A banquet back at the hotel in the evening was followed by a trip to a show down-town where Tina Turner topped the bill. She was terrific. As always.

CHAPTER 16

On the following morning, the agenda switched to Stork Delivery, a division of the group that was enjoying rapid expansion thanks to a world-wide upsurge of interest in surrogate motherhood.

Kicking off early, delegates at the conference were first given a briefing on a cluster of small islands in the Red Sea, sitting out from the coastline where the two countries of Egypt and Sudan meet. Three of them were Cyrano Zafros's private property and had been developed over the past four years as Stork Delivery's breeding base.

He invited Wendy to give a brief history, then sat down as she stepped up to the microphone.

"Global Enterprises started it all off when it bought the first island back in the early-seventies," she said, "to build a holiday centre for swinging couples. The location was perfect: totally self-contained and miles off the conventional tourist track, with endless sun and bright blue water.

"It became a plush get-away with room for three hundred couples and only ninety minutes from Cairo by air. Up went various new buildings and in came the swingers."

It made good money in those early years.

Wendy continued: "So Global bought the neighbouring island in order to tap into a somewhat similar trade, that is to say holidays for single 18-30 year-olds wanting sex and sunshine. Another hotel went up, fitted with even more luxuries and built at rock-bottom prices using cheap labour brought over from Sudan.

"Those two markets peaked and then started to drift backwards. Stork Delivery spotted this and knew it could do better, so it took over the lease on the two islands from Global Enterprises and developed them further again, investing an additional $10 million dollars. The result of this extra capacity means that today, there are 600 rooms on Akhmin and 1000 on Hafcriznic.

"The Golden Adona is the current name of the former hotel on Akhmin. Here, girls live two to a room, which gives us a total of 1200 breeders. They come from various Third World countries, the main attraction being our offer of free accommodation and adequate food - it's as simple as that," Wendy said, mostly for the benefit of the newcomers to the SuperSires' team.

"They regard the money they get on top of that as a bonus. Girls, from Brazil in particular, clamour to come because they know the alternatives - prostitution and disease – only too well. By contrast with pimping back at home, we offer free medical attention, in-house entertainment and a cash payment of $250 per child born.

"Half of the girls in the Adona are now in their third pregnancy with us: in other words they ask to stay on. Another item to note is that they all opt to carry triplets, since that earns them an extra $500.

"Our other hotel is The Sheik's Magic Veil and here there are 1000 girls. They are ova-providers first-off, while after that they go on to be embryo-hatchers, a switch of track that gives us more breeders.

"As the regular faces here already know, Stork Delivery supplies the needs of three categories of customer.

"First, infertile women who are stuck with no prospect of their own offspring.

"Second, high-flyers who are so rich they can't find enough ways to spend their money and when they do, they like to show it off.

"Third, women who hate pain, who simply wants to avoid nine months' of increasing discomfort, knowing that it ends with the final agonies of childbirth.

"A good way of looking at all this is to recognise that in the years after giving birth, every woman will hire a baby-sitter sooner or later; it's just that women in the third group I've just listed here merely start the process that much sooner, well nine months sooner to be more precise."

"It's called Rent-a-womb," piped a voice from the third row.

Wendy continued: "At the Veil, they have every luxury and it all comes free: swimming pools and saunas, hair styling and manicuring. Our cinema runs films and we get the latest ones, to be sure, while the smaller studio we have puts on video recordings and repeats of popular European and American TV programmes.

"We are enjoying an upsurge in popularity of our rent-a-womb concept such that we now have plans for a third hotel, dubbed by a working title of The Red Sea Hilton. It will open next year and recruiting has already started."

Wendy took a breather, handing over the microphone to her deputy, Beth.

"Last year, to give you some basic statistics," she said, "Stork Delivery recorded 100 single births, 100 pairs of twins and 2500 sets of triplets. Mortality was minimal: even with our accent on triplets it was only 3%.

"To give you some comparison with other parts of the world, the average mortality figure in low income countries is 6%; in low middle income countries it is 4% and in middle income countries it is 3%. So we can be proud, in fact very proud, because in practice giving birth to triplets, as we do, comes with no end of additional problems.

"How do we achieve this? Because we employ good quality gynaecologists."

The background painting went on, with Wendy nodding for Beth to stay at the microphone and deliver more.

"Obviously all new breeders are rigorously examined," she explained.

"We reject 45% of applicants because of infections of one sort or another. In the main, they are girls from the poorest countries.

"Which helps, in part I think, to explain our steady shift towards younger girls.

"Newcomers are kept in isolation while we run a whole string of tests and it is only after they are given a clean bill of health that they move into the established team of breeders.

"And now to some of the lighter and more curious facts about Stork Delivery... "

But before she had time to continue with any of that, it was coffee time. Everyone stood up, then moved across to the array of tables at the side and poured whatever took their fancy.

Dr Ruby Stones, chief gynaecologist, enjoyed this opportunity to break from her normal routine on the Red Sea islands, to fly over to Miami and mingle. It was refreshing and helped her update herself with the various happening elsewhere round the world.

Two batches of cows and heifers were due to arrive on the islands in the coming week, one from Thailand, the other from Britain. How were they coming on? Were there any problems she should know about?

She caught up with Janjira, head of Stork Delivery in Thailand, and after that, by squeezing between various chattering groups, she found Jackie who was Janjira's counterpart in the UK.

"And how is your next group?" she asked.

"Oh hello," said Jackie with a smile, turning to face Ruby. "My group? Well the twelve women have had children already. None are currently pregnant. That leaves the thirteen heifers, and by jove they so young, all teenagers with several of them under sixteen."

"Well that's fine with me, just as long as we get the parents' consent," replied Ruby. "I'm more than delighted to have youngsters, girls aged between 13 and 18, because biologically that's the perfect age for child-bearing: the pelvic muscles are so flexible and they relax much more during delivery. Yes, give me a well-grown fourteen-year-old any time."

She checked her watch and thought it about time she tracked down the third person on her 'must have a chat with' list. Ruby was a cheerful, capable woman of about forty-five, with gently-curled brown hair, parted somewhat to the left of centre, which made her appear slightly manly and rather authoritative. She wore green jeans and she rocked endlessly on her heels, both while talking and while listening.

Christina came across with a coffee-pot, offering top-ups, but Ruby spotted the lady in charge of shipments and decided that this was the moment to hive off to inquire about an overdue supply of prostaglandin.

Jackie held out a cup and Christina poured. "I hear that we have a liner party of 'wanna-be parents' making its way across the ocean right at this moment," said Jackie. "How many couples are on board?"

"Seven hundred and sixty."

"My, my," said Jackie.

"Yes, a veritable legion of ladies, every one pretending to be pregnant and genuinely tubby, but all wearing, in reality, one of our special cushions, specially padded and contoured. Then next news, in just a couple of weeks' time and with their cruise 'holiday' all over, it will be back home again and exiting their home port with not just a nice tan but - surprise, surprise - a child.

"Telling everyone 'yes, it popped out rather earlier than we'd planned, all happened while we were away' and then 'want to have a peek at the little mite, looks just like his dad, don't you think?'"

Jackie took another biscuit. She was resplendent in a red and grey two-piece suit, a crisp white shirt with a lace-decorated collar, and a thin red leather tie. Christina wore a fetching sleeveless top with a big rose emblazoned on the front in ultramarine, white trousers and white high-heeled shoes. She was both beautiful and business-like.

Jackie glanced round, checking that no-one was close enough to hear, then said quietly: "Well, we got something on Charles and Diana yesterday," she whispered.

"Yes, I thought that and I have a plan," Christina replied. "The two of us settling down in a quiet corner with Hana for a few drinks sometime soon would seem like a sure-fire way to learn more."

Changing the subject, she then asked: "What are you doing for holiday this summer?"

"I'm not sure, yet."

"But?"

"My two girls want me to take them to Italy again."

"Oh, you are lucky that they want to be with you, doing things."

Jackie smiled and glowed inwardly. "And you?"

"Julie, you know, the one from the Nat West, phoned and she wants to come rock climbing here in America, so I've said yes, do come."

CHAPTER 17

Back in Suffolk, a lot of people were badly shaken by the loss of Fleur. Bruce hide the way he felt for the sake of Ysanne and Louis who were already suffering enough.

Nellie was in hospital and things weren't looking good on that score because, laid flat on her back for weeks on end, she got a bout of pneumonia to add to everything else and couldn't seem to shake it off.

Sandra, from across the road, made regular visits and agreed to step into Nellie's place when it came to supporting the two kids. Dawn Piper, one of the badminton crowd at Great Bealings, stepped in, asking if she could move into the bedroom in Nellie's place for free, in exchange for providing back-up duties whenever needed. She was out of work, having been stabbed in the back by Rentokil and was plotting vengeance.

They knocked a hole through an internal wall between No 8 and No 10, the result being direct entry between the two houses. Sandra and Dawn used it right away, while the prospect of using it herself once she got home cheered Nellie up no end.

Mary called round of a morning to make sure the kids got off to school whenever needed, while Sandra kept things ticking over at teatime.

A few weeks after settling into this new routine, Horace Makepeace's will was printed and it named Fleur as his chief beneficiary. She was to receive

£250,000. It was such a surprise that the story earned a double-column headline in the East Anglian Daily Press.

Apart from Nellie and Sandra, Dexy was the only person who knew what was coming, Fleur having let him in on the secret weeks, if not months, before.

A consequence of the news was that Bruce worked out who had bought Kathy's shares and who had made an anonymous investment in Hotpolarity. It was Fleur.

News of her inheritance brought visits from a few greedy-grabbers and one of them was Waveney, her first husband.

"I got rights," he insisted, pushing through the door without knocking. "I'm taking them. They come with me."

"Let them choose for themselves," suggested Sandra who was inside at the time.

"I'll get the law, the authorities," he threatened. "Not natural them living here with a strange man."

"That's rich, coming from you," she snapped back. "And what have you ever done for them? If it's rights you want, how about started with what you owe Fleur?"

"Up yours," Waveney bluffed. "I don't owe her nothin'."

"How about five years' maintenance. At £30 a week, that comes to £8,000 in all, now pay up or get!"

Waveney got. Never to return.

The next such charmer was Alison, Horace Makepeace's daughter. She blew in in the same fashion as Waveney before her, shouting and full of lip.

"The scheming slut," she hissed. "She robbed us of everything. That money is ours!"

It took a while, but as Alison continued to screech, Bruce worked out who she was.

"That bloody tart screwed for his money and took the lot."

"Hold on, loose lips," he said. "Let's get the facts right. Your father Horace Makepeace, a top London barrister, left a will which clearly said all his money was to go to his second wife and you're going to tell me the name of his second wife, aren't you? Come on, it was… ?"

No reply.

"On the other hand, his house was left to his first wife Doris, the lady who is your mother. Are we agreed on that? A house worth £480,000 according to what the papers say. Leaving her with such a splendid roof over her head seems more than generous, if you ask me."

"The randy little bitch who... "

"… who was his second wife. Are you listening? Whatever she was, he married her!"

Sandra came through the door at that point, saw Bruce was struggling, and took over.

"Listen, Pissy-Missy they made a pact: he divorced your mother and married Fleur but, as per the arrangement between the three of them, nothing changed on the surface As far as your mother's friends in the Lord-and-Lady Snooty set were concerned, Horace was still at home with Doris, superficial at least.

"As a result of that, she could still appear to rule her precious roost, the £480,000 abode that goes by the glorious name of Ampton Quarter."

Alison wouldn't back down. "She paraded herself to Woodbridge Round Table, offering it to the three highest bidders."

"Four," said Sandra. "They're not all that rich in Woodbridge, dear. But forget that, the question you ought to be asking yourself is why did your father top the bids?"

"He didn't."

"Oh yes he did and I can tell you why, because he'd not been getting anything at home for five years."

"If he was paying then why would he marry her?"

"The usual answer to that question, my dear, would be that in marrying, the male believes that he has acquired exclusive rights to the female's crutch and the juicy bits within," said Sandra. "You know what men are, especially ones with money. But in this case you'd be wrong, it was something else."

Alison was quiet so Sandra continued.

"Surprise, surprise, after a couple of forays, he started to feel too old and wrinkly to get his clothes off in front of her. So what was it then? Why did he marry her? What was he after? I'll tell you what it was, he wanted a place with peace and tranquillity to practice his cello.

"A room, even just part of a room, no more than that because he was fed up with the carping he got at Ampton Quarter. The first time was here in

He played music and Fleur listened on her own

this house but it was such a squeeze that after than she brought him through into Nellie's next door and he played music and Fleur listened on her own, and sometimes both Fleur and Nellie listened, and sometimes neighbours from up the road came and they all listened.

"It made him so happy you would not believe. So is happiness worth all of £250,000? Well, having seen him change with my own eyes, I'd say yes.

"Young lady, if there is another world after this and if your mother comes back as a fish, then I hope she gets to be a carp…. because she'd be perfect, she has it in her to be the biggest carp the world has ever seen."

"But she stole my inheritance!"

"Go, get out. See a solicitor if you're not happy."

"You'll hear more from me," she shouted at the doorway as she left the house.

Sandra turned and looked at Bruce and wished she'd been less factual, given the current situation. He looked back at her and just shrugged his shoulders. She had hoped for a better response, a faint smile perhaps, something that might suggest he was still on board, but no such luck.

"She said she was a bigger mess than me but wouldn't say how come," he told Sandra. "Now look where we all are."

"Bruce, you've been a right lad ever since goodness knows when," she said. "You might not want to hear this, but whatever Fleur has been up to over the past few years, you'd have done much the same if you'd been female, been a young woman still in her teens and stuck at home with two youngsters."

He didn't seem convinced so she continued.

"Listen, Bruce, it's a man's world. You guys, you can just wander off when you feel like it. But it's one-sided, it's so one-sided. Go get yourself pregnant and you'll know soon enough."

He opened his mouth as if to say something but nothing came out.

Ysanne must have put the music on because it was Planxty and the song was Arthur McBride and he knew it was her way of saying don't be mad with mum.

***

Days ticked by, then weeks, then a month, then more months after that and still all they could do was watch the post and hope, thinking all the while 'where, oh where, is the parcel from Areej that could end all this?'

And why was there no news from Fleur? Was she alive? Was she safe? And where had they taken her?

The suspense went on and on: autumn slipped past; Christmas came and went; then in next to no time New Year went sailing past. Bruce was keeping a count and knew that she'd been gone over a hundred days and still not a single word.

But then it happened.

It was a Tuesday morning. Ysanne was ready, costume and towel neatly packed in her swimming bag, while Louis, satchel bobbing on his back, was kicking a harmless foam football around the sitting room. Bruce was upstairs getting dressed.

They all heard the same sequence of noise: the postman's footsteps outside on the path followed by the letter-box's flap's familiar squeak and jangle as a letter was pushed through. Even as it floated down to land, there was already a rush to get there first.

Ysanne recognised the writing: at last, word from her mum. Bruce sat down on the steps next to Louis and they both listened as she read out the letter.

Dear Louis, Ysanne, Bruce, Nellie and everyone else at home,

My love, kisses and kindest regards. How I miss being with you all. They say I can write, at last, but I fear I won't be able to say too much.

I rise every morning hoping to hear news that the book from Areej has arrived so I might be sent back again to Woodbridge, to you. I can't write about anything in this letter that says where I am. They warn you won't see me until you have word from Areej.

Unless I obey I can't write at all. I do miss you. Please, please write back soon as they say I can have news from home. The address that you should use will be written on the back - it's a licensed collecting point. They'll only collect when it's safe, though.

Any news of Ysanne's piano results? How's Louis' diving? What's Nellie like - keeping well? I'm fit and I'm alive. I do love you Bruce. That's all they'll let me say.

Bye now. Do write. Please.
Fleur
I miss you.
xxx xxx

Just getting the letter, brief though it was, was exciting: it brought her closer. She was alive, she was somewhere! The children went off to school, Louis bouncing all the way, Ysanne smiling and holding her head up high for the first time in months. Bruce was also beaming when he arrived at work.

The kids both hurried home at tea-time to write to their mother telling her all the things that had happened since she had been taken. They started cheerfully, but by the time they had finished they were both crying.

"Oh, I miss her so much," Ysanne cried. "I wish she was here right now."

"So do I," blubbered Louis. "I'd tell her how bossy you've been."

"I haven't!"

"Yes, you have."

Later that night, when they'd settled, Bruce also wrote. He wasn't accustomed to writing long letters but he took his time and told Fleur everything he thought she should know, everything he thought might cheer her up: that he was still coaching tennis but had given up active competition for the time being.

Then news that *Hotpolarity* was ticking over nicely, followed by a bit about Nellie but skipping over her current health problem, then on to how Sandra and the neighbours were looking after Ysanne and Louis who were fine, though he then qualified a little that to let her know they were missing their mother big-time.

Plus the bad news which was that there was still no package from Areej.

The letter ended with: "*I think of you all the time. I long to hold you and tell you how much I love you.*"

By the time he had finished everything, putting his words along with the children's all into a large envelope and then sealing it all up, he just lay lengthways on the sofa and went to sleep with his shoes still on.

He woke three hours later, had a large whisky and went to bed.

Following this breakthrough, letters came and went but they were painfully spaced out, with Fleur only being allowed to write once every few weeks. Even so, they were a lifeline. The writing got longer and more detailed. After the basics came the more personal things.

Bruce searched for clues but it was like looking for a needle in a haystack. No secret message, no un-Fleur-like phrases even, that might hold a hidden meaning. The only vaguely odd thing was Gillian.

First, she asked Bruce to pass her news on to Gillian, then later asked if Gillian was still running, still coping with the high hurdles. Each and every letter referred to Gillian, who had been a good school friend once, true enough, but now was quite distant as she had gone off to teach the piano in China. So why mention her at all?

Eventually he thought something might add up if he asked her if she could help put two and two together since at this stage anything was worth a try.

The trouble was that she now based in Australia having married a high-rising medical guy who had been entrusted with completely reshaping the Australian army's pharmaceutical procedures. They met in Hong Kong after he'd heard to her playing the piano and was immediately smitten. The snag was that no-one, not even Nellie, could exactly remember his name: while she thought it might be Luke, that was little more than a guess.

Ysanne then had a brainwave and saved the day. "I'll get Mum's old address book. Gillian's phone number's still there. I've seen it. I can remember Mum ringing her once, a long time ago."

Sure enough, the number was there. They rang the international operator and got put through… but the wrong person answered.

"That was the maid," Bruce explained. "Gillian's been in hospital apparently and has now gone off with Luke to recover. Seems that they'll be cruising round the Barrier Reef for a bit longer. Anyway, the maid promises that Gillian will ring us when she returns."

"But when will that be," moaned Ysanne.

Almost crying, Louis turned on his sister.

"Soon as she gets back, dummy!"

"Okay, you guys," Bruce warned. "Knock it off."

It was three weeks before the return call came, by then Gillian and Luke were back in Sydney, spending a couple of nights with friends before tackling the final flight back to Adelaide.

Gillian was excited, that was clear right from the word go and she got straight down to business.

"Yes, yes, I know why she's asking for me, it's because she's putting messages in the letters, a secret system we invented in my bedroom, back when I lived at home in Rivendell. We were girls, about nine years old then. Listen, have you got the letters there in front of you now?"

"Yes," replied Bruce.

"Right then, get the first one. Look at the top and tell me exactly what the first line says."

"It says '*Dear Louis, Ysanne, Bruce, Nellie, and everyone else at home*'."

"Right, now then, count the words. How many are there?"

"Ten."

"Okay, good, now start reading from there and find the first word with a letter 'i' in it."

"Got it. '*Kisses*'. She starts off '*My love, kisses...*' "

"Stop. Lovely, that means K is the first letter of the message. Now count the next ten words after '*kisses*' and what do you get?"

"You get '*all*'."

"You want the first letter again, so that's an A. You've got KA so far. Count another ten words from 'all' and.... "

They moved on but lost hope because they found themselves working closer and closer to the end of the letter yet all they had to show was a string of random letters with no apparent meaning: with twelve letters listed, the message, for what it was worth, read:

KAFRFAIYUMIS

The result was an all-round collapse in confidence... but then hope suddenly surfaced as the full fifteen-letter message read:

KAFRAIYUMISLAND

The *ISLAND* element from the final six letters was clear enough but the stuff before that offered so sense, however it stood firm even after a double check.

"Move on. Read me the next letter," urged Gillian brimming with glee.

"Here you go. It starts '*My darling Bruce, and my wonderful children Ysanne and Louis*'. That's ten words again."

"Read on from there and tell me what is the first word after that with a letter 'i' in it?"

The repeat letter-by-letter, de-coding process confirmed that the theory was good.

Ysanne read out the new message: *EGYPTARMEDGUARDS*.

Her mum's third letter was a long one and ran to 315 lines.

Its message said: *STORKDELIVERYBABYBREEDINGCOLONY*.

The fourth revealed: *TRIPLETSINAPRIL*.

And that was it, with no more letters to work on they were all done and in total they had the name of some foreign island, a connection with Egypt and a warning about guards, plus a puzzle over triplets.

Trying to put things into some sort of perspective, Bruce walked down through the town and took the footbridge over the railway, then forward through Whissock's boat yard. The footpath led to a seat.

It faced across the water to the Tidal Mill with its quaint old wheel and safe-harboured water, its white-boarded walls and cheerful red-tiled roof. The last time they sat there they had kissed: this time he was alone.

After two false starts, he worked out what he wanted to say in his reply while at the same time weaving his own secret coded message into the letter by using the same formula as the one that Gillian had revealed.

He told her: *GOTMESSAGEWILLHELPMAKINGPLANSNOW*.

***

Luther turned up at the tennis centre with a second lad who was a new face, threw his bag across at a chair without even looking across to see where it landed, then walked straight over to Bruce who had his back to him as he was leaning over the desk at reception and talking to Tracy.

Luther tugged at Bruce's sleeve and butted in, saying: "I've brought Tog. He wants to help."

At his side was a cheeky-looking white youth. Freckly, with ginger hair snipped into a crew-cut. Some longer bits at the back had escaped a ruthless home trim and they stuck out as if in permanent shock.

"He's in his second year at university, the one at Manchester," Luther announced. "Comes from up Stone Lodge, from this end of Holcombe Crescent. He's wizard: he can do anything. Just ask and he'll do it. Won't you Tog?"

The wirebrush nodded.

"What do you mean he can do anything?" Bruce asked, puzzled. "Wizard at what? Tennis? Juggling? Artexing wet plaster over police-car flashers?"

"Tog's our Calvin's friend," the youngster replied, "I told him you're in a mess and he wants to help you." There was a pause before he added: "He's a computer hacker."

It turned out that he was the real deal, for sure. They did a trial run to prove he could access confidential information such as bank statements and private accounts. It didn't seem to worry him that this stuff was illegal... just the opposite, he loved beating the system. He told them that his mother played poker for money, she was good, but he found hacking more exciting, more challenging.

They all sat down in a quiet moment and Bruce quickly warmed to Tog so he went straight to what he saw as being the start of his problem: the container wagon that came to Debach airfield with illegal immigrants on board.

Who owned it? There should be paperwork at Felixstowe docks in the customs office perhaps, that might hold clues but when Joe, his dad, had tried to find it, he'd got nowhere. Someone had already covered their tracks, cleaned away the traces, the paper traces that is.

"No problem," Tog said, smiling. "Just give me two days."

He was back two days later as promised, saying he would need some back-up help.

The result was that the following night a five-man team set out from Thurleston: Bruce and the young wizard together with backing from Ossie, Hal and Floyd. They made their way down to the docks and found the Fred Olsen office: Ossie did a neat damage-free job on the door and they were in. Tog led the way, heading straight for the computer upstairs.

"All shipping agents have a direct computer link into Customs and Excise: someone might have torn out the relevant pages here at the port, but they'll not have cleaned the slate back at HQ, that's across in Rickmansworth, should you be wondering. There's a FCP80 system at Felixstowe Customs, so I'm told, and it should be easy to slip into that from here: then we'll get it to push data up front for us to read. Data from Rickmansworth, that is."

He then went quiet and got to work. Like a programmed ferret, he was everywhere: searching desk tops, unlocked drawers, ledgers, files and even notepads. He hummed while he hunted about, his ginger bristles bristling, his whole demeanour electrified. Suddenly he jumped in the air and shouted, waving a crumpled sheet of paper in his hand that he'd just fished out of an unlocked drawer.

"This is it," he exclaimed excitedly. "We're in. See, the code-word... CONTAINERCAT. Right boys, stand back."

Tog was now up and running. The entry code went into the computer and the FCP80's entire world opened before him: he flipped back through various manifests, looking for two crucial dates.

"Here they come," he shouted, after a while. "This is what we're after. Look, this is the first container, the one that your girl Areej came in...

"...and this (he flipped the screen through the four menus that followed and then clicked right and down once again)... this is the one you followed up to Yorkshire a month later. They both have the same details. Write this down Bruce. They were booked in from Rome by Skentex Worldhaul and the sea freight charge of £4700 was paid by Skentex RoRo. The declared cargo was Formica tops and the agent at this end was Skentex (UK). Thank you, customs records, thank you very much indeed."

Tog sounded like an expert and Bruce wondered where he'd got all this background/foreground/all-round knowledge from. "You're chuffin' great, man," Ossie said to Tog. "A chuffin' marvel."

"There's more we could do if you fancy it," the young lad added, his mind still on the move. "Records in London for those Skentex divisions should yield shareholder names, directors' addresses and all that. If you wanted to look?"

They certainly did.

***

So soon they were at it again: Bruce and Tog along with five Thurleston GPs this time for extra backing. The target was Drumshang Tower, a swish modern office block on the South Bank, straight across from the Houses of Parliament in the very heart of London. From the roof you could see the goings-on in Jeffrey Archer's penthouse which was just across the way.

It was mid-afternoon when the hacker and his backers arrived.

"How do you know this is the right place?" Tog asked Bruce.

"Dawn told me," he replied. "She knows a journalist guy who works for the Financial Times and he told her that another guy on the same desk is now with Kroll. That's an outfit that does forensic accounting, so fraud and money laundering is their cup of tea.

"Then she hived off and comes back with her contacts book. Man, it's vast. Turns the pages and finds the writer guy's name, points to it and we kick off from there. We get to the Kroll guy and he buys in. We owe him a big drink."

Bruce said: "Kroll hire guys from MI5 and Mossad and such like, don't they? Or so a guy at tennis once told me."

"I could do with meeting this guy for real," said Tog. "A job with an outfit like that would get mother off my back: she thinks I'm turning into a bit of a bum."

First off, Ossie went in on his own, carrying a toolbox and clad in brown overalls. He took directions at reception, as bold as brass. Once down in the Tower's basement, he set to work, changing a lock on a door that opened out onto the backstreet.

At nine o'clock that evening, soon after the cleaners had left, the team returned with Hal taking the lead. He checked around, then unlocked the door and Tog was the first in. Bruce was close behind, followed by Gripper, Peffpeff and Half-breed. Ossie, the decoy, brought up the rear.

Drumshang Tower was much bigger than the Fred Olsen office in Felixstowe, but even so Tog wasn't going sky walking; he knew exactly what he was doing, having learned the day's password from the computer department earlier with a wild, but plausible, cock-and-bull story.

"What is the password, then?" Bruce asked, curious to know.

"ARNOLD216."

"Really?"

"It's as simple as that." Tog grinned.

"Care to explain the theory?"

"Later."

"What's that you're doing now?" Hal asked.

"I'm knocking on doors, getting replies and look...," Tog babbled while pointing, his face shining with intent. "The password's got us in. Aha, so they've an IBM System 6000 up aloft have they, with GXR. I've only been in one of these once before.

"They're well defended: you've got to pretend to be two people, both an attacker and a defender. That way it shows you the traps before you walk into them. Anyway we're where we want to be - it's yielding up, it's relaying impulses down the wire and I'm recording them onto this floppy disk. It's called dumping the files.

"Best to get ourselves out of here quick, then read through its memory bank later, when we're back in Ipswich as what we're getting is quite a big haul so it should be juicy, juicy."

The whole task was over rather quickly; wires disconnected and portables packed away and in next to no time Hal was out in the street again giving them the all-clear. Ossie put the original lock back on the door to clear their tracks and they all melted away into the night.

Overhead, Big Ben coughed and then struck.

It was still only eleven.

***

The plunder yielded some startling discoveries as Tog had quickly jumped sideways from just Skentex Worldhaul and Stentex RoRo related data, to then investigate a string of coincidences which put Lady Seckford in the frame for a lot of unsavoury activity.

There had been a lack of concrete evidence up until this point about her goings-on, but now, Tog's investigation brought everything out into the open.

He'd shaken the tree and the facts had fallen out. They were a rich crop indeed.

"That was fun," said the wire-brush wizard, laughing. "Much better than juggling or what was it you said, *artexing police-car flashers*? Cool. I like that idea. Anyway thanks for calling me in, Bruce."

"Go on," urged Bruce, taking out his wallet. "Have an extra hundred quid. You earned it."

"No. Five pounds an hour is what we agreed, so we're all straight."

"Okay," Bruce conceded. "If you're happy."

"Right then, to business," said Tog. "I've put Lady Seckford's accounts through the printer, and here's a hard copy for you, it's all yours. The picture is this, she's either involved in, or herself running, a mass of companies. Some of them are pretty dubious. There's two I particularly like... yeah, here they are, *Crystal Angels* and... *Ring Miranda*... supplying girls as escorts for foreign businessmen, starting at £500 a night. Just imagine what they get for that!

"But the one you want to know about is *Stork Delivery*," Tog said, guiding Bruce through a stack of print-outs.

"I'd put her total net income at eight million a year," he said calmly. "Out of that, *Stork Delivery* is making her a profit of one-and-a-half million, while *SuperSires*, which is closely linked to it, is adding three of the eight million... she must have a bigger finger in that pie."

"What exactly is this Stork Delivery?" asked Bruce.

Tog chuckled: he was beginning to enjoy being centre-stage.

"They contact childless couples," he explained, "asking if they want a baby, making around forty approaches each week. Look at this and see. The staggering fact is that 50% say yes. Imagine, a fifty percent positive response - wowee, that is good going. Now then, how do they manage that, you ask? Well, I'll tell you how.

"They've got an insider, someone working for the Department of Health and Social Security up in Newcastle-upon-Tyne, who pulls lists out of the big DHSS computer for them. This... (pause while checking a read-out)... Ursula she's called.... gets £1200 every month in exchange for an updated printout. It works a dream... I've hacked in myself for a closer look.

"Look, the last time round, Ursula gave them a list of every woman in the country earning over £14,000 a year, who's aged between 26 and 44, with a husband on the dole and with no family.

"At first they only approached women over 30, but each time they've brought the age down, demand has grown, in fact it's boomed. They identify their market accurately and they are, if we're totally honest about it, supplying a need."

"Could you get us one of those lists?" Bruce asked, thinking ahead.

"Easy."

"So if we wanted to reach one of these couples first, perhaps, we could do so, could we?"

"That's right."

Tog latched into Bruce's thinking right away and came back with his own contribution. "Another tack would be to feed a name of our own in so that it appeared on the next list they produce. That way we'd get a call from them."

Bruce nodded. It was a nice idea.

"What sort of detail does Stork Delivery have on its child-buyers?"

"It's all here," replied Tog, pointing to the pile of paperwork. "Name of husband and of wife; full address; name of bank; name of branch and bank account number. You'll spot that they require a basic £1000 in advance.

"Then, for an extra £500, they'll reveal the child's sex in the sixth month of pregnancy, and for £2000 extra there's the option of choosing a boy or girl, right from the word go."

Bruce was amazed. Tog had sliced through Stork Delivery's secrets as easily as cutting a slice out from a hot pie.

The only thing still missing was the custard.

CHAPTER 18

A mud-splattered pick-up juddered to a stop after bouncing along for more than a mile and the driver said: "We'll have to get out and walk from here, she'd never get through that hole ahead, it's massive."

"It must be a gamekeeper trap," chirruped Louis. "I know it must."

Bruce looked down at the eager face. The lad was all excited as he was going to meet a real, old-time poacher.

"Ready to walk?"

"Yes. I'm off" replied Louis, making a big leap from the vehicle. "Come on. Try to keep up."

He ran ahead. Ducking through tangles, the two of them worked their way towards the forgotten world of Boyza and Moll. When the house appeared, Louis stopped and gazed ahead. The door was off its hinges, propped against the wall at an angle. Moll shouted welcome and in they went, along a stone-flagged passageway leading to the back.

The couple had just killed a pig and with one half already trimmed and jointed, Boyza was working vigorously at the second side. Moll's space was covered with saltpetre, ready for the next joints of meat as they got passed across, one by one. Behind her were flicks of bacon, rolled and finished and packed into old pillowcases.

Boyza looked up. "We're nearly done," he said. "Plenty of fry going spare if you want to take some with you."

Moll told Bruce to get everyone a cup of tea, then scuttled off to the cellar and came back carrying food. Louis dived in first. "This is lovely," he said. "Is it custard?"

"No, but close, lad," answered Boyza. "We calls it beastings pie."

"After a cow calves," Moll explained to Louis, "she don't give normal milk, not for the first four days, see. She gives beastings instead, thick like this, full of special stuff for her young calf, to protect it and get it going.

"Country folk all used to make beastings pie, but farmers today mostly feeds half a bucketful to the new calf, then throw the rest away."

"What a waste," Louis offered.

"Me, I think second and third day's taste best, then fourth day's is less so good and you needs an egg for to thicken it up. Making's easy. I adds salt and ginger, then pops it in a slow oven. Bit of nutmeg on top and she's ready."

"Tell you what, young lad," said Boyza, "there's a job needs doing. Would you square up Nettle's box for me? She's my dog.

"She's due to pup anytime and the space in the shed where she always has her pups needs a good clean-up. Throw the old straw out and get her some fresh water."

Louis nodded: he was keen.

"Here, take this bucket. You can fill it from the trough. There's fresh straw stacked behind some sacks of dried sugar beet pulp."

Louis bounced off along with Moll who wanted to show him the way. "Lad couldn't wait," she chuckled on her return. ""That's all about it here. I'll boil a couple of pans and scrub out the backus table."

When they went to see how Louis was doing, they found him sitting in the straw having fun with Nettle. He was twiddling away at one end of a dog-chewed package while the dog tugged at the other.

Boyza explained that the dog goes down the lane every morning, the postman gives her the letters and she always brings them inside except when her pups are kicking inside her. Then, she takes them away and hides them before chewing them to bits.

He pulled a letter from inside the envelope and said: "This one here. It's from the girl they brought to the airfield that day, the one when all this started. She says I'm to hand something on to you. Come on, let's be indoors. There's better light in there." Once inside, they read the message properly.

Areej wrote that she had posted it to Boyza because she remembered Bruce talking about him and he'd seemed the perfect person to send black book to because he lived in such a remote and private spot... and he would be able to ask Bruce to come over unseen and collect it.

Bruce flicked through the pages of the book: they were full of data and comments on tests and recordings.

So many entries and so much detail.

"This is it," Bruce shouted, waving the book about just like it was a hard-earned tennis trophy.

He was back in the game with a trump card to play.

***

Cairo airport was scorching hot: even in the shade it was 35 degrees C, so for new arrivals it felt like stepping into a pre-warmed oven. Two individuals emerged from customs and stepped smartly through the waiting throng. As soon as they got through the exit they spotted a waving hand, it was the one that they were searching for and so they ran towards a car.

It was an air-conditioned Mercedes.

Holding the rear door open, Moaz ushered them both in, then piled in too. Amy found herself sat in the middle with her brother on her left. They both sank into the car's rich upholstery. It felt so good.

For Amy and Moaz this was new territory. She had bumped into him quite recently, at Tramps disco on a night when a bunch of girls out partying found themselves mingling with a bunch lads on a similar venture.

The two got on like a house on fire, more so when he learned that she was Bruce's sister, though he quickly realised he had to trim the tennis talk back to zero, the reality being that she had a zilch interest level in her brother's sport... on the other hand she loved kayaking.

Which was fine because it still meant that they could happily talk about fitness and such stuff.

Egypt was out of Amy's comfort zone. Her furthest ventures to date had been once to Ostend with her parents, plus with a trip to the Imst Gorge, Austria, much later with her kayak group.

Moaz squeezed her hand and smiled so she leaned towards him and gave him a kiss.

Cairo was packed which made driving through it mayhem. "Eight million people live here," he said. "I thought you might like to drive through Ramses Square. It is the very heart of the capital, like London's Pall Mall."

"Can we see El Mosky?" Amy asked, so he leaned forward to re-direct the chauffeur towards the Khan el-Khalili bazaar. Bruce gazed out of the window in fascination. "What's in those big sacks?" he asked, pointing. Seeds, beans and grains came the reply.

Eventually the Mercedes halted, allowing them to step into Cairo's exotic oriental bazaar, the largest in the Middle East. Overwhelmed, the two visitors made sure to keep close on the heels of their guide.

Bruce had got to know Moaz because they both played tennis.

The Egyptian had performed well as a junior, so well that he'd gone to America at the age of eighteen, enjoying full-time coaching from Rod Laver, a former Australian champion. He had built up his skills to the point where he was ready to join the professional circuit.

He'd been in the Top 250 for the past 30 months, and the latest computer printout put him at Number 112. The two had been friends for three years now, having first met on the circuit in Copenhagen.

Moaz was rich thanks to the efforts of his mother and aunt. The two of them had combined forces and cajoled Moaz's grandfather into reviewing a major discrepancy in their inheritances. The result was that he and his mother each now held 10% of Orascom Telecom's shares, a company headed by his cousin Naguib.

Naguib's father Onsi Sawiris was very much the family patriarch, with newspapers reporting that he was rapidly heading towards becoming a billionaire.

Moaz had plans for the future: he wanted to combine his tennis talents with business by setting up a holiday/tennis centre on the coast at Idku, ten miles east of Alexandria.

Once back in the car, they drove northwards which took them through Shebeen El-Kom on the city outskirts, then on to Moaz's apartment in Fuwwah, a small town sitting on the Nile delta. Once inside, Bruce met up with the team that Moaz had assembled for the coming venture, while Amy was greeted by Ann.

She was the daughter of the Beresford-Pierces, the girl who had been 'recovered' from the Moonies a few years back. Her parents, learning the saga of Fleur's disappearance, had told Vernon that they would be giving Bruce money, however much he needed, to mount a rescue. There was also the offer of making use of their links, if that might help.

It certainly did and it was Moaz who had got things moving on the ground, the result being quite a gathering of talent.

Three of the rescue team had served in the El-Sa'ka Forces, the Egyptian military commando division, all having been together its 31 Thunderbolt Brigade. Others had previously been with Task Force 777, Egypt's equivalent of the SBS.

Only one individual was still missing. He had first flown from London to Tripoli before making a follow-up flight eastwards. That saw him land at Cairo airport, the hope being that he'd stayed under the radar of any watching eyes.

Right now he was driving to Fuwwah in a Hertz hire car. The person in question being Tog, the hacker from Holcombe Crescent, Ipswich.

***

A dull-coated freight plane took off unobserved from a commercial runway near the El Nasr fertiliser plant, flew across the Red Sea to Saudi Arabia before landing at Mecca. Next, a drive of just over an hour along straight roads to Jeddah, a thriving port on the Red Sea, where the group headed for a private marina and boarded a pair of high-speed powerboats.

Bruce looked at Tog and gave a silent cheer as they pushed out onto the shimmering water.

The plan was to rendezvous with a luxury yacht called the Hathor which had been cruising for the best part of a week, carrying two dozen doddery holiday makers. Invited on board as a deliberate decoy, the group had flown out from Stansted and landed at Hurghada, a thriving city on the Red Sea coast.

Once loaded and on the water, the Hathor had been pushing steadily southwards, some 500 miles in all. As the yacht finally came into sight, Bruce looked at his watch and smiled: they had made rendezvous right on time.

Not only that but Zareeb, the yacht's captain, had a large chunk of good news to report: namely that the QE2 had steamed majestically past three days ago and so she should now be at rest, safely moored off Hafcriznic, the largest of the Stork Delivery islands.

"You were right then, Mr Tog, with your figures," said Zareeb. The young man nodded, smiling to himself confidently.

"There's no going back now," said Bruce, suddenly aware of being caught up in a fast-flowing forward tide, though one of his own making.

While crossing the Red Sea, the two boats had steered a south-westerly course before arriving in Sudanese waters. From here, the plan was to then head back north through clusters of offshore islands, giving a wide berth to the ones colonised and developed by 'friendly' Russians. Even so, despite with their raised level of prudence, heavily-armed patrol boats twice cut out to meet them, forcing them into wide detours.

Zareeb took Bruce and Tog on a tour of the yacht before showing the pair of them down below where their bunks waited.

***

Wednesday morning and Bruce was up in the chartroom being shown the charts. Sunlight streamed into the cabin as the Hathor bobbed about on the peaceful water. The maps showed blue-shaded fathom line changes, ragged coastlines and small sand-toned islands.

"That's where the fun starts," said Zareeb, pointing to a spot some way ahead.

There were six islands in all. The two largest, Akhmin and Hafcriznic, about a mile apart, were the most northerly. Kafrfaiyum lay three miles south of Hafcriznic. Four miles further south of Kafrfaiyum again were three smaller islands set in a triangular shape. The captain planned to sail into the middle of this triangle then drop anchor to give his elderly passengers a chance to examine the fish, as well as the opportunity to step ashore where the biggest attraction was the markintoma, the only white bat in the world.

All this was something of a subterfuge, for as well as the camera-clickers up on deck and leaning on the rails, there was also a less-than-innocent raiding party hidden down below.

Masud, their leader, had with him plans of the buildings on both Akhmin and Hafcriznic, teased out of various Government officials in Cairo and Sudan. His up-coming task was to get Tog onto Hafcriznic in order to gain access to their computer and avail everyone of certain secrets hidden within.

"Look, there she is," Masud said, pointing Bruce's attention towards no more than a speck in the far distance.

It was the QE2 and she was at anchor some way to the east of Hafcriznic, waiting for the stork to deliver. A large pontoon had been ferried across the water and was now bound firmly to the side of the ocean-going liner where it would serve as a stepping-stone in a few days' time, as 760 couples descended side ladders and onto it as anxious, childless twosomes, then returning to the vessel just one hour later as gleeful threesomes, as families at long last.

The very thought of babies brought back Fleur's message, the one that said: *HAVINGTRIPLETSINAPRIL.*

Masud waited for dark and then, five hours into the night, he sent out two canoes with four men, chosing Zuberi, Edfu and Chigaru to accompany Tog. Everything was deserted when they eventually reached the liner. Two of the four stepped silently onto the floating pontoon, Edfu leading the way and Tog close behind. The pair climbed upwards, then onto the open deck and silently made their way across to a passage door which would lead to Room 641, their destination for the night.

Down below, Zuberi and Chigaru waited the agreed length of time then pushed off and paddled the two canoes away into the dark.

Edfu cautiously opened the cabin door next morning once the breakfast bustle had subsided and made his way back down to the pontoon, again with Tog close at his side. The pair queued along with about thirty others, all waiting for a small boat which was shuttling back and forth between the liner and the island as a ferry service.

They were on dry land in next to no time. Once ashore, Tog chatted nonchalantly while they walked from the pier towards the Magic Veil hotel. "Nice place," he said, as they mounted the broad steps leading into the cool interior. "Here, you go in front Edfu since you know where we're going."

Having the building's layout in his head, Edfu led the way to the administration office. "Temporary power loss on board last night," Tog announced to all and sundry, but to no-one in particular, as they entered. "It wiped out some of our figures: it's mainly the food and drink inventory that's gone... looks like two disks need re-programming. I've got them here."

A girl working at the third typewriter on the right stopped typing and assumed seniority. "Oh hello," she said as she stood up. "Follow me."

She led the way towards a door down the passageway, opened it and told them: "There you go. It's all in here - just help yourself because I'm busy. But do give me a shout if you need anything else."

"Thanks," replied Tog easily as she walked away and left them to it. Edfu shut the door.

They were on their own, free to access the computer system and its secrets. Tog had no interest in the ship's food and drink inventory, what he wanted was Stork Delivery's list of girls having babies and he found it.

Flipping quickly through screen after screen until he was a good third of the way through the alphabet, he then slowed to a more detailed name-by-name crawl.

"Almost there," he muttered. "These must be the end of the G's. Guiffre and Guilfoux. So then we move on to H….. here's Hadley… then bingo. Hainault, F! Yes, we have it!"

"Oh, oh," he cried, looking across at Edfu. "Yes, the lady in question is indeed having triplets... or should I say she was having."

"Meaning?" said Edfu. "Explain."

"To use their somewhat basic terminology, Cow 2107 gave birth to three offspring last Saturday."

"Mr Saxon's heirs?"

"Hardly. She's been gone ten months."

Tog hunted into various other menus. "This sure is some place," he declared. "They must have had 900 births in the last few days. All pre-sold, every single one booked to an anxious buyer, or should I say to two anxious buyers."

He asked Edfu to check that no-one was coming, then said: "Now to run off a printout of Miss Hainault F's details."

He keyed in the appropriate instructions and the printer whirred, its top sheet of paper moving rapidly through the box's green lights and noise-emitting mechanism.

SIRE: SUPERSIRES BULL No 173
PREGNANCY CONFIRMED: 25 NOV
CHECKED: 17 DEC
PREGNANCY NOTES: NO COMPLICATIONS
BLOOD PRESSURE: NORMAL THROUGHOUT
DATE OF PARTURITION: 6 JUN
MALE SIBLINGS: 2
FEMALE SIBLINGS: 1

M1 BUYER: RONALD AND JODY SWARTMEIN, DALLAS

    ACCOUNT NO: 63741/FH1
    PURCHASE PRICE: $19,000   (dollar transaction)

M2 BUYER: ANGUS AND JENNIE MCDONALD, PERTH,
SCOTLAND

    ACCOUNT NO: 63826/FH2
    PURCHASE PRICE: £11,000   (sterling transaction)

F1 BUYER: DES AND ANNA ROACH, SHREWSBURY,
ENGLAND

    ACCOUNT NO: 63827/FH3
    SEX-SPECIFIED EXTRA: £4,000
    TOTAL PRICE: £15,000 (sterling transaction)

SIBLINGS MOVED TO GROUP 21:   7 JUN

POST NATAL CHECKS ON DAM: 7 JUN
    8 JUN
    10 JUN
    12 JUN

SIBLINGS MOVED TO GROUP 35:   12 JUN

Tog moved on, calling up the Action List menu. After a brief hunt, the relevant page appeared: the daily roll-call listing the mothers who need to be brought to the clinic for examination by Dr Stones or one of her gynaecologists. There were 37 names on tomorrow's list as it stood right then, but moments later there were 38 as Fleur Hainault's name had been keyed in and was now making up the extra.

"Well, that's the essentials done. Anyone coming, Edfu?"

Edfu looked.

"All clear."

Tog continued his hunt, enthralled by its revelations. He took a closer look at Kafrfaiyum and saw that they were holding four prisoners there: three suitable for breeding and one infertile. Just then the girl from the third typewriter walked in. Tog hit ESC-S-M-ENTER, in quick succession and the screen instantly changed.

"Ah, the golden girl," he said, bubbling with charm.

"The name's Karen," she replied, "and I've brought two coffees."

"Oh, lovely. Thanks very much."

"I do like men with freckles."

"Mine are nothing to shout about," said Tog, feeling suddenly embarrassed: he viewed his body as a disaster zone, a major flop and had zero experience of being sought after.

"They need more sun. Come over again tomorrow, will you? I've got the morning off."

"Alright, you're on."

"What were they doing out there last night?"

"What you mean...the party-before-the-pop? It was a riot: fancy dress costumes and a couple of bands."

Karen leaned against the door, explaining that admin staff couldn't get across to ship parties. Tog realised she wanted to chat and was ready with more banter but before he had the chance to start spinning yarns, Edfu chipped in. "Hey, Michael, son," he said. "It's close to lunchtime already. We need to get this inventory back, or people are going to go hungry."

"Spoilsport," grumbled the hacker.

Pausing at the door, he turned and blew Karen a kiss.

"See you then."

"Tomorrow. Come early and we'll have a swim."

Edfu and Tog spent the rest of the day hiding under Teri and Pete's bed in Room 641. At midnight Zuberi arrived and tapped a coded sequence of knocks on the door. It was time to go and they left with a silent wave to the couple they left in bed reading.

Teri got up and crossed the room, then locked the door behind them.

***

Bruce hardly slept a wink all night and first thing the next morning he declared: "I'm coming with you in one of the boats. I simply must." But Edfu shook his head.

"No," he replied. "Too dangerous. There will be guns and shooting. You stay here where it is safe. We are professionals and this is an active mission. Don't worry, we will return with the girl."

The sun rose, brilliant as ever, a blistering, circular orb that climbed slowly but relentlessly up through the infinite blue sky and the sea warmed again after the overnight chill. Here, every day seemed exactly like the previous one, a never-ending blaze with not a cloud in sight. Did it ever rain?

Things were on the move by seven as people started stirring; there were noises in cabins and mumbles through walls. This being an extra special morning, the old folk had been briefed as to what was going on so they kept out of sight and well out of the way.

What's the hang-up, Bruce wondered, the sun's up, we're up - what are we waiting for?

Powerboats were checked and ready. Bruce wanted to get a move on, but for this stage of the operation, Edfu was the man.

The sun got hotter and the attack force were seen making final personal provisions: bullets in packs, water and hats with brims in position. But still they waited. Nothing stirred up front. No go. No lift-off. Nothing.

Then at last, at long last, a message from the man embedded on Hafcriznic as lookout saying that two small boats had put out; they were leaving and heading south for Kafrfaiyum with two men on board each one

That was quite a shock and it threw the plans.

Edfu gasped. "It should be one boat, they never do two so we have a problem. One boat with two on board should be a tea-party, but this. We don't have enough cover. This could all go wrong."

He had four men dug in and hidden on Kafrfaiyum, covering the exit point. "They're our emergency attack but now the odds have changed. If they split the passengers into groups which one will... "

His voice tailed off. "Stay right there," he instructed Bruce, then walked off so that the revised plans were made out of earshot.

By the time this change in the anticipated situation surfaced, Edfu's two powerboats had been long gone and were already way out at sea, travelling west towards the coastline of Sudan before diverting north. Well out of sight, they started to swing round in an arc until the far off island of Kafrfaiyum appeared in their sights in the far distance.

Its only building stood next to a sandy inlet on the north-facing shoreline. A tree-covered hillock, held in place by strong-rooted palms, screened it, blocking all views to the south.

As the powerboats got close, they throttled back and then stopped, half a mile to the south. With binoculars, the men on board could just make out Kafele's aerial, a valuable communication stick, lashed to a palm tree on its south-facing side. It was now a case of waiting.

The boats were motionless, just gently bobbing about on the water.

"All four guards have gone in," Edfu said, repeating the latest message fed over to him.

A pause then more news from the on-site sandbags.

"They're coming out," reported Atsu, in an urgent speaker hiss.

"All the guards have appeared. And they're bringing out girls, loads of them. No way we can make out... ."

Bruce waited anxiously. Come on, come on! Say it!

"Hold one they've singled one out. She's getting onto one of the boats on her own. All the others are being led onto the other. We need to see her face. She needs to turn."

She, whoever she was, must have then turned because the next news was: "Yes it's her! She fits the photographs: the girl on her own is Fleur Hainault. "

"Thank God," breathed Bruce.

The flow from the observation post continued.

"Another guard has come out and he is getting on with her. A fresh one! There are three guards on the Hanault boat... confirm, three... and they're moving. They're off. They're on the sea. All on their own. It looks like she's a special, the one they've sent the extra boat for. Her on her own. They must have been told to keep a close guard on her.

"The second boat is going to be way behind because it's only just starting to load up and it's slow progress so we can go ahead with the plan, it will work, the others will be so far behind it'll be all over before they realise it's even started."

"Good," said Edfu. He leaned over and switched channels. "They're all yours," he instructed. "Move in."

Laszlo and Rich, the two Canadians leading the next phase, were more than ready and their craft, lying side by side, came to life as the massive engines of the CUV powerboats roared.

Both were the identical model of the one that had won the Class 1 Powerboat World Championships only a couple of years earlier. Italian boat builder Cantieri Uniti Viareggio fitted two 8.2 litre marine Lamborghini V12 engines in each making them close to untouchable when out on the water.

By conventional standards, Silver Spray, the boat now ferrying Fleur across to Kafrfaiyum, was fast. She was fairly flying along, skimming the surface when the guard upfront spotted two approaching powerboats gaining on them from behind. He yelled, pointing, and the three guards all turned to face back to where they could see men laughing, fooling about like silly pranksters.

The verdict was that these must be some of Moving Cloud's friends out for kicks. As the splashing and wave-slapping came nearer, ribald shouts and raucous laughter could be heard. The guys behind seemed to be having a hell of a good time. One of them, in a pink and blue floral shirt, seemed to be about to jump from one boat to the other.

"He'll never make it."

"Not at the speed they're going. It's not safe."

Then the Honeybird, the yellow, white and grey boat on the nearside coughed and popped, lost her rhythm and slipped back.

It left the gaudy Kingfisher, decked in a dazzling blue and orange trim, free to fly. It soared away into a long lead.

The men on the Honeybird shouted across to the Silver Spray, as the gap narrowed. Their boat's engine was still spluttering but its crew were still laughing and silly, asking for a tow, for a spare can of diesel, for a push, for a shove, for the time of the next bus.

A half-empty champagne bottle was raised, flourished and shaken, releasing a spray of fizz. Laszlo, dressed only in a pair of yellow Bermuda shorts, brandished the champagne bottle. He looked mighty annoyed and very drunk. He was neither.

"Damn," he hollered to the men on the Silver Spray. "Five thousand dollars we had riding on that. First into the pool at the Golden Adona collects the lot. And what do we get? Mucky fuel!"

Tarek, the guard at the helm, popped his eyes in wonder and disbelief. He'd never gambled more than two hundred piastres in all his life, and even then he'd lost.

"Still that's the way it goes," Laszlo shouted, still acting as the Honeybird drifted closer.

Helpings of honey-smacks had put Tarek at ease and he stood grinning all over his face.

"Any chance of a tow?" shouted Laszlo.

Tarek looked for a rope.

The other two on the Silver Spray, however, were not completely taken in by the jolly display and one of them, Taqy, tucked in behind Fleur, just in case, which in turn set off Wasim too. "Go away," he yelled. "Go away now."

Taqy grabbed Fleur and pulled her back towards him but Laszlo just stood there and held up his hands to show he was unarmed. The tension eased a little and Laszlo spotted the chance to get a message to their prisoner.

"You carry without us on then. We'll just hang around here and wait for help," he shouted across. "Micky'll be back before long." He turned and leaned over an open hatch. "Hey, Woodbridge," he shouted into the hole below. "Let's you and me take a dip. Come on, show yourself on deck woman."

Across on the Silver Spray, Fleur pricked up her ears. Woodbridge, was he shouting Woodbridge? And woman? Well, she was the only woman around. Perhaps it was code. Never mind perhaps, it must be... and suddenly, for the first time in months, she dared to hope.

"Come on, Woodbridge woman, what's keeping you?"

Then the truth hit her full on: Woodbridge wasn't down the hole on that boat over there at all. No, the person in question was on this boat and... SHE was Woodbridge. The man on the other boat was sending her a message. She was sure of it.

Chapter 18

Laszlo turned to Wasim and grinned.

"The theory was to go in together on the count of three, but I can't wait forever," he yelled in an amiable tone while marching over to the side of the boat.

He stood on the edge then shouted: "Get ready. Here we go. Three, two, one... Geronimo!"

The guards watched closely as Laszlo dived forwards and then plunged into the sea. Fleur saw her chance, broke free from Taqy and jumped away from him. The startled guard dropped his gun and grabbed her again but with a second wrench, she pulled herself free once more and in an unseemly tumble, she splashed down into the drink.

So far, so good. Instinct told her that she must stay under for as long as possible, so she struck out, swimming deeper and deeper. Taqy grabbed his gun from the deck and started strafing wildly but his blitz came to a halt when a single shot rang out: it came from the Honeybird and it sent him crashing backwards, clutching his chest.

"I'll take the boat, Tarek!" Wasim yelled. "You shoot the girl when she shows."

Fleur broke the surface, coming up with a rush, urgently gasping for air.

Tarek raised his gun but a third Canadian on the Honeybird by the name of Robichaud, put an end the threat by raising his gun faster. Tarek crashed heavily against the side of the boat. Wasim reached for the throttle to escape but he also took a bullet and his day was over as well.

Suddenly silence ruled. The scrap was over.

Laszlo climbed out of the water at the same time as Fleur was being hauled on board. She was shaking and gasping, but she was safe.

The Kingfisher swept off in a large arc, making its way round to the back of the island where it was out of sight to make a pick-up... the land-based lookouts heard it coming, waded out into the water and climbed on board.

Then both powerboats went racing back to their base among the uninhabited cluster of small islands to the south. It had worked out after all.

They approached the beach, cut their engines and then drifted to a halt. Overwhelmed with delight, Bruce swam into the sea to greet them. Fleur spotted him and took to the water herself. They had found each other at long last.

CHAPTER 19

Kingfisher sped off across the water first, cutting a straight furrow of foam, towards Saudi Arabia which formed the eastern flank of the Red Sea, while Honeybird, the sister powerboat finished loading. It left soon after, though not at such a breakneck pace. After all the commotion and now left on its own once more, life on the Hathor returned to normal.

The Kingfisher's destination was Algalh, a small coastal town fifty miles to the south of Jeddah, the plan being to then travel north by road to Jeddsh and fly back to Egypt from there, returning to the El Nasr landing strip with a minimum of fuss.

The surprise attack to free Fleur, the Stork Delivery hostage, was over before it had begun. It was only when the second boat, loaded with the other 37 women, drew close to the floating remnants of the first boat, more than forty minutes later, that anyone realised that something was badly amiss. It triggered a lot of hasty messages.

After guards on the various islands had pooled what information they could gather, one of them called the mainland. That done, all they could do was wait for the backlash. They knew it would be painful and it would be coming soon because everyone knew full well that Moving Cloud, the top man himself, was somewhere hereabouts in person.

But they got it wrong, totally wrong, because there was no stormy aftermath, there was no thunder… the feared reprisals never came.

That was because Cyrano was entertaining and doing it in quite some style.

***

His palace was full of guests invited in for the annual extravaganza where the highlight was what they dubbed as 'the big gamble'. This was a game of chance where the stakes were phenomenal.

Last year, a young Dutch lawyer who'd crossed swords with Cyrano was the sacrificial pawn. He'd had to survive out in the desert for as long as possible. The first of the vultures dropped after twenty three days and six hours and that was the agreed marker moment so Kenneth Nwodo, a rich Nigerian, won as his estimated time guess was the closest to the reality.

He scooped up the pot which ran to two hundred million dollars.

The question on everyone's mind, right now, was what would this year's challenge be? Cyrano always came up with a great 'staying-alive' scenario. It was rumoured that a new name in sport was being built up for something, hints having been dropped already in order to build up interest.

"Come on, Zafros, tell us more about the cabaret," urged Luigi Rizzi whose father had struck it rich in Malaysia back in the day and who now lived in luxury in Italy. Rolling in money, he wore scent and jewellery and had a hankering for young girls.

"Yes, Cyrano, when do we see the formbook?" Kirk Straffman added, a cash-loaded Californian oil mogul with a decorative Brazilian wife and a valuable collection of rare cars.

Cyrano smiled, rubbing his hands together.

"Patience, gentlemen, patience."

"You said we could anticipate action very soon," Luigi reminded him. "Could that action happen today?"

"Indeed, it could," replied the host. "In fact, it is happening right now."

He told them a little of the background regarding an unchallenged escape and a Red Sea chase, one which was currently in progress, then pressed a button so that pictures appeared on the big screen to the rear of the VIP lounge. They noted that the powerboat involved had passed a buoy and a clock was running as a result, all of which meant that the race was on.

"You chasing them?" asked Straffman.

"Yes, well sort of yes, just to check they don't go deviate from the plan," answered Cyrano. "We know where they intend to land because we tapped into their agenda. I don't want them caught, just a little push now and then, perhaps, to keep them up to speed. I do have a boat that can match theirs should it come to that."

"Ah, yes, the Topaz," Straffman said.

"Where's the finish line?" asked Castlemaine, a burly horse breeder from Australia who was dubbed as Four-X by several of the group. He felt it was time to start making calculations.

"Ah, yes," replied the host. "The finishing line is at the entrance to the harbour at Algalh and the distance from the red starter buoy is 120 kilometres: you'll have to work out for yourselves what that is in miles. I can tell you that there is no wind and the sea conditions are calm. What entry fee do you suggest, gentlemen, for this first look at this year's selected player who goes by the name of Mr Saxon? He is on the boat speeding towards us like a moth to a flame. Do we agree that the winner takes all?"

"Six million apiece," growled Bunker Lacey, the big Canadian grizzly who'd made his fortune mining aluminium ore.

"'Bout right for me," said Straffman.

"Lift it, take it to ten million," suggested Lou Yin, hoping to up the stakes. Once part of the emperor's family in Thailand, he had skittled off to the West where he enjoyed a rich life-style thanks to the plunder he took with him.

"If this is just a warm-up, what's the big one, Cyrano?" asked the horse breeder from Oz.

All got in return was a mysterious smile.

"We'll see."

Voting over, the majority opted for stakes of six million dollars and the twelve big spenders each pushed their pile forward without so much as a blink. The pay-out would hand one of them seventy two million… with this gamble just the starters.

Threadneedle leapt into the air when the winning time was announced as his prediction was within a minute of the result. He was a rogue from Essex who managed to slip away from his desk on the London Stock Exchange with a vast illicit gain from rigged futures trading just as inspectors pushed through the door having uncovered his dirty deeds.

He handed two million dollars back to Cyrano as a thank-you gesture for him staging such an impressive 'opener'.

Zafros smiled and saw that this was his moment; his guests were in the right mood for the announcement.

"Gentlemen, gentlemen, please...," he said in a loud voice. "Now that your gambling senses have been stirred, allow me to whet your appetite further by making two small introductions."

He gestured towards the back of the room where there was movement as a pair of guards presented themselves accompanied by a boy and a girl.

"These, gentlemen, are children you will see more of in tomorrow's drama," announced Cyrano. "Their mother will also be taking part as she is Mr Bruce Saxon's little lady. Haas collected them to ensure that our tennis star performs with commitment." He turned to Louis and Ysanne, smiling expansively.

"Beautiful, aren't they?"

"By the same father?"

"Yes."

Luigi was intrigued and full of questions. Cyrano tried to answer them but struggled to explain the technicalities of how exactly a white mother and a black father could produce such a big difference in the colour of their two offspring, namely a near-black daughter and a near-white son, though he managed to remember some of the basics of what Dr Stones had told him on several occasions, which was that just over different 100 genes are involved, according to some, while others would put it way higher than that, at 900.

"Ruby herself thinks 500 genes are at play," he said "They are melanosomes, she tells me. I'm more than interested because if we could find a way to control them, or should I say be the first to manage to control them, then we could make a lot of money."

Straffman and Castlemain moved over to collar Haas in the hope of wheedling out more information about Cyrano's upcoming challenge as they couldn't quite marry the different elements of the hints that had been offered of a tennis player and a family being involved with a setting that was said to be out on the ocean.

But Haas played a straight bat and they found themselves none the wiser.

CHAPTER 20

It was early the next morning when a helicopter arrived: flying in from the sea, it circled just the once, then settled on the lawn in front of a fabulous pavilion situated on one of the Dahlek Islands that sit in the Red Sea a few miles off the coast of Eritrea.

Leaving his guests indoors, the owner came out to meet the two new arrivals himself. Guards immediately released the female prisoner and she rushed ahead to greet her children who were being paraded provocatively fifty yards in front her.

Not so for the second prisoner who emerged next. In his case he was prodded and steered away to the left, towards an ornately-roofed garden sun-house where he climbed a flight of wooden steps, walking between two guards, then stopped at the top and took a moment to register his surroundings.

Beyond the two rows of trees, he could see the island's private harbour with a string of white yachts bobbing on blue water.

A guard gave him a poke in the ribs, making him look ahead to where a man sat waiting for him.

"You know who I am?"

"I assume you must be the guy with the rather daft name of the Moving Cloud," Bruce said, "Why am I here? Why are those two children here?"

Two men pulled him down and handcuffed his wrists to the chair so that he was helpless to resist when a syringe was emptied into his right arm.

Haas then arrived. "Truth drug," he said, in a matter-of-fact tone.

Bruce felt curiously relieved.

With a nod from his boss, Haas's questioning began.

"Have you got the book?"

"Yes."

"Why didn't you tell us? We promised you an exchange."

"Have you seen the condition she's in?"

He didn't have to say who.

Cyrano to his friends, Moving Cloud to others, he liked the duplication.

"It was her own choice," he declared, economically. "I had offers from friends of up to £5,000 for a night with her, but she wanted to have babies instead, she preferred to be a cow. Her choice, my son, not mine."

"That was no choice," Bruce roared. "You are just evil."

"You play with words, young man, when you're here to play something quite different."

Bruce kept quiet. Reason told him he was in no position to argue.

"So you came running to Moaz, your friend, hey? And where did that get you? To Cairo to meet your team, indeed a good team, I must commend you on that. But you brought Ann, your sister. You brought a weak link, weak because she keeps a diary.

"Full of glee, she sets off on her exciting African venture, follows the Nile way, way inland. Gets to Uganda and finds white water at Jinja. Hurray, she goes out splashing her paddle without a second thought, day after day. And what does she do? Leaves her diary in her room. Where is she staying? Oh, I can tell you where, at Wildwaters Lodge. Her brother leaves messages and updates and she writes them all down."

Cyrano chuckled. "She made it so easy," he said.

But he was done with the skirmishing.

"Haas brought the four of you here, because... well, because you put up such a commendable struggle. The search for the black book has been good, it's kept my men on their toes. That said, you've cost me dear, yes, you know that, but I've put the Saxon expenses down to entertainment because it's been your preparation for the test and I'm pleased to tell you that you've passed that with flying colours."

He paused and took a deep breathe, looked at Bruce, then moved closer.

"I have bad news, we found the book," he announced.

He said it slowly and solemnly, savouring the sound of each separate syllable. Bruce's heart sank.

"My men tracked it down."

The last hope was gone, but Bruce tried a final bluff.

"Where was it then?" he said.

Cloud ignored the question, so Bruce turned to Haas, who stared back and said nothing.

"I don't believe you've found it," declared the captive, his spirit suddenly returning. "So we can do a deal - the book in exchange for Fleur and the children. Let us all go and I'll tell you where it is."

The Cloud was contemptuous. Standing suddenly, he slapped his prisoner across the face. "There is no deal, fool. I have the book: you are here, boy, to jump to my tune."

He pointed towards the yachts and back to the mansion. "Look," he snapped. "Look at all this and then listen to my words.

"My friends are gathered here, drawn together from all parts of the world, for my famous festivity. They have come to expect something imaginative, exciting and memorable. And they will not be disappointed, boy, for I have planned an extra special treat. YOU!"

Bruce tried in vain to tear himself free.

"Save your hands and stop being a bore," Cloud said impatiently. "My friends and I like to bet big money, but not on routine boyish trivialities like cards or horse racing. What we enjoy is a survival fight, a man under threat, struggling to save himself."

Bruce didn't like where any of this was leading.

"But I have seen the book," he said.

"Yes, you have seen the book, we accept that," said Cloud. "But the reason you have been given the truth drug is to help us establish one fact. Are you listening?"

Bruce waited, wondering what was going to happen next. Haas looked at his watch and nodded. He'd administered it many times before: he knew it was circulating fully in the blood stream and had reached the brain.

Cloud stepped behind the prisoner, pressing his thumbs into Bruce's wrists to feel for any changes in pulse rate. Haas stood in front of Bruce, watching his eyes for giveaway signs.

"Have you made a copy of the book?" asked Haas, his voice as cold as ice.

Bruce thought quick and hard.

"No", he declared.

He never was much good at lying, even at the best of times. A tell-tale heat flush that was uncontrollable showed up and there were further signs at the wrists, where his pulse-rate increased.

"That was a lie. But don't worry, my boy, good liars are born not made," said the Moving Cloud. "So you made a copy, hey?"

"Yes."

"One copy or more?"

"More. Two copies."

"You made two copies?"

Bruce was lying but he had to try to bluff.

But Haas knew… the lie detector showed a flicker and there was give-away tint on Bruce's cheeks.

"Once more," he said, "this time the truth. Is there a second copy?"

"No."

Haas waited 10 seconds then nodded, they knew they had their opponent beaten.

Cloud exploded with delight. Speaking enthusiastically, he told Bruce: "Two things you should know. First: we found the black book hidden up in the space above the ceiling in your new office. Second: we found the copy you made back at your parents' house in a box of your old school books."

Bruce didn't speak. There was nothing he could say anyway. Not now. Even his insurance had failed.

"So, it's the big match for you, champ!"

Cloud was almost beside himself, his eyes bright with glee.

Bruce was crushed, thinking more of his failure than his future. The roof of his mouth had gone dry.

"What big match?"

Cloud laughed.

"What is it you'll be missing in a few days' time?" he teased. But there

180

was no reply.

"Think."

"Wimbledon."

"Yes, Wimbledon. And the local hero, Bruce Saxon, won't be there."

Cloud was a sadist. He was enjoying every minute of Bruce's discomfort. "You'd like to be there, wouldn't you, hoping to reach the final of the All-England Lawn Tennis Championship? But would you really try, give it your very hardest knowing that out here we have your lady - what is her name - Flower?"

"Go stuff your fat arse with light bulbs and sit down on them," snapped Bruce, trying once again to jerk loose.

"What a novel idea," beamed Cloud. "One to remember, Haas,"

"Indeed."

Turning back to Bruce, Cloud continued: "Well you're a lucky man because on Saturday you will be playing tennis and playing it like you've never played before. Win or lose, you'll know for sure that on this occasion you couldn't have done more."

Bruce said nothing so Cloud ploughed on. "The highlight of my little entertainment features you, dear boy. My friends and I will watch your moves with more than passing interest because we will be wagering a fortune on the outcome."

Bruce put on a brave front and spat at his tormentor. But Cloud ignored him. He glowed with excitement generated by his own cruel fantasy.

"My friends, collectively, have challenged me in a wager. It is somewhat ironic, I think, given all the irritation you've caused me, that I am offering them odds of two-to-one, but gambling etiquette must always rule. You do realise what these odds mean? They mean that I actually think that you will win and in doing so you will make me very rich.

"Therefore, I must minimise my chance of losing four hundred million dollars simply because you played without drive or motivation. Now, I think this is something you, especially, will appreciate: the sweet little flower's life will be in your hands. You play for her life!"

Bruce looked at the ground, his heart sank.

"The game will take place on Saturday, the same day as the Wimbledon final. It will start at dawn to avoid the main heat of the day. Even so, a long, drawn-out game, with the sun climbing in the sky, would be torture. The top deck of the QE2 has already been cleared and marked out. I guarantee a surface equally as good as the Houston Astrodome.

"The mothers will be busy down below in their rooms for at least an hour, if not two, so I can't promise you your customary crowd of fans, unfortunately. But not to worry as my party will be there, they will have flown over by airship… such stately transportation in a far-too-frantic world."

Bruce was really worried, although he tried not to show it. It was what the Moving Cloud hadn't said.

"What do you mean 'put her life in my hands'?" he asked.

Cloud spread over his seat, savouring the moment. The scenario was set and he had the 'star' eating out of his hand. He smiled, looking more than a little like Alfred Hitchcock at his most malevolent.

"Ah, yes… Fleur, your sweet Fleur, and her two darling little buds. They will be coming out to watch as well, in fact they'll have a first-class aerial view… "

The Moving Hitchcock paused, purring, as he portrayed the scene.

"They'll be up in the sky in a… in a cage."

Bruce groaned: it didn't sound good.

"Just picture it, Saxon… a helicopter hovering overhead… motionless, held on autopilot… a cage hanging below it with three people inside. Yes, you guessed right, Fleur and the little ones.

"Now this cage is quite special. The base is solid enough, but - surprise, surprise - it's detachable, held in place only by four stout pins, one at each corner."

Cloud was so pleased with himself, with his great it's-your-life-at-stake game of chance. He complimented his henchman, Haas, and told him his work was done.

Later, back in his cell, Bruce would put the pieces of this monologue together again and again, hearing in his mind the Black Cloud, Moving Cloud, Never-Ending, Horrible, Tormenting Cloud rant and rave.

When he closed his eyes he could see it all too clearly: the cage suspended beneath the helicopter, knowing that if he should lose three games in a row, at any stage, in any set, then one of the pins, by automatic relay, would drop out and the floor of the cage would loosen, would perhaps flap open. Even if they'd hung on to the last, when the fourth pin dropped along with the floor itself, at that point Fleur, Ysanne and Louis would drop down into shark-infested waters below.

Also, winning a lengthy, drawn-out marathon would bring no salvation for the fuel would run dry beforehand, sending the whole lot plummeting into the sea, captives and all: for them it was certain death.

"Tonight will be the worst." he recalled Cloud saying, "You'll be thinking that perhaps there still might be a way out, but by tomorrow you will realise there is no escape. The quicker you start preparing for the fray, the better your chances will be. Tomorrow you will be a changed man as you will no longer be fighting against me, instead you will be fighting for me.

"Use your days well, and your nights. Use your woman's warmth to gain rest and sleep, for you need all you can get."

With that they had all stood up and left him on his own.

He felt doomed, exactly the same feeling as Billy Bones had when Blind Pew gave him black spot, except this was no story book, it was reality.

***

For Fleur, it was a case of deja-vu: they had both been marched back in the very same room that she had lived in throughout the past nine months, for her entire stay on Kafrfaiyum.

During that time it had been peaceful, however: she'd had the room all to herself and she'd been free to wander out along the beach in the moonlight whenever she so wished. But not tonight. Everything was very different now: not only was the door was locked but men had been posted outside it as watchdogs.

On top of that a floodlight had appeared, plus she now had company as Bruce was there at her side, laid under the blankets with her. She held him close, knowing that she had to rekindle a spark, had to light a flame.

"He's got Sargis Harut for my opponent. The bastard."

"What did they say about practising?"

"I can use the court every morning from half past five until eight. Harut gets his two and a half hours on a night."

"Anything else?"

"I can train in the gym on the island," he told her mutely, sounding like a muffled robot. "Any time. It's air conditioned. Harut's already been here three days getting used to the court. That gives him a head start."

"But you've been practising all winter," Fleur said, trying to give him confidence, "and you said you've been keeping fit."

"I know."

"Well then, stop worrying."

She held his head against her chest and ran her fingers through his hair, then rocked gently to and fro, wrapping him in love.

"But you're at stake," he cried moanfully. "You could all die and for what...? For a sackful of sodding money and a laugh."

It wasn't going in the right direction and she recognised full well that she had to bring his spirit back to life as the only escape from all this was for him to rise to the challenge… he had to produce his best on Saturday against Cloud's man.

Sargis Harut, the man in question, had enjoyed a productive year having beaten Andrei Cherkasov in the final of the Swedish Open to become the first Armenian to pick up a major European title. He'd also won admirers in Australia, getting to the quarter-finals of the Open Down Under by stopping Kevin Curren and polishing off Brad Gilbert, before going out to Emilio Sanchez.

***

They settled more easily the next night: Bruce was calmer thanks, in a large part, to Fleur's soothing efforts, though there were still occasional outbreaks of fury and moments when he slipped back into remorse. He'd had a hard day's practising which left him quite tired and that was a big help.

Before lying down, he paced back and forth for a while. "I feel like a prize ape stuck in here," he said, looking down at Ysanne and Louis, asleep at last. "Have you decided what to tell them about the cage?"

"I'll do it tomorrow," answered Fleur with some hesitancy in her voice. "I can't put it off any longer: if I prepare them a day early then there's less risk of them getting hysterical when we're up there."

She made a space and whispered: "Come and lie down. Please. Keep me warm. I need you."

He lay down beside her and kissed her and she wrapped her arms around him, pulling him close.

"I love you," he said.

She nuzzled him affectionately, then her head sank against his chest. She was still weak from her own trials and tribulations but tried not to show it. The births had been tough: right now she needed peace but she was getting war.

"Before you ask, it's out of bounds," she whispered. "Also, though this might not be the best time to tell you, I don't think I can have any more kids."

"Don't worry about it," he replied. "This is just fine. You're warm and you're here… that's everything I need."

"Oh, I do love you," she said, with a kiss.

***

As they lay together cuddling and musing, Fleur said: "I still can't sleep yet so talk to me, tell me about that black book: what is it all about?"

"It all seems so something and nothing, I can't get what the panic is, I really can't," Bruce said. "It was just a string of ordinary names. I can't even remember them all, well perhaps the first few I can.

"David Normanton, born June 9, 1982 to a couple in Jesmond is the main one. He's right up-front. That's up north I think, either Newcastle or Sunderland, not sure. Next name Geoffrey Hooper, born two days later on June 11, 1982, a son for parents George and Isabelle Hooper.

"Then Alex McCann who was born the next day. Then, the only other one I can remember, so fourth, was Aled Hughes, born 14 June 1982 to Tegwyn and Eleri who live at 35 The Square, Uzmaston. In Wales I think. Is that in Wales? Perhaps.

"Put that little lot together, look for a theme and what have you got? My thinking? Four babies, all boys, born within the space of five days. Also… born to infertile mothers. The person compiling the information in the book said that they had inactive ovaries but they wanted a child and so they came to Stork Delivery for help."

"There's a lot of women who would give anything to be mothers," said Fleur. "It's a natural instinct."

She felt that he must be relaxing to remember all this detail.

He went on again: "The book suggests something fishy though. Nominally, the embryos implanted in these women's wombs were the result of a test-tube fertilisation, a combination of the husband's sperm with an ova from an anonymous donor.

"But in reality, according to the details in the book, these select few were being duped as these particular embryos that were inserted, were ready-fertilised and special, frozen and lying in store, just waiting for the right customer and the right time.

"The book shows that fresh semen of the dads was collected, yes, but was then ignored and the replacement stuff used to create each of the four boys has the same code number and the same name: Charles.

"And the eggs all came from the same woman and she has the name of...

"Let me guess... Diana," said Fleur, anticipating.

"Exactly."

Fleur yawned and snuggled closer.

"Go on, squire," she urged in a somewhat muted tone. "I'm still listening."

"There's a section later on about implanted embryos. There's notes after that about gibberellic acid, an enzyme that...

But Fleur wasn't listening. Her rhythmic sighs told him that she was asleep.

Once she was settled in his arms, it wasn't long before Bruce joined her in the land of nod. They slept for a couple of hours, gaining much-needed relief, until a clunk-and-clang from the door signalling the middle-of-the-night, routine guard-check woke them. Bruce looked up, then settled back down again.

"What is it?" murmured Fleur.

"Just the guards doing their thing."

"I'd only just got off."

"Me too."

"Hold me."

They'd been apart for more than ten months. Fleur rubbed her cheek against his, and sighed as his hands ran down her back, tracing over shoulders and curves in swishes and swirls. She stretched in response. She found his mouth, savouring the fullness of his eager lips. His hands were like gloves of comfort, easing the pain, though he kept them in check lest things went too far.

They then slept again, and slept well. For four hours. Even the following door-check failed to shake them.

"It's funny thinking about the end," mused Bruce as he next came to. "The odd thing is I don't mind... the thought of dying doesn't worry me anymore."

"Listen," she said, butting in. "If it comes to basics then I don't want you diving in after us. Right?"

"I've already decided that one," Bruce replied. "If you go then I go too. I couldn't live without... "

Fleur took his wrists, shaking him.

"Don't be a fool, of course you could," she said with emphasis. "You'd have to pick up the threads, one by one."

"I love you so much."

"I'm going to cry," she said.

***

It was still dark when a guard woke Bruce with a prod. He blinked, then gingerly unthreaded himself from Fleur who, at long last, was sleeping soundly. He tip-toed to the door and they let him out without making a sound.

Every chance to practise was to be welcomed since every second counted now. Cloud had brought in several practice partners and Bruce used them to the full, sharpening his skills, honing his match-play. He knew he had to be needle-sharp.

Each day he worked at it, relentlessly punching balls across the net, generating more kick in the second serve, seeking out more variety in direction. High lobs up into that glaring sun and backhands straight down the side-line. Then drop volleys off his toes.

Time flew by.

Physically, he was in good shape and those long practice sessions back at Thurston had helped keep his mental pressures in check. In fact they had been a tonic and he had taken delight in playing back-to-back sessions with all-comers.

Days slipped by and in next to no time it was the last night before... before what might well be the last day. Everyone tried hard, but they were only human. Louis and Ysanne sprawled over Fleur and Bruce, seeking comfort and relief, knowing they were too young to help. It look a long time but finally they fell into sweet oblivion.

Bruce carried them back to the other mattress, one at a time, then carefully spread blankets over them. While he was away, Fleur straightened their own bed and welcomed his return.

"I'm pleased they're asleep at long last," she whispered as he slid in beside her. "Ysanne in particular has been so frantic and up-tight about not being able to do anything to help save us."

"Well, we're all in the lap of the gods now," Bruce said, "so she shouldn't take it to heart."

Then, face to face, they melted into each other. "Your daughter said something this afternoon," Bruce ventured, sounding a little embarrassed, "that made me want to cry."

"Go on."

"She called me dad and said she loved me."

Fleur smiled.

"Of course she loves you," insisted Fleur, kissing his neck. "You should be pleased."

"I am," Bruce said. "You know I am."

They kissed. At first tenderly, gently...

"What was the verdict on the stitches?"

"They said I was fine. They took out all the non-dissolvers and said the rest would go in their own good time. I don't have to go back."

Bruce ran his finger across her lips, then kissed her.

"Is it too soon?"

"I'm still sore, but if you want... "

"Hush," he said. "No. Forget it, it's all right."

"Sure?"

"Sure."

"Know what?"

"What?"

"I still want to feel you inside me."

"OK then, when this is over, down at Martlesham Creek."

"Yes."

"Under our special tree."

"Sounds fantastic."

"Is that a promise, do we have a date?"
"It is… and yes we do."
Then they slept.

CHAPTER 21

The lights had already been switched on and were already shining bright when guards rattled the door and pulled back the locks because it was getting close to dawn. This was it: the day had finally arrived. No sooner had they stirred than Haas appeared at a distance, taking charge and ensuring there would be no last-minute blunders.

There was no privacy. They had to dress and share their last moments together under the cold stare of men who had entered their room. When they were clothed and ready, Ysanne was first to say goodbye, with tears, as she hugged Bruce... he wiped away her tears and kissed her.

"Look after your mum," he whispered, as he lifted her off the floor.

Louis waited his turn with a sad face. Bruce dropped to his knees, hugging the lad, no longer a bouncing bundle of fun.

"You too," he said. "Stay calm."

Then Fleur.

"I'll love you for ever," she whispered.

"I'll play my heart out."

She took a deep breath. "It's just another game," she insisted, "so go out there and think about tennis and not about us."

She's been so brave, Bruce thought as he watched her walk away without looking back: she wanted to, but even more she wanted him not to see her cry. Nor did she want to see the tears on his face.

Ysanne broke free, managed a few steps back, but then a guard stepped in and took her away to re-join Fleur and her brother as they all entered the helicopter's cage.

"Okay, Saxon, let's go," Haas said, giving him a push.

The Moving Cloud was taking no chances: he'd given Haas back-up for the walk to the small boat that would take them to the QE2.

Once up on court, Bruce looked around. Although the sun was emerging over the horizon, the floodlights were still switched on. He walked around the boundaries of the court to settle. Then into the middle where he twisted and turned, one foot and then the other, judging the tread of the AstroTurf, first here and then there, finding it a flick faster than real grass. Good... or bad, depending on your playing style.

Once his limbering-up sequence had got him warm and loose, he nodded to his practice partner and soon they were hammering away vigorously. Over on the other side, his opponent was doing exactly the same.

"One minute to go, gentlemen," announced the umpire. "Please make your final preparations."

Up in the gallery several of the roulette weals were already waiting, eager for the big event to begin. Flunkies buzzed about lining up chairs and settling bottles of bubbly into ice buckets. Binoculars were cleaned and focussed. Anticipation mounted. Cyrano raised his hand and gave the sign.

Drapes hanging all along the far side of the ship fell, revealing the 'prize': a helicopter hovering, motionless, seemingly just hanging in space. And there below it, trapped in a cage, were three humans, the Hainault family, like puppets on a string.

"Brilliant," exclaimed Bunker Lacey, as he spotted the crisis cradle.

"Hey look man, look at the sea below them," urged Straffman, nudging his neighbour. "Food mixers, ready plugged in and waiting to grind."

Bunker looked and quickly spotted the sharks, six of them circling in the water.

"Not the best place to take a swim," drawled the Australian horse breeder, adjusting his cushion. "Fantastic set-up! Looks like being a sure-fire humdinger, Cyrano. I'm even thinking it could well be the best ever!"

Cyrano smiled. His eyes moved across to the fortune stacked up on the table, though his thoughts were elsewhere: it was the agony of the forthcoming contest that gave him the biggest thrill. At the end of the day, he didn't care who won.

The umpire checked his electronic pad and pressed buttons. He'd been in control of tennis finals in Flushing Meadows, Paris and Rome, but this degree of sophistication was another level again.

"Time," he called and the game was on. It started fast.

For Bruce, it also started badly.

Sargis took the first game comfortably and then Bruce served: a double fault followed by another. He knew he had to settle down… and quick. But the merest glance up into the pre-dawn sky knocked rationale for six. Blinkers would have been a better idea.

It was a struggle to settle.

He was too brittle and tense, so he dropped a gear, taking a more cautious line, putting in the equivalent of two second serves, trying to work an opening into the game. Sargis anticipated this change and, already leading love-30, he pounced on Bruce's next 'softer' serve, took it early and sent it back down the side-line beyond the server's reach.

That made it love-40. Harut had already won the first game, so just one more notch, and, with his own service game to come next, there was the making of a three-game advantage within his grasp.

Bruce served for game point. Once again he was too cautious, hoping to rescue his dismal start through safety. Harut pounced, smacking it back hard, under the server's racquet and into the 'catch-all' curtain that ran round the back of the court.

Sargis wasn't here for fun: he was here to pick up money, big money, and the bonuses started with £50,000 for the first Pin Point he managed to pull and that tasty little 'extra' was almost within his grasp.

The third game got under way.

Harut served a clean ace. It clipped Bruce's racquet, then rocketed over the twenty-foot-high netting. The next two points started with second serves, heavily loaded with top spin. Both led to short, server-dominated exchanges. Harut hunted eagerly for the fourth point. He raced to the net, leapt up in the air and produced a mighty smash. Splat! And that was it. The shot was too good to catch: three-love to Harut.

The conventional scoreboard had been extended so that to the right of it there was a second frame with a screen and four red lights. One of them blinked and came to life, lettering pulsed onto the screen screaming:

PIN 1…. PIN 1…. PIN 1…. PIN 1

All eyes turned towards the sea, Bruce included. He didn't want to look, but he couldn't help it. The first bolt shot out. Once flung free, it fell fast and there were cheers from Cloud's gang of high-rollers. They were delighted. .. this play of his sure had delivered a lively opening act.

Bruce stared hard into the floodlit sky. He knew that while nothing looked different, he had just surrendered their first key and had to try harder.

"Time!"

Harut hung fire, dawdled and wasted time to let Bruce savour more fully the stressful situation. He towelled his racket handle not once but twice, before tested its tensions, gloating all the while over further pay-offs that he was sure were his for the taking.

He had already scooped the opening bonus. The second pin promised another £70,000 with an extra £20,000 on top of that if two pins dropped before the end of the first set. It was almost a sure bet, with Bruce still tumbling and fumbling, hurrying strokes and fluffing aces.

The score line stole on to read 5-0.

Bruce was in a lot of trouble, and the way things stood so were the three in the cage. One more game to Harut and the second pin would drop. Then what would happen to the cage's floor? Bruce knew only too well the challenge ahead. This was a service game he had to win.

He knew it was crucial to keep his mind on tennis and nothing else. He started to fight back. A good serve, a point won, a solid start. Points were no longer handed over on a silver platter but were contested to the hilt. His courage climbed as confidence mounted.

Standing 40-15 up, and feeling stronger than ever, he had got to game point for the first time. His first serve was too hot to handle, it was an ace-all-the-way, glancing on the ground before exploding back up, straight into the receiver.

The chance of two Pin Points in the first set had gone, the £20,000 bonus for rapid progress was lost: the score line was not 6-0 but 5-1. Harut went berserk in the next game and, as a result, Bruce was crushed.

First set to Harut: 6-1.

Chapter 21

The sun had climbed and there was the tingle of new-day warmth. Bruce wanted to look out to sea, but told himself he mustn't. He would only lose concentration. Instead he turned and called the boy across with drinks. Nervous tension had left his throat feeling parched. He was tempted to take another, but decided against it. Better to get on with the game.

The umpire called to the players. It was time to start the second set.

Back on court, Bruce plunged into a fine rally, bounding round the court with vigour and ferocity that more than matched Harut's push. He won points yet Harut smirked. It was driving Bruce wild. Why wasn't Sargis worried?

The answer hit him at 40-15, right out of the blue. A wobbliness, a dazed feeling. No-one else seemed to notice, but one look at Harut was enough to reveal the truth. Sargis was up to his old tricks again: spiking drinks. He was grinning like a Cheshire cat.

It was no wonder Harut smiled, for he was playing it crafty. Instead of putting Bruce to bed early, he was going to make it look good, knowing that only the players themselves were aware of the trouble he was in. Rallies stretched to ten or twelve shots, but really they were just cover. He let Bruce run out winner in his opening service game, but after balancing the score to 1-1, he skilfully steered the third game to deuce. Bruce twice had the advantage, but lost it both times.

Cyrano's gamblers cheered when Harut finally blew him over with an overhead lob that wasn't all that good, if truth be told.

Harut cruised through his own service game to open up a 3-1 lead, then kept the pedal on, inching along steadily until he was at deuce on ol' rubberlegs' service once again.

They were now in the pin vicinity for the second time.

A big first serve from Saxon shuddered into the net. A second serve followed suit. That meant advantage receiver. Harut took his time to settle, making Bruce wait. Play commenced and Saxon found himself hanging on, resisting the push. Ground strokes rained down relentlessly, firm and hard forcers, not killers, but also not kind.

Everything was at stake, Bruce's whole world stood sideways and he fought like a lion.

The rally had risen to twenty three strokes when Harut pulled the plug. With Bruce beleaguered back on the baseline, he conjured up a delicate lob with back-spin. The ball landed, stood in its tracks as it rose only modestly, then fell like a stone, leaving Bruce totally stranded.

Cyrano's crowd rose like vultures on a thermal, breaking out in gleeful anticipation. They watched the scoreboard for confirmation. First the conventional display appeared, showing Harut ahead in the second set at four games to one.

The second bulb of four in the red light zone went through its flashing sequence and after that the bright-light message on the screen returned, proclaiming:

PIN 2…. PIN 2…. PIN 2…. PIN 2

Bruce put his head in his hands. Yet he had to look. Up in the stands, he saw that the cruel cluster of gamblers had all moved away to the liner's rail-side with binoculars focussed on the cage and the sea and were busily taking side bets on what would come next.

Time seemed to stand still until the pin flew free. Then there was chaos. The cage shook on its string, it was all bounce and consequence, as the floor flapped loose like an open book.

The three prisoners screamed and held on to the bars of the cage tightly. Fleur had prepared Ysanne and Louis for the dangers ahead: she'd had them practice what they would, or could, do if the worst happened. To spread the risk, the plan was for them each to take a different corner, to grip their chosen bar and hang on for dear life.

They followed the plan, reached as high as they could as cage swung madly then slowly settled back down.

Ysanne knew without looking that, for her, things had gone wrong. She heard the pin below her slide out and felt the floor then drop from beneath her feet. She screamed, shut her eyes, and hung on for all she was worth.

As soon as the worst was over, she opened her eyes and remembered the drill: she mustn't look down, had to move across to the next corner without delay, to her Mum's corner. Louis was safe. His pin had held, like his mother's. Together they watched as Ysanne made her move.

Below them the sharks circled, eight in all, as life or death was hanging in the balance above them.

She wanted to scream. With no foothold, her body was all dead weight only held in place by her arms' muscles and by her hands' grip around the corner bar. "Move love," Fleur called gently. "Come on. Come to me."

Breathing deeply, she pushed panic aside. The drill, follow the drill. She knew it could be done. She must concentrate. And she must never look down.

"I'm coming," she cried, with a short gasp.

Fleur stretched out from her corner holding out her arm, shortening the distance that Ysanne would have to travel on her own.

"Take it easy," said Fleur, encouraging her. "You know you can make it."

She moved slowly, one bar at a time, pulling herself across the cage towards her mother, steady but determined. With each forward motion she drew closer. Hope was slowly rising.

"She'll make it," suggested Lou Yin across on the liner, his eyes sharply focussed on the dangle-drama. "Yes, she'll just make it."

Zafros's smile had a knowing smirk as he turned to his guest.

"Don't be too sure," he said, "because the next two bars are decoys."

Lou Yin's mask cracked in a grin.

Ysanne had progressed closer to her mother's outstretched hand. She knew that she needed all the help she could get because her fingers were so stiff from tension and painful from the effort needed to grip.

Then it all happened in a flash: the next bar gave way, like a bad tooth yanked free at the end of an invisible string, and worse still Ysanne's hand seemed stuck to it.

She was paralysed. "Let go!" screamed Fleur. "Let go of it!"

Ysanne finally got her fingers loose, and the bar dropped.

The fiends on the upper deck gasped while Cyrano's cameras rolled, recording every moment. This really was worth saving: only in the face of disaster do victims produce unbelievable acts of self-preservation.

The bar plunged down like an air-to-sea missile.

"It's hit a frigging shark," cried Castlemaine. "Look, it's harpooned the damn thing. Jesus, see that trail of blood."

Without thinking, Straffman leaned over the rail for a better view, then stood back sharply, checking that his white suit was unmarked. It was. He felt relieved.

Castlemaine and the other turrets around him forgot the tennis for the moment, focussing on the sea in anticipation of the unholy blood-bath there would be if the girl dropped. Seven hungry sharks homed in. Blood meant food, and the feeding was about to start.

Unable to see the commotion in the water down below, Bruce's eyes were on Ysanne as he prayed she would get across and reach the safety of her mother's corner.

"Don't look down," Fleur yelled, stretching out even further. "Stare at your hands for a minute. Count your fingers, go one to five until you get over the shock."

"But I'm getting weaker," moaned Ysanne. "I'm never going to make it."

"Oh yes you are!" Fleur shouted. "Come on. I'm waiting for you."

"But I've lost height. I've slipped down. I can feel the bottom of one bar already."

"Come on."

"Oh, mummy," Ysanne gasped. "I can't hang on much longer!"

"Come on!" urged Fleur. "Another bar, darling."

"Come on, Ysanne," Louis yelled. "You can do it. You can! You can!"

Ysanne obeyed, reaching out across the gap left by the breakaway bar.

"It's a big stretch," she grunted.

"I know, I know. Just do it!"

"I'm scared," Ysanne wailed.

Fleur's voice was more silent prayer than speech: "Do it, baby, do it!"

Ysanne released her trailing hand and grabbed the next bar with both hands and.... and it too gave way and plunged downwards. With nothing to support her, Ysanne followed it, flapping like a struck gull. Fleur and Louis screamed as their eyes followed her long descent.

Still shouting, Ysanne hit the water hard and plunged below like a heavy stone. Silence ensued as the sea circled over her.

Then, just as suddenly, she broke the surface, spluttering and gasping for breath as she began to tread water.

"There she is! I see her, Mum," shouted Louis.

Fleur breathed a prayer of relief: "Thank God."

Bruce ran to the side, straining for a clearer view.

The ring-siders on the upper deck couldn't have cared less what happened to the girl. The ones who had bet that she'd be the one to fall first cheered. The others paid up, drowning their loss with a further fill of bubbly.

Ysanne bobbed up and down, gasping, trying to remain calm. She looked for the sharks. They had gone, chasing after the stream of blood already in the water, but she knew they'd return all too soon. The liner reared up like the sheer face of a mountain, its polished steel cliffs offering no hand-holds whatsoever. Her only hope, and a distant one at that, seemed to be a light yacht some way to the south. It had a dozen or so croaky old-folk on board and all of a sudden they had come to life, waving and shouting encouragement. It was a long way to swim but she had no other choice. Surely someone would rescue her before her strength gave out.

Cyrano spotted the small craft and its cluster of holidaymakers. He reached for the intercom to call for Haas to intervene.

"Just hold on there," said the horse breeder, deftly catching Cyrano's arm. "Let's give the young filly a chance. It's a fair few furlongs for her to swim to reach that yacht and who knows... "

He turned and offered bets and another side challenge was on.

Fleur was beside herself. She didn't know what to do. Ysanne down there in the dangerous drink. Louis petrified with fear, still with her in the cage. She watched, horror-stricken, praying for a miracle.

"Look, Mum," Louis cried, pointing. "A little boat is coming across!"

Fleur saw the yacht and recognised it. "It's the Hathor," she told him. That was good, except that everyone down there was so old: sure they were making a noise, but what could they do? If she'd only turned the other way and looked north, however, she'd have had much greater cause for worry because two of the sharks had now split off from the rest of the attack-pack. Finding themselves to be unfed, they had turned back and were now knifing their way towards... the swimmer.

Splash, splash, splash. She pressed on urgently.

On the yacht itself, two volunteers for the mission hurried and fumbled forward while others scuttled round like busy ants, helping to steady the little shore-boat that they had managed to launch. It was flimsy fibreglass but it would have to do. Driven to distraction by what they were witnessing they just had to help: duty is not a feeling that dims with age.

The sharks were getting closer. Fleur's heart was in her mouth.

Two pensioners now on board, one pushed clear of the yacht while the other tugged life into the outboard motor.

"How close are the sharks, Four-X?" asked Threadneedle, looking over Lou Yin's shoulder.

Castlemaine reported back saying:"The girl's fifty yards from safety. Sharks are sixty yards behind her but they're coming up fast, I'd say twice as fast."

Ysanne swam on. The movement of the small boat ahead made her kick harder. Then she turned and saw the sharks.

Everyone gasped. This was going to be close.

The cockleshell heroes lost valuable time trying to master the rudder, but then got it sorted and got back on course. They too saw the sharks and tried to pump more life into their rescue craft.

"It's going to be touch and go, Alf."

"I know. I know."

The craft bobbed on a slight swell and, temporarily, the helmsman lost his view. Ahead of him, Sandy took up his post right at the front of the small boat: he was kneeling over, paddle in hand, ready to do his bit as their craft bounced closer on the waves.

"Here she comes. Come on girl!"

"Keep going."

"Alf! Quick, the sharks!"

"I know. I'm not blind!"

"Block them off with the boat."

"I'm trying, Sandy, I really am!"

Sandy hung over the front as far as he dare, shouting to Ysanne.

"Get round this side and tuck in close. Then lie flat!"

The girl obeyed. Tucking in tight against the boat, she pulled her legs and arms up and made as shallow a float as possible. Losing sight of her dangling limbs, the first shark swept past inches from the front of the small craft while the second one swam straight under the boat. Then the two sardine seekers made U-turns and started back.

Alf and Sandy struggled vainly, pulling and tugging together on the oar that Ysanne was clinging to down below in the water. But she was wet and she was heavy. Turning for a view, Ysanne saw white teeth and fins looming nearer and nearer, and from somewhere within herself she found that inner extra strength: the sharks were almost on her when she shot out of the water with one last mighty heave.

Chapter 21

On the yacht behind, the crowd of old folk cheered: the girl was saved, the veterans of valour had won the day.

Up in the cage, Fleur sighed with relief, shut her eyes for a moment, then leaned out and touched a tearful Louis.

On the liner, Luigi Rizzi wiped sweat from his collar and liked his lips: he'd cleaned up, collected £80,000. But it had been close.

"Marvellous," declared Kenneth Nwodo sitting next to him.

Cyrano smiled. What a splendid day this was. He had Saxon going nowhere and the fun was growing by the minute, what a plan this was.

A snigger from Harut brought Bruce back from the netting at a good pace: there was no time to linger even over a grand escape like the one he had just witnessed down on the sea below.

Time to get back to business.

***

A call from the umpire brought both players back to the game and Bruce discovered that the break, unwelcome as it was, turned out to have at least a bit of an upside as when the action kicked off again, he had thankfully found his good legs again.

He fought furiously and, now trailing 4-1 down, re-joined the battle with a vengeance. The next two games went with service and the score moved on to 5-2, which left Harut serving for the second set. But now not only was Bruce holding his own service games, he was pressing Harut on his and the score in the next game stood level at 30-30, then level again at deuce. It returned to deuce three times and after those quick walkovers earlier on, this was an altogether different kettle of tennis.

They were in their longest game yet, stretching to eleven minutes. Bruce ran out winner, taking his first game from the Harut serve. He followed it up by holding his own service game, which narrowed the score to 5-4. They then went into another marathon on the Harut service that lasted over ten minutes, a blistering session that finally ended with a pair of clean aces.

"Harut wins the second set by six games to four," announced the voice on the speakers.

"Harut leads by two sets to love."

As the sun got hotter by-standers started to appear as oven-fresh

201

mothers hidden away within the lower decks of the QE2, stepped out to promenade their new babies, bonding with them in the sunshine. Arriving up aloft, most of them started off by taking in only a mere glance or two but then a growing number stayed on as they found themselves gripped by the match's slightly strange tension.

Next came more eyes again, this time from across the water, from the Queen Juliana, a dirty freighter that had been at rest some distance away to the north east for the past two days. It blew a cloud of fumes and nuzzled closer. It had passed on the Thursday afternoon, belching black smoke and just limping along slowly before grinding to a complete halt. Its current movement was laboured, showed that it was still not cured.

The Juliana came to a stop just when she lay parallel to the QE2: it made such a contrast with the larger, cleaner, ocean-going liner, so resplendent with white flagging and gold paint trim. The distance was not too close and the shouts were almost out of earshot, but its crew could clearly see and enjoy a bit of much-needed entertainment.

Bruce found a new strength in the third set: swept backhands, loaded with top-spin, meant a rough ride for Harut at the far end. The array of strokes widened with a push to the left, then a push to the right, then left again... strength sappers to alternate corners... The honours went to Saxon, he took the set with a score of 6-3.

Cyrano was content as the game was beautifully balanced: two pins gone; three sets played; and Sargis Harut just ahead, holding a modest lead. The umpire proclaimed:

"Harut leads by two sets to one."

Cyrano glanced at the private console to his right which contained the time register.... it said *2 HOURS 8 MINUTES 40 SECONDS.*

"How are they for gas?"

"Enough for another six minutes," replied Cyrano. "But there's a reserve tank, and she's programmed to switch over automatically."

"I think I'll take bets on them running out of fuel before the game's over," announced Threadneedle, spreading his chest.

The loose affiliation of millionaires sat back. Threadneedle started doing sums: the boy was in the bubble, but could he make it burst?

"If you wish, we can all watch the countdown to the very moment when the fuel runs out," announced Cyrano. "It's behind the masking tape on your right."

A hand reached out to uncover the hidden data but was checked by one of the guests.

"No! No!" chorused several voices, each high on suspense. "We'd rather not know!"

"I don't think the Englishman is going to make it," Bunker Lacey said to his neighbour.

"I think this too," replied Lou Yin. "Which means we can clean up proper and good."

It was getting hotter in more ways than one.

Harut felt the heat rising… and it wasn't just the blaze of the sun. It was greed that was bringing him to the boil.

True, he had netted £120,000 already, the payment for winning two Pin Points, but he was out for all he could get, and he still resented having missed that additional £20,000 earlier on. The drugged drink hadn't quite worked, but he had a second dirty plan.

It was time to raise the anti.

Trailing 3-0 down in the fourth set and swamped by Saxon's upsurge, he started his nonsense by disputing a line-judge's verdict. Then, having got nowhere, he turned in anger to the umpire. But the umpire was having none of it and turned the appeal down flat. Harut wouldn't give up though. His claims grew more and more agitated.

A warning was issued but still Harut kept on protesting. Next, a penalty point was deducted. "The man's lost his trolley," thought Bruce, impatient for the game to continue.

His opponent stood below the umpire, waving his racquet and shouting louder and louder until he pulled a ball from his pocket and hurled it upwards towards the umpire who put his hands in front of his face and ducked. The throw missed him by a mile.

But it wasn't the umpire he was aiming at: his target was the third red button, the one controlling the next cage pin, and his aim was spot-on.

The gallery-gamblers rose as one, cheering lustily. Their hullabaloo was magnified by the coarse crewmen on the freighter who hollered across the bay, also yelling for blood. Not so the crowd who were stood watching close round the edges of the court itself, the proud mothers and fathers of surrogate offspring, they just stood and gasped in silence at the happenings they had strayed upon. It was so unreal.

"Look," yelled Rizzi. "He's hit the pin button."

A foul move. Cyrano's finger rose immediately and hovered above the over-ride button. It was now or never...

He could have blocked the badman's move but he didn't. Not one iota and so there was no cancel. In truth, he was rather delighted that the inevitable tipple had just shifted that much closer as shown by the third of the red lights which started flashing.

With his back to all this action, Bruce hadn't the slightest inkling of what was going on. When he spun round he discovered everyone had already pushed across to the side of the liner again.

The doom chorus broke out:

"Five... four... three... two... one."

"God Almighty!" Bruce gasped. "They're at it again."

Red lights flashed, firing off their early warning for the third time, then the word-screen section came to life, the message-maker part shouting the next alarm:

PIN 3.... PIN 3.... PIN 3.... PIN 3

He ran, crashing into the netting at the far end just in time to see the third pin shoot free from the floor of the cage. It flipped and fell. The helicopter held firm and rode the storm that followed despite the cage below swinging madly from side to side. From a distance it could have been a cloth duster being held out from an open window and madly shaken, gripped only by a flimsy, one-corner squeeze.

New fathers arrived up-top and they were not at all happy, shouting their strong disapproval at what was happening, but the gamblers only chortled and more fresh side-bets were dreamed up and odds shouted, fast and furious.

In response to the noise from the fathers, loudmouths on the freighter cheered even more madly for Harut who, sensing their value as a weapon for his cause, made an appeal for them to be shipped across so that they could make an even bigger row. His request was given consideration... and then it got the nod.

Up in the cage, the loss of the third pin caught both of them unprepared: Louis had one of his hands round at the back of his neck, shading it from the blistering sun; while Fleur was in a mental blur, just staring at the underside of the helicopter, looking for hope.

She screamed.

"Louis!"

They'd taken a gamble: guessing that the pins were coming out in rotation, they were positioned together at the same corner. Fleur knew the risk of doing this but had said nothing: if they fell, at least they'd go together. The blessing was that Ysanne was safe. She gripped the bars tightly while Louis hugged her round the middle, holding on for all he was worth.

The bucking and kicking finally eased as the weight below re-centred. Fleur felt about for a foothold with the end of her toes and yes, it was there and no, it hadn't gone.

"We're alive," she gasped. "We did it. We picked the right corner."

Louis said nothing.

"Put a foot down, Louis, and stand on mine. Then the same with the other."

Louis did as he was told, then looked up, helpless and frightened.

On the liner, Bruce ran across to the umpire. "That's ridiculous," he yelled as he climbed the ladder. "You've got to call the whole thing off."

But a guard took a hold of his shirt from behind and growled in his ear, saying: "That's far enough, Saxon."

The gallery agreed with the protest, but only in sarcastic, mocking tones...

"Very unfair. Naughty boy."

"Oh no... not sporting."

"Smack his wrists."

The Moving Black Cloud stepped forward, looked down at Bruce and shrugged his shoulders. "It was just one of those things," he yelled. "You are in a high-risk game here, Saxon, and angry players sometimes boil over."

The new parents didn't agree and began to chant: "Unfair.... unfair.... unfair."

Bruce lost control, throwing down his racquet and swearing angrily while the gamblers watched with satisfied smiles on their faces as they sipped champagne and soaked up the sun.

The chanting from the crowd got louder: the parent-part strongly favoured Bruce, whereas Harut's imported counterweights, the boatload of roughs brought from the freighter, were turning into a mess, arguing among themselves rather than staging a counter-chorus.

And that annoyed him: they had to do what were brought over to do, to back him, fully and more vocally because they could throw Saxon's game and be a more valuable advantage than they were right at the moment.

Seeing that it all seemed to be going the wrong way, he shouted: "I want that crowd of women out of here."

Cyrano ignored the call and with Bruce belatedly back on court, the game continued.

Lou Yin pointed to the clock. "They're going to run out of time quite soon," he told everyone, "so none of this noise stuff matters much, one way or the other."

The observation triggered more information from the circus master.

"The chopper's actually been running on its reserve fuel for the past three minutes," he announced. "When we reach the last ten minutes, the count-down figures will automatically turn from green to red as the alarm registers. At that point, if you agree, we'll take the cover off and watch for ourselves."

"Forget all that, I want see that Saxon beaten fair and square, never mind the fuel," said Lou Yin.

Straffman, however, was more interested in the very opposite: he wanted the drama of seeing the helicopter go crashing down while they were still in play.

"Any which way is a win, be it fair and square or dirty and round," rumbled Four-X. "Just bring it on."

Questions about the exact rules surfaced, so some of the finer details got aired once again, one of them being, Cyrano declared: "You all win if Saxon forfeits the match... I mean to say he may, perhaps, and this is by no means certain, he may choose to dive in to save his darling lady before... "

He suddenly had a further idea and added: "We could, of course, make it difficult for him to take that plunge: we could offer him an incentive to keep playing even if the floor does drop, or even if the helicopter runs out of fuel and the sharks get their long overdue feed."

"Now that would be cruel," said Nwodo, the man who scooped the pot the previous year.

"But brilliant," added Straffman. "Let us all - how do you say? - kick in, then, to make it worthwhile."

Cyrano took the lead: "How about two million each from all twelve of you, plus myself? That makes twenty six million dollars in all, enough of a tempter to give the boy a sizeable problem."

That met with nods all round.

Standing on court down below, Harut made a further appeal about the crowd and this time Cyrano agreed that they had to go and for two reasons: first, the women's chants had become more like protests and they were growing louder; second, because as Haas had just pointed out, they wouldn't like the sight of what was increasingly likely to take place within the very near future.

As a result, orders were given, guards started rounding up onlookers and herding them down below deck. Not surprisingly some resisted, the ones who were most keen to stay and watch the match. "Don't worry," said a new arrival, "because you can see it all on the giant screens down in the ballroom… someone has started beaming live pictures for us to see."

This was true and Cyrano was the one who had set it up. He wanted everything recorded so why not share the fun all round the below-deck parts of the liner, he'd thought, and while he was at it, why not also beam live pictures onto the screens they had installed over on the two islands as well.

After all, it was all going so delightfully well.

The parents with new-born were easy to gently induce to make their way down into the ballroom where they settled into the plentiful seats waiting for them. The freighter yobbos, however, were a rather different matter. Despite their easy-rolling merry state, they set some of the guards on edge because they proved rather difficult to manage: they realised that their restricted manpower fell short of requirement.

As a result there was a little incident that none of them noticed.

It happened when an individual standing near a life-belt stepped aside, allowing rowdy rejects to push past him. He put out a hand and slipped a piece of paper across to one of them. There was a string of code written on it. The exchange was impossible to spot given the way a crowd of bodies just happened to be packed all around him at that very moment… thought that might have been stage-managed and quite intentional.

On court, the game continued, but in peace and quiet. With the crowd gone, Bruce was aware of the gallery's every move: the chink of glasses, the shuffle of waiters scuttling up and down stairs with dates and olives, caviar and crab sandwiches. And aware also of the five cameras that were rolling and turning, capturing the moment.

He found it hard to settle and his 3-0 lead was whittled down in next to no time. Harut took advantage of the upset caused by his underhand move and pulled himself back into the set, levelling the score at 3-3.

Winning three games on the trot should have triggered another pin to fall and earn him more money in the process. But his call was rejected and he was told that this three-game run would merely cancel out the ill-gotten gains he'd already made thanks to his earlier ball-throwing misdemeanour.

That verdict helped Bruce settle. Service games were locked, in-hand and secure. Aces couldn't be trumped.

The score line moved on and soon it stood at 6-6.

The tie-breaker seemed endless, but it ended with Bruce finally winning at 15-13. It was the longest tie-break most of those on the QE2 had ever seen. Up-top gamblers held their breath; down-below parents were mesmerised; guards dropped their guard; even the Cyrano was engrossed.

Away over the water at a distance from the busy happenings, the cage dangled motionless, as did Fleur and her boy... for them it was deadly silence and suspense.

Slumped in his chair, panting, Bruce sighed with relief as the scoreboard made it official.

It was two sets each.

He mopped up a flood of sweat with a fresh towel, then sat up in abrupt fashion knowing he had to push on. "Win the match and they are safe," the Moving Cloud had told him, but how good was the bastard's word? Just one pin remained. There was no room for error.

He looked at the big clock: they had been playing for over three hours. The chopper was running on its reserve tank, which meant there couldn't be much fuel left. He stood up and took a last swallow of water, swished it around in his mouth, then spat it out.

He was on court and ready but true to form his opponent made him wait knowing that the delay ate up more time, burnt more fuel.

"Time!"

This was it then.

CHAPTER 22

Britain stood still as activities all ground to a halt because the man who'd let his fans down by failing to turn up for Wimbledon, their hero, their one big hope, well he was here, back in action. No-one knew quite where 'here' was, but wherever it was he was there and wow, was he was playing.

The press had hunted for weeks on end, searching high and low, but he had just vanished, gone off the radar, just couldn't be found. Tabloids fuelled a verdict that he'd just bunked off with a woman, a former girlfriend, and the pair of them were on a yacht somewhere, swanning round the world, living it up.

Millions fully believed the story, fans and supporters felt badly let down, but then hello… all of a sudden he was back, the man himself. How could it be? Not just back but he was live, he was on the box and in full colour and playing tennis as if his very life was at stake.

Which it quickly became apparent it was.

At the BBC, switchboards were flooded with calls, lines jammed as they had been ever since the first pictures appeared. The first four-minute teaser that went out was very unofficial, in fact downright illegal and, not surprisingly, the top brass were highly annoyed. But then when it went off air, just disappeared, the public's response was immediate, a massive clamour from people wanted more of what they had just seen and not a return to gardening.

The top two, that is to say the Director and the Controller, put their heads together fast, since the air-wave pirates told them that they had the first offer and if they pulled the plug then fine, they would go to ITV and Channel 4 instead. It was a quick decision, to the point and pragmatic: the bad-boys' broadcast was boosting the BBC's ratings big-time, so it could stay.

That bridge crossed and in order to draw in additional viewers, they gave instructions to flash a message on BBC1, the sister channel, at two minute intervals saying:

TENNIS ON BBC2 NOW.

LIVE COVERAGE.

BRUCE SAXON IN MID-OCEAN DRAMA.

The response was fantastic: by half past eight of a Saturday morning, the corporation's automatic monitoring and censoring system recorded a count of 12 million, and the figure was still climbing at a serious rate of knots.

Early-bird live-wires roused bed-lingering parents. Village bread queues just evaporated. Tuned-in housewives phoned neighbours and friends. Baskets of wet washing were dumped and left abandoned. People got off buses and walked out of hairdressers.

Fans in the overnight queues around Wimbledon, thirsting for the afternoon's final, packed in tightly round anyone further along the pavement with a portable TV.

Saxon fans dropped everything as the word travelled fast.

Nobody knew where the transmission was coming from, but the unscheduled broadcast won massive approval.

About this time, a conversation took place between two men, one in London, the other on a liner in the Red Sea.

"Midge made it!" Dexy shouted excitedly into the phone. "He's got us through to American TV. I've just had him on the line and, boy, do they love it. He says they're getting out of bed by the lorry-load! He's in Chicago and their clocks are five hours behind us."

"Time for phase three then," Tog replied. "It's time to tap into ITV."

"You're on."

"They have such poor blockers they're asking to be challenged."

Dexy laughed. "Byter's inside the London Television Centre already, just waiting for our word to go. He's tapped into LWT's signal pattern and reckons they'd never find his link in a month of Sundays."

"Do that and then run the words, man," urged Tog. "To everyone. The sooner the better."

Thus it was, then that at 8.37am precisely, a breakfast-less audience blinked as a curious message started rolling across the bottom of every picture screen in the land.

ATTENTION PLEASE. ATTENTION...

BRUCE SAXON HAS DISCOVERED SOME SECRET INFORMATION..... BECAUSE OF THIS HE AND FRIENDS OF HIS COULD DIE.

WE BELIEVE THAT BY MAKING THESE SECRETS KNOWN THE THREAT WILL BE LIFTED.

THE FACTS ARE UNCOMFORTABLE.... SWITCH OFF NOW IF YOU DON'T WISH TO SEE THEM.

There was a pause, then the announcement continued.

AN INTERNATIONAL FRAUDSTER KNOWN AS THE MOVING CLOUD HAS TAKEN A FAMILY HOSTAGE.

TWO OF THEM ARE IN THE CAGE UNDER THE HELICOPTER.

YOU CAN SEE THEM ON YOUR SCREEN.... THE THIRD ONE HAS ESCAPED.

BRUCE SAXON MUST BEAT SARGIS HARUT AT

TENNIS OR ELSE THE TWO OTHERS WILL DROP INTO THE WATER.

THE MOVING CLOUD WANTS THEM ALL DEAD BECAUSE THEY KNOW HIS SECRET.

HE BREEDS BABIES. HE HAS COLONIES OF GIRLS ON TWO ISLANDS.

THE ISLANDS ARE THOSE ON YOUR SCREENS. THE GIRLS PRODUCE 8000 BABIES A YEAR. THEY SELL AT £10,000 EACH.

THE SECRET IS THAT A BOY NAMED DAVID NORMANTON BORN ON 9 JUNE 1982 IS THE TRUE HEIR TO THE BRITISH THRONE.

THREE OTHER OFFSPRING BRED FROM CHARLES AND DIANA WERE ALSO BORN BEFORE 14 JUNE.

THEY WERE ALL BOUGHT FROM A BREEDING COMPANY CALLED STORK DELIVERY BY INFERTILE PARENTS WHO WANTED CHILDREN.

NONE OF THESE PARENTS KNOW THE TRUE IDENTITY OF THE CHILDREN THEY BOUGHT.

PRINCE WILLIAM IS NOT....

The flow of words stopped in mid-sentence.

Viewers blinked at this overlay of words, this non-tennis information, but for most of them the reaction was 'so what, let's get back to the match'.

Dexy gave out a big sigh of relief: his duty was done.

Putting the message out there for the world to digest was the least he could do for his housemate. That second photocopy of the book's contents, the one he'd persuaded Kathy to run off without so much as a word to Bruce, the one which he had later slipped down the back of the village hall noticeboard at Great Bealings for safe keeping, had turned out to be vital.

On that morning when Bruce had first told him of his plan to take the black book in to work to run off a spare copy before hiding the lot, he saw the need right away for a little extra so he'd phoned Kathy and she'd had agreed with his secret request. The two of them did the handover on a day when Bruce was over at Thurleston.

***

The technician in overall charge of television monitoring appeared on deck, whispered a message and then walked away, returning to his control panel at the centre of four live screens down below. The information he imparted produced a mixed effect. On the one hand, yes, the overlord very much liked the idea of the whole world watching, while on the other, he did not like being invaded and out manoeuvred.

So he picked up a phone and spoke to Haas, instructed him to track down and punish the individual who had somehow penetrated his private sanctuary here on the high seas.

That said, it was little more than a light aside, deal with and immediately put out of mind so that he was able to settle down and watch the tennis through to the end.

Because Cyrano was absolutely revelling in his tense production. His 'tame' man in the match, Harut, stood to collect £500,000 if he emerged as the outright winner.

On top of that there were the pins.

Harut already had £200,000 in his pocket thanks to the three that had popped out, leaving a further £200,000 'bonus' to be added if he could only knock out that fourth pin.

In all, a lot of money was still up for grabs, enough to make a man very greedy.

For Bruce it was do-or-die by the moment, not only for himself but for Fleur and Louis. He knew only too well how close to the brink he'd been in the fourth set, during that marathon tie-breaker. But that was in the past, it was over and done.

All the gamblers were looking on. They had arrived by helicopter in two waves, first the early birds who had been watching from up-top from the very start, then the second group who had opted for a more leisurely start to the day. Now it was time for everyone to change places: those at the back stepped forward and replaced the individuals who had commandeered the best seats up until now.

There was Nishikawa, a multi-millionaire from Japan, and last year's winner Nwodo, a man who had fled his country of birth with a truck-load of gold and now lived in Monaco.

In the next seat along was Rusnak who had swiftly left Poland on a false passport after collaring a handsome tally of Communist Party funds.

Settling down next to Rusnak was Aschmoniet: he had acquired a string of mid-Pacific islands through bribery and who loaned the largest one out as an American airbase. He had numerous signed portraits of Richard Nixon thanks to 'under the counter' deals made with the former power-broker.

Finally, Paul Howard. His father landed up in America back in the Thirties, buying a tract of sea-bed off Galverston at give-away prices. Within months he'd tapped into a never-ending supply of oil. Paul's daughter Molly had a priceless saxophone all made from gold but she preferred the sound of one that she had bought for forty nine dollars in a junk shop. It made Paul very angry and the two of them now never spoke.

This second-half team might have got up late and missed the first call, but right now they were enjoying the best of everything. "Time, gentlemen," barked the umpire. "This is the fifth and final set."

The soft centres of the gamblers up-top spread round the mahogany-and-brass rail as they leaned into it, anticipating the fortune they might well win... indeed, their chances were rising rapidly by the minute.

Cameras rolled, taking in the action, following every movement. Editing and splicing would produce a first-class documentary that afterwards would run and re-run.

As the fifth set got started and the legion of television viewers all round the world soared by the minute, no-one on the QE2 realised the phenomenal drawing power the game was having. Sixteen million were watching in Britain by this stage with a further fifteen million in America.

Next on the numbers list were Australia and New Zealand, followed by Brazil and then Japan. All linked in. But out of this multitude of scattered humans, only four people really mattered: the two tennis players who were locked in battle, along with Fleur and Louis, whose lives depended totally on the outcome.

Both men had been ready even before the time call sounded, eager to get on with it and bring things to an end: Bruce, desperate but determined to save the two he loved; and Harut, eager for money, for a bigger cash prize than he had ever won in his entire life.

Games passed without tantrum or dirty trick from the far end and without a fault or drop in concentration on Bruce's part at the other. They were playing the best tennis of the day and were proving to be an even match as at the end of the first six games they were locked dead level at 3-3.

Rusnak went public with the odds he was offering on the chopper running out of fuel and dropping before the game ended.

That brought the off-court, over-the-ocean risk into a fuller focus and eyes turned to the dangling cage and its two distant figures.

By this time Fleur was both scorched and parched, and she realised that she was going to faint before very long. There was no respite from the sun and if she didn't have some relief, however brief, she wouldn't be strong enough to help Louis when needed. The chopper, beneath which they dangled, cast a shadow over part of the cage and, by leaning over to the right as far as possible, she was just able to escape from the sun's direct rays.

She stayed there in the shade, head bowed, until she felt some of her strength return. Then, she gathered Louis in her arms, protecting him as much as possible from the cruel heat. Louis looked up, smiling sadly.

On the tennis deck of the QE2, the contest continued. Games were tense and gripping and every stroke took its toll. But there was no give and so eight games into the final set, the score was tied at 4-4.

Neither player had given an inch and after three hours and fifty minutes on court there was still not a whisker to choose between them. The countdown clock showed that the helicopter's reserve fuel tank was getting ever-nearer to being empty.

Bruce sensed that he was running out of options. He mustered a mighty attack and a string of aces were fired off like cannonballs, giving him a 40-love head start. Bollocks to caution, Bruce thought, as he went all out for a quick kill. But his 'double first serve' tactic misfired and two line calls both echoed the same verdict…. "out".

That made it 40-15.

He didn't dispute the calls, so eager was he to get on with the game. Tossing the ball high, his intention was clear: to launch another rocket, another ace, only this time make it good. Harut took a gamble, anticipated it was going to be a backhand and had his racquet out, half raised and ready. But the ball came straight at his midriff, fast, leaving no time to adjust.

"Game to Saxon," declared the umpire. "Harut to serve."

With the score standing at 4-5 in Saxon's favour, Harut knew he had to hold the next game otherwise he would fail, losing 4-6.

He glanced up at the gallery where a curtain had now been draw back a little, enough to reveal a timing sequence. Realising that, of the two players down on court, he was the only one privy to the details revealed showing a count-down based on the scant amount of fuel remaining. He smiled: the read-out was saying:

8 MINUTES 8 SECONDS.

With a smirk on his face, he re-tied his laces and straightened his socks, using delay actions that were only interrupted when the umpire demanded that he commence play.

Uplifted, Harut served quickly and sent Bruce an ace that the receiver couldn't handle.

Bouncing the ball before his next serve, he again glanced at the clock, gloating over the fact that Bruce, from where he stood, couldn't see any details of the imminent deadline. He realised that he held all the remaining trump cards.

His next serve, although no ace, was hard and accurate. Bruce parried the fiery offering but struggled to find a good return: a struggle it was… good it was not! Harut smacked the ball back with both angle and thrust, a winner all the way.

He ambled back to his baseline and prepared for the next serve. Bruce sprinted across to the side, towelled his hands, and was back in position before his opponent was ready. He sensed that time was running out and that the only answer was to gamble everything.

As another accurate first serve came hurtling at him, Bruce stretched his body to the left, his racquet raised and ready. The commitment was total, the risk was enormous as it left him off balance. But the result was that with just time to angle his racquet properly, he met the ball and sent it back. It was a lovely return, catching the server completely flat-footed. The server had no hope.

"Thirty-fifteen," boomed the official.

Harut glanced at the fuel-clock and delayed his approach.

6 MINUTES!

Harut's next serve was called out. The follow-up was loaded with top spin. Bruce moved round and took it on his forehand, smacking it firmly back at the server, to his far left-hand corner. The eager Armenian got to it and drove a two-handed backhand to the receiver's baseline.

A splendid safety shot, it landed midway between the two corners, cutting down the range of angles that the Saxon could pick from.

The ball then went up and down the centre-line time after time: every shot from both players was controlled, defensive and safe. Harut was quite happy with this but Bruce, feeling to be pinned down by time, was not.

First, he broke the tied-up-and-tied-down central situation, pushing the ball to Harut's furthest edge and outback instead. He repeatedly found those most-distant corners, alternating one with the other, then sliced heavily so that the ball dropped just over the net.

But Harut anticipated and raced in. Dipping while still on the run, he mustered a delicate soft return. Bruce lunged forward but Harut read the Bruce's racket angle and re-positioned his feet, but a last-minute flick of Bruce's wrist caught him on the hop. Finding himself going the wrong way, he lost his domination in the rally. As a result his lofted over-head pass hadn't enough depth and Bruce buried it with venom.

"Thirty all."

Harut's door was being battered, but he still had the serve and there would be no tie-breaker, this being the final set. The fuel-clock had a new message:

4 MINUTES 9 SECONDS.

A minute later they were still level, this time at deuce.

Harut checked the clock and smiled.

The rat-pack gamblers in the stands checked the clock and smiled as well.

Cyrano smiled without even needing to check the clock.

Bruce couldn't see the clock but even so, instinct told him there was precious little time left and the next rally was already on.

All was fine until he was hit by a moment when his emotion got entangled with his concentration, a bad mix. When these two ingredients combined they lifted the lid on a box marked 'Too Costly'. The ball bounced slightly higher than he anticipated and stumbling to respond to the extra rise, his return was over-hit, landing well beyond the line.

Now they had a game.

His opportunity for match point had gone.

Over-zealous and rather wild, the server put his first serve into the net. Gambling everything once again, Bruce raced towards the second offering, took it low and deep, hacking it back at Harut, straight at his body. It caught him in two minds, between forehand and backhand and that split-second of indecision cost him dear. Bruce pounced on his return shot and volleyed it past the server.

"Deuce."

Harut produced a tremendous first serve. It should have won the point... only Bruce was gambling once again, anticipating it would zap down the centre-line. He managed to reach it, rasping a return back hard over the net to catch the server napping. Harut made an instinctive lunge and achieved a touch, but only enough to send the ball soaring high and sideways such that it flew out of court.

Nishikawa caught it, then passed it to Howard who rolled it in his hand, treasuring the moment, his touch of such a memento, then threw it back.

Lou Yin glanced round at the fuel-clock and the movement of his head caught Rusnak's eye. "Hey!" he shouted to the rest. "Just look at the time!"

ONE MINUTE.

"Holy cow," gasped Straffman, brushing his wealthy but anxious nostrils. "What a fabulous end."

"Advantage Saxon."

The much travelled ball was back with Harut who looked it over as he walked back to the baseline. He decided against it and took another from his pocket, bounced it over and over, then rocked forward, then bounced it again and rocked back.

The universal verdict was that this could decide it.

Saxon stood at championship point and the gallery were on their feet as a staggering four hundred million dollars hung on the next few seconds.

Play commenced.

Harut's first serve was ferocious, but it was also too long. The electronic eye bleeped to give an impartial 'over-run' verdict.

"Out," called a linesman in support.

Behind them, the fuel-clock moved on.

46 SECONDS

Harut didn't like the verdict.

"Play on," said the umpire calmly. "Second serve."

Harut froze, a statue of indecision.

"Play on, Mr Harut," said the umpire. "I won't tell you again."

Harut complied, threw the ball up from his left hand and as it fell his flashing racquet knocked it out of its skin. It was a cracker of a second serve… but Bruce was already out prowling.

His backhand was good; it had everything - power, bite and cut. The server raced across to the right, took Saxon's return early and played it as a half-volley on the rise.

38 SECONDS.

Ashmoniet's eyes sparkled; this tension was wonderful. Lou Yin squeezed the rail; Threadneedle clenched both his fists. Bunker Lacey moved over to the far side, anticipating the helicopter's imminent crash. Straffman followed him, binoculars already pressed to his eyes.

Bruce met the return and fired it back. Sargis retrieved well, sending a backhand flashing down the side-line. Bruce took it fast, punching it back.

Those watching round the world who knew the game recognised that the server was still in the stronger position. His string of forcing shots were played in sequence to both sides of the receiver such that Bruce was diving all over the place, intercepting brilliantly but barely holding on.

The two athletes had hammered away for three hours and 46 minutes, producing some of the most gruelling tennis imaginable. On top of that, for the last hour at least, they'd had the extra burden of toiling under the sun's blistering heat. But now, time had run out.

19 SECONDS.

Departure time had almost come.

Up in the viewing gallery, the cruel cast of big spenders were on Ecstasy Island, twitching with a mix of blood-lust and greed. Around them, guards forgot their duties as they too found themselves locked into the tension. Up high, cameras panned into every corner and soaked up the moment.

Below deck in the packed ballroom there was hush and total silence. Not even the new babies cried.

Thanks to Dexy, Tog, Midge and others, the whole world was watching, riveted by the happenings on this distant outpost that was both hidden and exposed. Three hundred million bit their nails as they goggled and gasped. Never in the history of television had there been anything as tense as this.

Pictures flicked and changed, producing a pastiche of action and imminent disaster. There was play and weary players, there were hostages and sharks, and there were moments of amazement when mountains of money filled the screen.

With the final seconds ticking away, a fresh message took shape in the server's head, one which said never mind winning, just hold the line as there's plenty enough pay-back for caution and control. Make sure you don't lose.

Bruce, however, had to gamble. He was madly rash.

Harut saw him scorching forwards to the net in his blind panic and sent up a lob high over his head. It looked like this could be it as it had 'winner' written all over it. But the charging bull ground to a halt, spun round and chased after it.

No time for fancy footwork, he just had to leap in the hope of meeting it. He soared in the air and made contact, surprising both himself and the watching world.

Four more shots followed, with the screw steadily tightening, until Saxon once more found himself at full stretch on the rack. As a result, he played a soft return that came gift-wrapped and shining.

With a mighty heave, Harut launched a blast, sure that he'd found his golden moment, but Bruce wasn't done. His brain took it all in... the opponent's stance and pose... the feet... the racquet angle... the lean... the shoulder and the wrist... and the verdict...

....a cross-court shot... to the side... to the backhand.

It triggered instantaneous action.

He took a mighty gamble, took a dive which took him fully horizontal.

The server's head was already in the clouds. He'd done it. He'd won it. But he was riding on a false assumption. Misjudging the Englishman's spirit and endeavour, he was totally unprepared for the fleeting cross-court return.

He watched in horror as the ball passed him by.

It was way out of reach.

Bruce crashed to the deck, spread-eagled and spent. He was the clean and outright winner. Gasping for air, he lay flat, face-down with his eyes closed. Waiting and hoping but still not certain until at last came the official announcement... he had done it.

"Game, set and match to Saxon. He wins 1-6, 4-6, 6-3, 7-6, 6-4."

CHAPTER 23

He lay there for a short while, face down and motionless, just letting the words sink in, before slowly pushing up off the ground and turning to the masters in the gallery. He'd done it, he'd risen to the challenge and was the worthy winner.

But his jaw dropped and he gasped at what he found... because it amounted to nothing, there was no visual reward. No, there was just an empty space. There was not one single person looking down, sharing his hard-earned victory. Instead, there were backs and shoulders all topped with a row of away-facing heads.

Everyone was gazing out to sea. "What the hell's going on?" he gasped.

Then reality struck as he realised that his victory must have come too late: Fleur and Louis must both be in the drink.

Gone.

He scrambled to get up off the floor and onto his feet, then ran for the ladder only to find it blocked off by an imposing guard. Lashing out with his racquet, he sent the man's gun flying and the noise of that made guards standing up at the top raise their weapons, ready to shoot.

But Cyrano raised a hand to stop them. "No, no, don't fire!" he called. "Let the man come up here. Join us and see for yourself. We have the best view from up here."

"What's going on?" snapped the baited English mouse.

He pushed his way through the press of bodies and reached the side of the ship, then shouted in dismay for the helicopter was done: its engine was coughing and spluttering. The cage below flapped wildly but it was already empty… Fleur and Louis were nowhere to be seen.

"It's the fuel tanks, dear boy," Cyrano gloated. "Just stand here and watch her go down. She'll plunge like a stone any second now."

Without any life-giving diesel fuel and simply sucking in air, the engine cut out and died. The gamblers roared approval as the helicopter fell from the unfeeling sky, tugged down by the weight of the cage beneath it.

The metal mish-mash hit the sea then splayed out and briefly formed a mad-tangled bobbing wreck. "Where's Fleur?" screamed Bruce. "And where's Louis? What have you done?"

He grabbed at arms and shirts indiscriminately, pleading for information from anyone.

"They abandoned ship," said Bunker Lacey lazily. "Fell together, don't you know."

"You were busy," said Ashmoniet.

"Perfect timing," Castlemaine slobbered. "Just perfect."

"They got out just before the chopper hopped it," Howard told him. "They somehow sensed that their time had come."

Bruce pushed his tormentors aside. "Where are they?" he shouted, leaning out to sea and then turning back. "Where are they, you bastards?" Having worked Bruce into the state he wanted, Cyrano took over the script.

"It's like this," he said, simulating concern. "They dropped just seconds before you dumped Sargis, so they could still be down there. Perhaps they're on the other side of the chopper-remains at this moment, searching vainly for some handhold.

"Suppose, just suppose, that they're safe. Think Saxon, just imagine. There's so many things that might be going on. The sharks, for instance…"

Bruce was frantic and he surged towards the filthy black raincloud, but stopped short when the rat drew a gun. "No closer," he ordered. "That's far enough, Saxon."

"You've killed them…"

"Quite the opposite you poor, deluded fool, they've fallen in because of you, not me. But why so gloomy, they may still be out there, mouths in and out of water, gasping for life, holding on for their hero, hoping he'll come charging over the waves on a white steed."

Cyrano laughed and Bruce broke, lunging at the evil force only to find himself pinned back by guards blocking his way.

"Easy now Saxon and just listen because I'm going to make you an offer which might change your decision as to what happens next." Cyrano motioned to a waiter, who revealed a silver tray piled high with gold bars and packs of paper money, worth in all, twenty six million dollars.

"This could be yours, every bit of it," continued Cyrano. "All you have to do is let them go: just turn your back while the remains of the helicopter sink and the sharks clear up. Your choice, Saxon. Every single one of us has contributed to the pot so there's a fortune here and it's all yours for the taking."

Everyone watched, rubbed their fingers in delight at the teaser they had generated, but Bruce wasn't listening, he was oblivious to their words as his eyes were out on the ocean, hoping to spot signs that might signal survival. He saw sharks circling and searching, which might just mean they hadn't eaten yet.

But why didn't he see Fleur or Louis?

"Come on, jock," Threadneedle said to goad him into a decision. "You can't turn your back on all this money. It's a no-brainer."

After that came more clatter-trap, more clutter and fluster talk. "What if they are out there, after all," mused Straffman right in his ear, "and what if the kid's just lost a foot, or half a leg."

Having wound him up tight, the question was which way would he go? He didn't need to think: there was only one choice. He had to save Fleur. He had to try. He might as well be dead otherwise.

Cyrano read his commitment, his decision and smiled inwardly. Time to add further torment. He beckoned to the waiter who nodded and walked forward holding up the dazzling temptation. Cyrano's cameras kept tracking, so the eyes of the world were still on the tension.

Livid with anger, Bruce kicked out, hard and high, and the tray flew out of the man's hands, scattering gold and money everywhere. He turned and spun away, ran to the side of the liner, opened a short section of rail, stepped through and dropped into the sea.

Cyrano was nimble and moved forward quickly, ahead of the others. He came to the same spot, then stopped and peered down. Without turning or looking round, he switched the tone of his voice to that of an official commentator: "Saxon's hit the water and surfaced. He's starting to swim."

The news brought everyone forward, their necks craning for a better view. Cyrano dropped the bolt back into the hinged portion of the rail, restored safety and then turned back to the sea for a second look.

A waiter, or at least a man dressed as a waiter and who was stood back at a distance, put down his tray of melons and ginger-dip and moved forward. He got close to Cyrano and put a hand on his sleeve, then without showing any emotion whispered in his ear: "Listen, my name is Izod.

"I was in love with a girl called Areej. We were going to marry but you had her killed. I vowed then that I'd get you and here I am. We're going in together. Now."

Ogilvie pulled the bolt back out once again and the short rail section swung free. He kept on pushing as hard as he could. "Help!" screamed Cyrano, resisting for all his worth and hitting out blindly. "Help! Help me!"

Haas saw the battle on the brink, drew his pistol and fired. Ogilvie felt a searing pain in his upper chest. But Areej's voice was still there calling him and he managed to tear Cyrano's hands away from the rail. Clasping Cyrano tightly, he made a last push and the pair fell, cartwheeling madly downwards through space.

Recognising the problem, Haas leapt overboard seconds later, anxious to save his boss. A big man who had been masquerading as one of the noisy yobs from the freighter saw the three bodies take the plunge. "This one's mine," he roared as he pushed the others aside and plunged in after them. This was no passing fruit gum: this was Gripper, a king-pin among the group of Thurston GPs. That meant there were five down in the foam.

Bruce was on the move, striking out ahead of the other four, searching frantically for Fleur and Louis and oblivious to the commotion behind him. But then one of sharks turned and singled him out and he was suddenly filled with fright as here in open water there was no hiding place.

It was too late to turn back and he couldn't reach the floating chopper-island, still bobbing tantalisingly on the waves some way ahead, so he flipped over and floated... and hoped.

The ruse worked.

The shark's attention now switched to new pressure waves that were reaching its nose's sensors from the thrashing going on further behind: it swept past Bruce and locked on to the foursome who were closer to the liner.

Cyrano was the nearest but as he was the first to see it coming, he managed to work his way back round so as to be positioned on the downside side of Ogilvie's weak body.

Haas was feeling relatively safe right at the back of the little group until Gripper swam up from further behind. Clamping his hands around Haas' neck, he pushing his thumbs inwards like steel wedges and forced a gap between the bones. Then there was a snap and Haas's neck was broken. His head fell forward. Loose.

The shark first hissed past in exploring mode, then turned to come back to take Ogilvie, or part of Ogilvie, for lunch. Gripper plunged below the water, re-surfacing with Haas's body held aloft. He flung it towards the monster: it cleared Ogilvie's head, landing with a splash just ahead of the incoming rows of teeth. There was a brief wrestle before the shark made off with a leg in its mouth, bitten off at the knee.

Cyrano pushed away from the floundering Ogilvie, heading south, away from the sharks and danger. He had spotted the distant yacht and his eyes lit up when he saw the same little boat that had rescued Ysanne earlier putting out once again. Safety, he thought.

Gripper's instincts were split. Ogilvie was spitting blood and he kept sinking, so he should stay... but that meant Cyrano was getting away. He reached out and grabbed hold of his mate. "Are you alive man?"

"Yes," gasped Ogilvie, looking dimly at the big man. "But I'm finished. You get out of here before the sharks come back."

"No way man," Gripper shouted. "They let me be a GP and it feels good. You know what it stands for, yes? You one too, man, and we stick together."

"No! No! Go! Look there's one already... "

Treading water as he supported Ogilvie, Gripper glanced back over his shoulder. Sure enough there was another shark coming all right but there was also help and it was closer at hand.

Hal crashed down into the water with a red lifebelt. "You're a bloody nutcase, Gripper," he screamed as he surfaced. "You know that?"

"You didn't have to come."

"Bollocks. I got GP fever too."

Gripper laughed. "You look after the lad then," he retorted, "and I'll sort this great sodding goldfish."

He kicked away, bobbing towards the monster. "I've come a long way for this," he muttered, unclipping a steel bar from his waist. The bar was four feet long and over a quarter-inch thick. "Come on you beauty, come put me on test."

He paused as the shark side-slipped past him, its cold eye giving a long unnerving stare. But he didn't flinch, just waited as the killer turned and then came in, mouth open and ready to eat. Spray splattered the muscleman as he was swept under the water, but by then the steel bit was in its place, across the inside of the monster's gaping mouth.

Gripper strained, pulled as he'd never pulled before, as he was dragged along under the surface. Teeth cracked, broke off one by one, as the bar started to bend, as its two ends slowly came round. The heaving from below went on and on until a steel circle was almost formed. Still the ring was tightened until, at last, the monster was well and truly muzzled.

His work done, Gripper shot to the surface, blowing and gasping for breath.

He punched the air with both fists.

"I done it!" he yelled madly. "Man, oh man, I sure done it!" He knew he'd achieved something that would become folklore among those who pump iron because, shaking its head in jaw-locked frustration, the shark was done. It had been beaten by a strongman and it made off.

The noise of winches at work up above meant that a lifeboat was on its way down to help rescue those in need. A second shark which had also been heading Gripper's way, switched direction: the revised item on its menu came in the shape of Cyrano.

The Moving-but-Slowly Cloud had been in command for so long, protected from first-hand danger himself, that he'd forgotten what fear tasted like, but now, glancing at the shark behind, panic flooded in. He was exposed. He was no longer top dog.

His swimming slowed as he became more and more exhausted until, with his power spent, he was virtually stationary in the water; by the time the Hathor's little shore boat reached him, the shark was no more than fifty feet away and closing in fast.

He threw himself at the boat, hands clutching at the cord that ran all around its bows.

"Help me!" he screeched. "Quick! I don't want to die!"

"Are you the man called something Cloud?" asked an old lady, leaning over the side of the boat.

"Yes! Yes, I am!" he roared, practically screaming. "But call me Cyrano. Be my friend and help me. Pull me out!"

The shark was getting close. The old lady reached for a paddle and stood up.

"We've come all the way from England," she said in a loud, proud voice. "They invited us pensioners onto the Hathor to act as decoys for if and when you sent people to search it. But, listen here you, I didn't come all this way just to find birds and white bats, Mr Filthy Black Cloud, I came to find you. This is for what you did to my sister. Her name is Nellie, not that you'd likely remember."

A paddle came crashing down on his left hand. He let go his grip and the hand dropped into the water. He brought it up again but it was still writhing in pain. "And this is for what you've done to all the others," she added as a second blow came raining down, breaking the grip of his other hand and ending his chances of survival.

Cyrano floated free. She nodded to Franklin. It was job done and the little boat turned round.

As they headed south, back to the safety of the yacht, Eleanor never looked back, not even once.

***

Meanwhile, all hell had broken lose on the QE2 where there were guns, bullets, fists and knives. The shake-out didn't last long because the liner only had a weak defence-line since the prospect of an attack such as this had been totally inconceivable.

By contrast, in the other camp Masud and Zuberi had fielded a much stronger team this second time; having been outplayed once before they were not going to let that happen again.

The fireworks soon died down and the Ipwich crowd helped 'the big boys' to tie up loose ends.

CHAPTER 24

With a loud bang, the windows of the helicopter cockpit suddenly cracked and splintered, showering the sea all around with a cloud of glass confetti. With loss of this buoyancy bubble meant that metal spider-work that had rested on the sea surface since falling out of the sky, was unable to spin out life any longer. It sank fast and was gone from sight in less than five seconds.

It left nothing: Bruce's eyes scanned the empty waters in vain, through those ripples still close to the centre, then the ones already inching away.

But there was nothing. No visible hand, no bobbling head, just nothing.

No matter where he looked, Fleur and Louis were nowhere to be seen. So that was it, then.

Certain that they were either drowned or devoured, he knowing that he'd done everything possible and this was it, he could give up. They were gone and the fight was over; he could close his eyes, switch off and die.

***

But he was wrong: in the living world not all that far away, there was still a final act playing out.

Helicopter re-enforcements had come sweeping out from the islands, driving low across the water, forcing Masud to defend his position. He had anticipated that it might come to this and his three choppers emerged in response.

They had been hidden under the camouflage covers on the Queen Juliana's deck.

Nebankh Ezzat, head of GIS, the Egyptian intelligence agency, already had had concerns over Cyrano Zafros for several years: the man had twice already posed a threat to vessels passing up and down the Red Sea and the ambush leading to the death of three former El-Sa'ka Forces men as they delivered the couple into the harbour in Algalh, was the final straw.

The result was that Ezzat had thrown both money and resources at removing this plague once and for all… plus it was good experience for his men at resolving a hostage situation.

Masud also called his second sting-strand into play: the Honeybird roared into life, broke cover and appeared from the far side of the Juliana, flashing out over the foam and coming to the rescue, while hard on the Honeybird's heels came the Kingfisher.

The plan was for one of these two to take on the gun-boats that were heading out from the pier on Hafcryznic, while the other raced in to rescue Bruce.

The Kingfisher took out one of the marauding craft but then lost power, her fuel pipe riddled by bullets, leaving the team on board watching helplessly as its attacker, the second gun-boat El Khorg, sped past, and bore down on the long-suffering swimmer in the water.

With Cloud's boat on full throttle and heading straight towards Bruce, the Honeybird needed to change tactics, so Laszlo racked his power handle full back so as to put his boat between Bruce and El Khorg and deflect the attack.

But the Honeybird's surge of speed turned into a disadvantage as she could only turn in a wider circle which gave the more manoeuvrable El Khorg the chance to nip back in and take a second bite at the apple… which was to run its propeller blades directly over the swimmer's head.

Bruce saw what was coming and although he had all but given up on life, he couldn't quite face going out in such a gruesome fashion, so he took a deep breath and plunged beneath the surface. A hull flashed past directly overhead, followed by propeller blades that missed him by inches.

Then it was all over: El Khorg broke off from further assault because of incoming fire from the Honeybird and beat a hasty retreat. The danger removed, the Honeybird turned and made a bee-line for Bruce. It came alongside him and Laszlo shut down the engines while Kafele leaned over the front rail, shouting to the man below:

"We're here Bruce! Hold on!"

But he was a lost soul. "I lost her," he roared. "I lost Fleur and I'm not coming back. For me it's all over!"

"But you haven't lost her. We've got her."

He bobbed in the water motionless. His eyes were glazed and he had a fixation that was blocking rational thought, a fixation that was staving off their incoming messages.

"I can't come," he gasped. "I've got to go on."

The exhausted swimmer made to push off on his own. Laszlo leaned over next to Kafele and screamed at him: "Hey, listen you great frigging pillock! Look at the boat over there. See, it's picking up people from out the water. Look, will you, you stupid wedge! Listen man, we sent in frogmen with spare oxygen tanks. We caught them and held them underwater, out of sight of that lot, until it was all over."

No response.

"Hey, are you listening? We've saved them, both of them, your woman and the kid too. Both are alive!"

But Bruce wasn't listening. He was already halfway to another world. He saw sharks coming in for him once again but this time he didn't care. Fleur was on her feet, jumping up and down in the distance, signalling for all she was worth, but he never saw her. He was done.

The two men knew they had to act. Both scrambled down the outside of the boat, hung out over the water with just one foot each back on a step, then reached out, straining to pull Bruce closer.

The sharks were here already, three of them and all with mouths open wide. The two dipped over together. One caught Bruce by the ankle just as the other snatched him by the hair and together they yanked him upwards and out of the sea, gripping ever so tightly. It was real close: his nose, face and various other body parts came crashing against the side of the boat as the snap of teeth sounded just inches below.

***

Louis stood frozen. He was left motionless, mouth agape, clinging to his mother's hand. Although it was all over, he was still wobbly at the knees, back blistered and burnt, he stayed close, his tear-stained face pressed against her body.

His sister was also heading their way: the frogmen who had saved her earlier were there to help as she stepped across to the boat, sobbing with relief and happiness, and flung her arms round her mother, crying: "I thought you'd gone for ever!"

Ysanne kissed her brother. "I've brought some cream," she said. "Can I put it on?"

Louis nodded and raised no objection… it showed he was still very raw.

The Honeybird arrived, shut down its engines, drifted up alongside and Bruce saw them all. He wanted to reach out and touch, but he had nothing left as the four-hour marathon was taking its toll... that and the blistering heat, the endless tension and the swim. He was washed up, totally spent.

Fleur saw he was about to crumble, so as the two boats touched, she made the first move by jumping across and taking him in her arms.

Then he passed out.

But he did that knowing that they were alive, that they were all alive.

***

Finally, it was all over and four happy people were heading home: their flotilla sailed northwards, steadily making its way up the entire length of the Red Sea before reaching Sharm El-Sheik where quite a contingent stepped ashore. With the protective escort team staying close at hand, they were escorting overland to Cairo then a follow-up spell as they savoured their first real taste of comfort by staying in Moaz's apartment for a couple of nights.

Next news they were off and in just a few hours they had landed at Heathrow.

Then back to East Anglia, to streams and willows and green pastures, to thatch-cap houses with pink plaster walls. They rolled round the edge of

Ipswich then up and over the Orwell Bridge where the river way down below them somehow felt like the last barrier before reaching home.

Onto the far side… and this was it; they were back into Suffolk with its sandy soils and knotty pines.

The rescue sequence down below the waves was Louis's favourite subject and he must have told Bruce, Ossie, Floyd and everyone they met on the way back, every minute detail at least a dozen times.

"You must have been frightened when you were up there," Bruce said as Martlesham masts came into sight on the right. "I know I would have been."

"I shut my eyes and clung on to mum," he confided.

It was a fine and sunny, mid-July afternoon when they got back to Woodbridge to find that the whole place had gone bananas… what a home-coming.

There was cheering in Pyches Road, bunting in The Thoroughfare and more crowds in Wilderness Lane. People packed pavements all the way from the boatyard to the ageing seed house until, at last, they turned the corner and swung round into Florida Way.

The open-top car, on free hire from Rex Tate, crept along in its lowest gear because the place was pandemonium, a bustling sea of welcome, of hats and flags and well-known faces. There were balloons and banners hung from houses, fizzy drinks and chocolate fingers, open windows, party-time and cake.

Bruce and Fleur stood squeezed close together, waving back to the crowds.

"I feel like a princess," said Ysanne as she spotted known faces in the crowd and squealed with delight. "Look there's Haerlwin. And there's the two Vicky's."

"There's Scott and Dean," yelled Louis, just as excited, "and Edward Hanania."

"Half the school's here."

"Mr Crissell."

"And Mrs T-B."

There was Billy and Sandra, and Tony MacDonald. There were folk who had walked over from Grundisburgh like Johnny Walker and the lads from the green. And Sheila from the shop, and Linda with a baby, and Heidi and Kelly and all the netball team.

Bruce leaned closer and whispered something in Fleur's ear. She threw her arms round him and gave him a hug.

"Yes," she said. "Yes, oh you are a darling!"

A wild cheer broke out from the welcome party as the kiss went on and on. It was the biggest, tenderest kiss ever.

Louis tugged at his sister's blouse impatiently.

"What did he say?" he asked. "I couldn't hear."

Ysanne's face lit up, beaming with a huge smile.

"We're going to have a dad," she said. "We're going to have a real dad."

The End

Printed in Dunstable, United Kingdom